ANGEL WING MINISTRIES PRESENTS

....

REDEEMING GRACE

CARRIED BY ANGELS SERIES

BOOK NUMBER 4

Brenda Conley
Angel Wing Ministries

COVER DESIGN
CREATED
BY

BRANDON ANDRINA

Carried By Angels Series...
Book 4...REDEEMING GRACE
Copyright © 2013. All rights reserved.

All scripture quotation, unless otherwise indicated, are taken from the HOLY BIBLE, NEW INTERNATIONAL VERSION R. NIV R. Copyright C 973, 1978, 1984 by International Bible Society. Used by permission of Zondervan. All rights reserved.

Scripture references marked KJV are from the HOLY BIBLE. Authorized King James Version.

Please note that I have chosen to capitalize certain pronouns in Scripture that refers to the Father, Son, and Holy Spirit. That may differ from some Bible publishers' styles.

Library of Congress Cataloging in-Publication Data
Conley, Brenda
Redeeming Grace/Brenda Conley
ISBN-13: 978-069236518 (Angel Wing Ministries)
ISBN-10: 0692365613

DEDICATION

This four book series belongs to all of the broken women who live everyday with the grief of losing a child to the lies of abortion.

God sees your brokenness and wants to restore you. He is in the restoration business. God loves you.

Do not let satan tell you differently. Satan wants nothing more than for you to live a lifetime of brokenness. He is a liar who comes to kill, steal and destroy. He will never have a victory unless you give it to him. He has already been defeated. A high price was paid for your freedom. God gave his Son so your freedom was paid in full. Jesus himself went into hell and took back the keys so satan could have no control over any area of your life.

There is no sin, nothing you could do, that is too big for our God to forgive. He does not want you to live a life carrying a load of regret or guilt. He made a way through His Son, Jesus Christ, to lighten your load and give you hope. In fact, He will pick you up and carry you when the road seems too long...When you are too weary...When you have gone as far as you can...When you can see no hope at the end of the day.

If you still feel burdened from the choices you have made, today is the day to lay them at the feet of Jesus. He is just waiting for you to come just as you are; broken and spilled out, surrendered to Him. Feel the freedom only He can give. Run to His mercy seat and live with joy. Jesus is just waiting to change your life. He wants to give you a life everlasting full of love, hope and peace; the peace that surpasses all understanding.

By ourselves, we will never be worthy. Through Christ all things are possible. He loves you so much that He laid down His life for you to live a life of abundance. He created you for a purpose. God knew that purpose even before He brought you into this world. Seek Him. Find Him. Live for Him. He loves you. Choose Him and find the freedom that only His love can bring.

For His Glory,
Brenda Conley
Angel Wing Ministries

ACKNOWLEDGEMENTS

How do I say "thank you" to all of the people in my life? It is each of you who have encouraged, taught and blessed me with your love over this journey with Noelle and family. I couldn't have done it without you.

To my family at Hillside Learning and Behavior Center, to the amazing children we are privileged to love everyday and their wonderful parents, I send you my gratitude. I have learned life lessons from everyone of you.

To my own children. You have challenged me, loved me, showed me the importance of living everyday to its fullest and brought me great joy. Words can not express my love for you. Each of you have become amazing people. Thank you for loving the Lord. That obedience has made all of our lives above and beyond.

To my grandchildren. You are the flowers in my garden, the stirring in my heart and you hold me captive. I love you more everyday and am thrilled to watch you learn about the love God has for you. I can't wait to see the adults you will become as He molds you into your best. Follow His every step for your life and live in joy.

Ron. Here we are again closing another journey in our lives. As I put Noelle to rest, I am thankful for the times you have understood my need to follow God's timing. Those times when your dinner wasn't ready when you got home because of hours behind the computer that day. Or your understanding that I needed quiet time to finish whatever God was laying on my heart at the moment. Thank you for your patience; but mostly thank you for your love. The future looms bright ahead for us. Our three year plan looks better every day. I can't wait to see where God is taking us next. Love you Baby. You're my best.

To all of the wonderful people who help to make all of this possible. Brandon Andrina who creates my beautiful covers and fixes my technology snafus. My Writer's Guild who shares important information. To those who help with editing, my sister Barbara Merchant, Sunday Petto, Jan Westendorp and Gail Conlan; thank you for cleaning up my mistakes.

To all of you...I have said it before and I will say it again...God is why I write. Without His lead, there would be no words. It has been my pleasure to bring you His message of hope. Don't take my word for it though. Pick up a Bible and find a lifetime full of love and wisdom. See how much He really loves you. Nothing can compare to the real deal. Find Him waiting for you in the pages of His word. He has a special message, created just for you that only He can deliver. He is that personal. Let Him love you.

Finally, to the four women who God sent my way and who started this journey with me. I hope Noelle's journey has brought healing to you. I pray your burdens have been laid at the foot of the cross and you have claimed the redeeming grace and mercy that only the blood of Jesus can give. It was not by accident God brought us together. It is not by accident He shared your stories. Your willingness to be transparent allowed God's message of forgiveness to reach millions of broken women who have walked in your shoes. Thank you for your courage.

TO GOD BE THE GLORY,
GREAT THINGS HE HAS DONE

Be captured,
Brenda, Mom and Friend

STORY CHARACTERS

Naming the characters in my stories is like giving birth to my own children. I have always thought it important that they have strong names that will serve them well through life. I decided it was important that I share with you why I chose the names of the people that you will meet in this story.

Noelle--(French origin meaning "born at Christmas time) She is a broken 19 year old. The oldest daughter in what was supposed to be a wonderful family. If asked, they would tell you that they are Christians; however, Christmas, Easter and marriages sum up their church life experience as a family. Noelle and her sisters attended summer Vacation Bible School programs and you will see how the Word of God is faithful. You will walk with her through a life changing experience. See how God made a way for her through all of it. All she had to do was look at His hand guiding and directing her path.

Brad Conroy--(English origin meaning "one who has broad shoulders") A hard working 22 year old who's life is about to change as he follows his heart into an area of God's leading. Brad is faithful to wait upon the Lord and wise enough to honor his father and mother.

Eyan Conroy--(Gaelic origin; form of John meaning "God is gracious") Brad's brother. Twenty years old and ready to embrace the world. He is looking to branch out into the world of the unknown. Living on the farm is not in his future. His passion is to reach the lost for the Lord out on a mission field somewhere adventurous.

Angelina Conroy--(Greek form of Angela, meaning "a heavenly messenger; an angel") Her name represents the part that she will play in Noelle's life. A survivor. She is full of wisdom and willing to walk through the ugliness of her past life to help save the life of an unborn child.

Terran Conroy--(Latin origin; Man of the earth) Angelina's husband and Brad and Eyan's father. A wonderful man who left this earth too soon. They miss him desperately. He lives on in the character of the boys as they grow into the men he would have wanted them to be.

Genie Smith--(English origin; form of Jean meaning "God is gracious") Noelle's mother. Trying to heal from a broken marriage. Her main focus becomes her girls.

Gale Smith--(Irish origin meaning a foreigner) This was the husband and father to Genie and their daughters. His leaving caused a hole in their family that left them trying to figure out who they are. He really did become a foreigner to them.

Aunt Debbie--(Hebrew origin; in the Bible a prophetess) Genie's sister. She loves her sister and nieces and wants only to help support them.

Nissa Smith--(Hebrew origin meaning "one who tests others") The middle sister. Thrust into becoming the protector in the home. Loves her sisters desperately and is the peacemaker in the family.

Anaya Smith--(African origin meaning "One who looks up to God) The youngest of the three girls. Anaya and Noelle have the closest bond of the girls. She feels Noelle's pain the most.

Michael Dunn--(Hebrew origin meaning "Who is like God") Genie's boss. Watching this family walk through fire and come out on the other side with a deeper relationship with the Lord will touch his life.

Chelsea Dunn--(English meaning "From the landing place for chalk) She is the devoted wife of Michael Dunn

Pastor Travis--(French meaning "To cross over") Brad's youth pastor. He will be helpful in showing Noelle the way towards healing through Christ.

Michelle Jordan--(French origin and feminine form of Michael meaning "Who is like God") She apart from anyone else will be able to come along side of Noelle. They will become friends through an understanding of brokenness.
Shawn Murray--(Irish origin and a form of John, meaning "God is gracious.") Shawn is laughter when times get hard. There is always a smile waiting from him.
Delmyn Whitehall--(English origin meaning a man of the mountain) This is a troubled young man. His life was full of money and no responsibility. There has been no accountability until his world comes crashing down around him. This man will represent an amazing opportunity to practice forgiveness.
Keefe Whitehall--(Gaelic origin meaning a handsome and beloved man) A hardworking man who had amassed a small fortune for his wife and son to share. After all what good was the money he had made, if he couldn't share it with the people that he loved. Admitting that he may have spoiled his only son Del a little, he believed that he had also taught him to be a good man.
Shauna Whitehall--(Irish origin. The Feminine form of Shaun; meaning God is gracious. She loves her son. He has been her baby for 19 years and she would lay down her life for him. Always looking the other way, she sees Del as perfect. She believes that every boy needs to sow a few wild oats before settling down. It will make them a better husband when the time comes.
Tempo (Teo) Mohan--(Spanish meaning a godly man) An attorney who's path will cross with Delmyn's. That crossing will have an impact on the young man's life and his own. A hard working, man who wants to make a difference in this world. Believes that Christ will bring you out of any adversity that you find yourself in, if you will surrender.
Laura Lynn Lyndstrum--(Latin meaning crowned with laurel; for the laurel tree) Prosecuting Attorney representing

the State in the rape trial. Laura has a personal interest. Her secret will be uncovered in preparation for the trial.

Judge Owen Marshall--(Welsh/Gaelic for of Eugene, meaning a wellborn man/a youthful man) A defender of right and passionate about the laws of the United States of American. He came out of hardship and battled to overcome. Fair but firm.

Pastor Preston--(English from the Priest's town) Eager to reach the lost; but weary from good works. A family man with teenage girls; he struggles with his feelings for the situation that he finds himself in.

Professor Lee and His wife Patty--(Lee is English for "From the meadow" Patty is English and is feminine form of Patrick meaning of noble descent) This couple plays an important role as they are used by God to bring our family closer together.

Grady Yost--(Gaelic; one who is famous; noble) This is the Director of the new office that Genie will be working for. He is a man of character and strength; a good man.

Emma Rae--(Emma--German; One who is complete; Rae--English; Form of Rachel, meaning "the innocent lamb") The innocent is a perfect name for this child. She is one of the lucky ones in this Country. A life saved by God.

Embrace these characters as they share the word of Jesus Christ with a waiting world. Each one of them has a story to be told.

FOREWARD

I read *SAVING NOELLE* and *PERFECT LOVE*, and have seen three constant truths presented in these books. Two are the truths of mankind since the beginning of time. They are themes as old as the dirt from which we were made. Choice and Fear. We did not have the opportunity or the ability to be present with Adam to scream "NO" as he betrayed the Lord Creator and his wife, Eve, by disobeying God's command in the Garden of Eden. So we have lived with his consequences. After his sin, he hid in fear from the only One who was able to save him from the choice he made. So it has been with us.

These books present tried and true Biblical concepts of our everyday lives. The choices we have made every day determine the destiny of our existence. Sometimes we have trusted and obeyed the Lord's instructions with our decisions and choices and sometimes we haven't. Sometimes decisions have turned out well and other times decisions have turned out disastrous.

The third constant truth is the Lord who created everything that is visible and invisible. He loved us and wanted to be intimately involved in our lives, especially our choices. The Lord tells us through his servant to ***Choose you this day who you will serve. Joshua 24:15*** He clearly states in this statement that we choose to either align ourselves with God or align ourselves against God with Satan.

If we ask the Lord to help us make the our decisions, we know He is with us. We know if His decision is for us to go through the deep waters of great troubles, He will be with us. If His choice is for us to go through rivers of difficulty, we will not drown. If His choice is for us to walk through the fire of oppression we will not be burned up and hell cannot consume us. Life here on this earth can be a constant battle with the enemy of our souls, satan. He only wants to kill, steal and destroy us by the choices he lays out in front of us each day of our lives. God wants us, like the characters of these books,who are just like you and me, to trust Him. He loved us so much He gave Jesus, His Son, to die for us and deliver us from the consequences of Adam's choices and ultimately our own.

Choices, fears and consequences have the potential to weave such a tangled mess of our lives when we do not trust the Lord and obey His words.

Beloved, Brenda Conley has written these books from the heart of the Father, who loves you. Listen to His intervention in the lives of the characters. He is waiting to be asked to intervene in your life also. He wants to show you His *saving and perfect love.*

A servant of The Most High,
Genie Garcia

WITH IN ME LIES

"I can do this"
She breathed as the car squeaked to a stop.
He would understand, she
Thought as she shut
The ignition off. She
Grasped the cold
Steering wheel as the world
Slowly began to swirl and twirl, relentless
White leaves from winter's eternal tree encased her.
She couldn't see, clouds
Escaped from her mouth, like she
Was talking with God.
Then she felt him
Move and fight in her
She could hear his screams
Not unlike her own, thoughts
Impregnated her mind
And birthed a fire ablaze in her heart
That thawed the frozen streams
Behind her eyes and caused them
To flow with certainty
One hand on her ferocious heart
The other straining to brush heaven's door
Head high
Mind calm
Shoulders free
Car in reverse.

Taylor Laird
College Sophomore
Age 19

INTRODUCTION

We are here. Noelle's journey has come to an end. In book four you will see how God brings the story full circle. Who am I to question God; however I wondered why he ended book three, FORGIVING FREEDOM, the way He did. I'm frustrated when movies and books end and leave you hanging and you don't know how it all worked out. That was what book three felt like to me. I thought we were at the end of the journey, yet it didn't feel like closure.

Then one morning God woke me up at 5:00 a.m. That's our communication time. I don't know why, it's always just been that way. If He wants to tell me something, He wakes me up at 5:00. That day He gave me book four, REDEEMING GRACE. As I went to the computer and began to type, I learned why He did what He did.

So I promise you will see His closure at the end of this book. You will understand why He continued to weave a specific character throughout all three books; yet He never developed that character. Again...I didn't understand why. God knew where He was going and now so do I.

In REDEEMING GRACE you will see His hand of love and we will learn of His plan for forgiveness. Most important, we will see His grace and mercy and what happens when we practice his ways.

EPHESIANS 2:4-10
But because of His great love for us, God, who is rich in mercy, made us alive with Christ even when we were dead in transgressions--it is by grace you have been saved. And God raised us up with Christ and seated us with Him in the heavenly realms in Christ Jesus, in order that in the coming ages He might show the incomparable riches of His grace, expressed in His kindness to us in Christ Jesus. For it is by grace you have been saved, through faith--and this not from yourselves, it is the gift of God--not by works,
so that no one can boast. For we are God's workmanship,

***created in Christ Jesus to do good works, which God prepared
in advance for us to do.***

You see sin came into the world and as hard as men tried
they could not help themselves. They continued through history
living in a state of conformity to the world. When we live in
sin we are slaves to satan. All of us are naturally children of
disobedience. We were created to be children of God and heirs of
His glory. He saw the need we had for a savior and He sent His
Son Jesus Christ to carry our sins to the cross. Where, because of
His obedience to His Father, He willingly climbed onto that cross
for a once and for all victory over satan. From that point on the
only victories sin can have over our lives are the ones we allow.
God and His Son paid a high price for our freedom and we should
learn how to live in that freedom.

God's eternal love fountain flows grace and mercy on us,
His children. His love is great and His mercy is rich. The grace
that saves us from sin and wrath is free. It is God's grace and
favor on us, the children He loves. This gift of salvation from the
Father can not be purchased by works. We can't earn it. That's
why it's a gift.

The Bible tells us this gift is not brought to us by anything
we do. God shut the door on any options for us to boast. This was
His gift to us. We receive it by surrendering to Him and asking
Him to come into our hearts. We lay down our lives of sin and
struggle and walk into a new and victorious life. By accepting
Christ as our Lord and Savior we are raised up into higher places
by Christ's grace. God seats us at the right hand of Christ. We
become royalty, children of the King; born into righteousness.
That's God.

God never intended we would carry the sorrows of this
world. He does tell us that in this world we will have troubles. Our
hope is in Him who overcame this world, which as His children,
makes us overcomers.

I stand in amazement of the price that was paid for us.
Jesus left Heaven, a place of beauty and peace, of which our

mortal minds can't even comprehend. He came to this world to die a tortured death. He did that for each and every one of us. My husband likes to remind me that Jesus would have made that trip even if we were the only ones on this earth. He loves us that much. He gave it all in pain and suffering so we could have love, peace and life eternal.

If you haven't given your life to Christ, today is not too late. He's just waiting for you to come to Him. His arms are opened wide and He wants to wrap them around you and cover you with His love and protection.

Confess your sins. Step into the light of the "Son" and accept His love. Get rid of a life filled with pain and sorrow. He has a plan and a purpose for your life.

For I know the plans I have for you, declares the Lord, plans to prosper you and not to harm you, plans to give you hope and a future.
Jeremiah 29:11

God is full of hope. He wants to share that hope with you. This world belongs to the ruler of the dark side. Satan and his demons were cast from Heaven. I promise, satan wants to steal any hope you may have. It would make him happy if you lived in brokenness and despair. He would steal your joy. That would give him pleasure.

Now God, He wants to be your companion. He promises He will never leave or forsake you. He will always be right by your side. All you have to do is ask. He won't push His way into your life; but He will come with open arms the very second you ask Him to come. He is always there, even when we choose to ignore Him. Just waiting. He is patient.

Today can be your day. If that's where your heart is please take this moment to pray with me.

Heavenly Father and most gracious God, I surrender my life to You. I ask that You come into my heart and be my Lord and Savior. I believe You died on the cross. I believe on the third day You rose from the grave. I believe You are coming again. I ask for the forgiveness of my sins accepting that Your blood has washed me white as snow. I acknowledge only through You can I be worthy; only by Your grace can I be free. I understand as far as the east is from the west You have removed my sins from me. They are buried in the deepest sea never to be seen again. I believe when You look at me You see me pure and sinless; and that I can rest assured knowing I will spend eternity with You. Thank You Father for loving me. Amen.

Congratulations. You did it. You have a future that belongs to Christ. God loves you. Don't look back. Look forward to your new future. Get your hands on a Bible and begin to read it. Let His word unlock the mysteries of this world for you. See what a good God we serve. Bury His word in your heart. His word is a road map for your life. Talk to Him daily. He is your daddy and a daddy loves to hear from His children.

Get ready. Satan will not be happy. Remember he does not want you living free. He thrives on bondage. Strengthen yourself so you are prepared when the enemy comes to whisper in your ear you aren't worthy. You are...Jesus said so.

Jesus came so you might have life and have it more abundantly. Enjoy your freedom.

So if the Son sets you free, you will be free indeed.
John 8:36

That's a promise from God's word. Grab it...Claim it...It was meant for you.

Therefore, if anyone is in Christ, he is a new creation; the old is gone, the new has come.
II Corinthians 5:17

God's word is talking about you. His book is full of love messages and He is sending them to you.

BE BLESSED. GOD LOVES YOU. SO DO I.

CHAPTERS

1. If I speak in the tongues of men and of angels, but have not love, I am only a resounding gong or a clanging cymbal.

2. If I have the gift of prophecy and can fathom all mysteries and all knowledge, and if I have a faith that can move mountains, but have not love, I am nothing.

3. If I give all I possess to the poor and surrender my body to the flames, but have not love, I gain nothing.

4. Love is patient, love is kind. It does not envy, it does not boast, it is not proud.

5. It is not rude, it is not self-seeking, it is not easily angered, it keeps no record of wrongs.

6. Love does not delight in evil but rejoices with the truth.

7. It always protects, always trusts, always hopes, always perseveres.

8. Love never fails. But where there are prophecies, they will cease; where there are tongues, they will be stilled; where there is knowledge, it will pass away.

9. For we know in part and we prophesy in part,

10.   but when perfection comes, the imperfect disappears.

11.   When I was a child, I talked like a child, I thought like a child, I reasoned like a child. When I became a man, I put childish ways behind me.

12. Now we see but a poor reflection as in a mirror; then we shall see face to face. Now I know in part; then I shall know fully, even as I am fully known.

13. And now these three remain. Faith, hope and love. But the greatest of these is love.

14. But the greatest of these is love.

EPILOGUE

THOUGHTS FROM THE AUTHOR

PRAYER OF SALVATION

Chapter One

I CORINTHIANS 13

1. If I speak in the tongues of men and of angels, but have not love, I am only a resounding gong or a clanging cymbal.

Michael Dunn hurried through the hallways that would lead him to the room of his Great Aunt Denise. *Why am I here?* He wondered again for an uncountable time today. He knew why. He had made a promise to his mother earlier in the week and had agreed he would stop in and say a quick hello. It was the only reason he had driven so far out of his way. Truth be known, the mother he loved had guilted him into this visit. Not that she had tried to make him feel guilty. He just knew what she was thinking.

He had tried to talk his wife and kids into coming with him. That would have made the trip more bearable. No takers. Now running through his mind were all of the reasons why they couldn't come. Every one of them had found excuses. All of them had busy lives. Well, to whom did they think they were talking. As Dean of Students at the University, his schedule was already so full he hadn't really wanted to add this one more stop. He didn't really have time for any of this. Especially when you considered this trip would cost him a good three hours out of his day.

Thinking about the time frame made him walk even faster through the halls that smelled like bleach and old people. In all honesty, if it wasn't for his mother's pleading, he would never come here. The smells always made him think of how life leads to the unavoidable. After all, it was appointed unto every man to die. Right? Those smells hit him the minute he walked in through the door. He referred to them as the smells of death. You know, the smells that remind you life slips away before you know it. The same smells that stayed with you long after you've walked away from a facility like this. He wasn't even sure if those smells were real or just a figment of his own imagination. That was why he hated the smell of disinfectant. To Michael Dunn it was just a reminder of his own mortality.

After all, isn't that why people came to places like this? Didn't they come to die? He never saw them coming here to live. They called it assisted living. Michael thought there had to be a better way to end your life than laying in a bed just waiting for someone to come for a visit. He pictured himself lying there, then taking his last breath on this earth.

That was when the guilt would creep in. If someday he would find himself in a place like this, he certainly would want someone to come for a visit; just for a few moments of reprieve in what had to be a completely tedious existence.

Okay Michael. You've made the drive this far. Stop complaining to yourself and make the most of this. You're about to brighten your aunt's day. She always was nice to you. Consider this your good deed and do it with a smile on your face.

Plus, it would appease his mother who, even though he was 58 years old, could take him back to those moments of his childhood. Just the tone of her voice as she scolded, "Michael"! Even though she didn't say it, he could finish her sentence with "Really?". Instantly he returned to those years before he grew up and became successful. There he was in the years of plaid shorts, white dress shirts, and the perfectly tied clip on black tie. Not to mention, the waxed hair laying so closely to his head that air could not possibly circulate through it. He chuckled thinking back on those early pictures where he would be so stiff; almost as stiff as his hair. He

2

wondered why no one but his mother and sisters were smiling. Along with him, his father and brothers all had the same look. They all seemed so somber you could almost hear the words as they were circulating through their heads, "Are we done yet"? Although not one of them would have dared utter that sentence; including Dad.

Even as his steps carried him closer to his aunt, he could hear his mother's voice. "Just how long has it been since you've taken time to visit your Great Aunt Denise? You know you were always her favorite and she never missed your parties or special events. She always brought you that one particular gift you had been waiting for all year. Honestly Michael, we don't know how much longer she's going to be with us and you owe her an occasional visit in her last days." He knew better than to argue. His mother was always ready to prove she was right about this matter. The truth...He knew she was right, even if going to the visit felt like a burden.

So here he was walking as quickly as he could through the hallway that brought him to the nurses' station. Michael hesitated before deciding to turn left. It had been some time since he had been here and if memory served him correctly he should make a sharp turn here. Pretty sure he had made the correct move, he made quick peeks into the rooms he passed. He didn't remember her being in a hall with so many men. He began to question if he had gone the right way just as he reached the suite at the end of the hall. His aunt had been in this room for all the years he had been coming to visit her; however, this didn't look quite right to him.

He read the sign beside the door and it said, "Mr. Smith." Obviously, that was not his aunt.

Michael started to turn just as something inside

3

of the door caught his attention. A sitting room separated the hallway from the actual living area. There was a second door opening into that room. Inside the second room was a man laying in the hospital bed all the way over by the window. It was a sad picture of a man, a young man. A man who appeared to be Michael's age. Then something familiar jumped in his spirit, a moment that gave him pause and in an instant he knew why. The man laying so very still in that bed was Gale...Gale Smith. His friend who had left his family. The man who walked away leaving no answers for anyone. He wanted to run before he saw anymore; but it felt as if his feet were glued to the spot where he was standing. He had to be wrong. It couldn't be true. What he was looking at had to be a mistake. It wasn't possible.

His mind began to scream, *Get out...Before he sees you...Get out.* He stood for only a few more seconds, though the time felt like it was ticking away ever so quickly. Then he turned and ran. Michael ran down the hall and out of the hallway that should have taken him to his great aunt's room. Instead it took him into a moment in time he would never forget. He had stepped into a nightmare of sorts. Just what the story was, he wasn't sure. What he did know was he had to get out of there before he was sick. He could feel the bile rising up into his throat as he ran down the halls and back out into the entryway that had started his journey into the black hole of reality. Bursting through the outside doors, he could feel himself gasping for air as if the trip back into the outside world had squeezed his chest so hard he couldn't breathe. Try as he may, he could not expel the sound that signaled a continued motion of involuntary effort made by his lungs. Then it came. More violently than seemed possible, his stomach emptied its contents

4

behind a nearby bush. Standing with his hand on the cold brick of the building as it held him in space, it came over and over and over again and then the end.

Forcing himself to pull air in through his nose and exhale it slowly through his mouth several times, Michael found the center of his universe. In those moments of repeating a very normal pattern of breathing in and out, he calmed himself enough to realize he needed to get to a safe place. Heading to his parked car, he quickly grabbed the keys out of his suit pant's pocket and clicked the button unlocking the doors. Climbing into the driver's seat and laying his head against the cool of the steering wheel leather, Michael began trying to convince himself that what he had just witnessed was not true. Yet, in his heart, he knew the truth.

What did it all mean? How could it be? Maybe his eyes had played a horrible trick on him? But no..it was true. He had seen it and the picture was playing over and over in his mind. With every frame, he was drawn further and further into the reality of what he had just witnessed. What he didn't know was what he was going to do with this truth. Realizing he needed some time to process the whole situation, Michael sat until the shaking of his hands subsided and he knew he would be safe to make the drive back into the city that held comfort and familiarity for him. He needed the noise of the traffic and bumper to bumper chaos that came with rush hour. His plans had changed and now he needed time to find the one perfect word that would right his world again. He had to find something that would put his center back where it was supposed to be, spinning perfectly on point. Something to erase the panic that threatened to capture him if he wasn't careful. He needed peace.

****

Gale's day had been like any other day. They were all the same now. The weariness of his reality spoke to him with the uncertainty of the future. Never different. Always the same unless he slipped farther away from life. Days were like that now more than not. He couldn't always tell if he had lost another piece of his body. There was so much gone at this point he didn't always feel the loss. Yet his mind remained strong and complete. Unfortunately, it was locked in a body he couldn't use. So he lay there waiting for the nurse to come and turn him occasionally or the therapist who would manipulate his muscles so they would not lock up and hopefully cramp less. He wished they would just leave him alone and let the process continue. Yet, he longed for the human contact even though he couldn't really feel it. Dying, and who knew how long that was going to take, was a very lonely journey. The good news ...His disease was progressing quickly. In the beginning he had studied everything he could find. What was the outcome of all of his searching? The doctors and researchers didn't have any conclusive answers. His didn't seem to be genetic and of that he was grateful. He couldn't have stood knowing he could have passed this unthinkable sentence on to those he loved so very much. For him to have to live with the knowledge he could have caused them to anticipate this in their future would have been a worse torture.

In fact, the love he had for them was how he survived each day. In the only part of his body that worked anymore was where he lived. Morning till night he relived the wonderful memories he had with the family he had loved so much. From his college days with Genie, through marriage, child birth, raising their children together, he replayed everyday, moment by moment. To make the days go faster, he would designate each day differently. In the morning, after all of his daily routines, he would decide today is a college day.

From morning through night, and often into the wee hours of early dawn, he would progress through those years trying to remember every moment. He was thorough. Pulling from the deep recesses of his mind he would put himself back into that time. Closing his eyes he would picture every fine detail. The mind is amazing; so complex and so complete. Using as many of his senses as he could, he would find himself back in time. Drawing deep inside he would find he could place himself in that moment and push through until he would know what it smelled like; he could hear the noises that were around him and almost taste the sweetness that existed.

Before this disease happened to him, there would be times he was sure he was becoming forgetful. Now he realized as the world around his life became quiet and all he had to focus on was his past, he could pull from his memory every moment of his life in detail.

There were even those occasional days when a new blast from the past would surface that he hadn't recalled yet. He wished he could express the excitement he found in that moment of memory. He would now have something else to focus his attention on for sometime. As he replayed the video of those memories, he could connect them to another memory and another until he would have a whole new direction in which to turn. The best days were when they were about his family. When, for whatever reason, a memory about one of them would slowly work its way up and became present. Building a day around that new memory brought him so much joy. It was those moments for which he lived.

By his own choice, there would be no new memories for him to create. He had closed that door. He had to do that for them. It was the only way he could protect them from this prison he now lived in. It was a prison he wasn't willing to share with those he loved so desperately. This wasn't a life he would wish on them. The biggest sadness he carried out of that decision was they may remember him with bitterness and anger. He hoped when he was gone it would make more sense to them.

Even so, he believed that would be better than seeing their pity and watching them observe him wasting away minute by minute. This way he was the only one suffering. This way he would die and someday they would move on and the pain of these days would not affect them. They wouldn't see who he had become. It would be better if they could remember him strong and vibrant. In their eyes he would be a hero, at least in his mind he had worked it out that way. He was refusing to think they were hating him for the lie he had planted. No, in his mind they had moved on with their lives and simply put him on a back shelf as if it was a wonderful time of their lives that had just come to an abrupt end. He liked to think they simply dealt with his loss as an unexpected death and then moved on into their future.

In his world he could envision anything he wanted. Who was going to argue with him? There wasn't anyone. He was alone...Until death did him part.

****

Genie was excited to be on her way home for the night. She had just left a conference center at the Indiana

University where she was working in an area that felt like she had been groomed for her whole life. Her title was Administrative Assistant to the Office of News Services, which was a long name for Jack-Of-All-Trades. She did everything from planning visits and tours for financial contributors to organizing special dinners in honor of people or events the University hosted. She liked to think of herself as a glorified schmoozer. Not really a word; just something she used to identify herself to the girls.

This week had been particularly long as she finished last minute details for tonight's retirement party that her office hosted for a professor who had been with the University for 50 years. He had come to work for the University straight out of high school and worked his way through his college years. She loved to listen to his stories. They were so richly filled with the history of this school. He had seen more change than anyone else who taught or worked on the campus. He called the others, "transplants". They came and went. He had watched buildings go up and buildings come down. He laughed at how ironic it seemed to tear down just to rebuild. His stories told of financial hay days and fiscal loss. He had seen it all.

As a professor of political science, even in his later days, the students still fought for a seat in his classroom. He was quite the talker and his years of insight, coupled with his quick wit, made his class a favorite. In short, his students loved him. They could see he genuinely cared for them. He had earned the right to speak into their lives; and they listened.

Because of his dedication and years of service, the University's Board of Directors would sponsor a retirement dinner and farewell. It was her job to plan the

9

extravaganza. She was loving every minute right down to the finest detail. This was her specialty. They had given her a free card. She had complete control over any decisions made. However, she had decided to enlist a committee of his closest colleagues to help in making the night as unique and memorable as they could. It couldn't have turned out better.

Genie had been excited about the plans. Everything had come together perfectly from the full seven course meal to the amazing entertainment. The University's orchestra couldn't have been better leading into a small play performed by the drama department about the life of a professor. Guest speakers had contacted her asking to have the opportunity to relay funny stories about happenings through the years. Others just wanted to offer words of encouragement; just as he had done for those he came in contact with. Yes...The night was a night the professor would cherish forever.

Genie never tired of activities like this one. She lived to organize. It was an area of her life that brought her great pleasure. This position at the University had filled a void in her life she thought would stay empty forever after Gale had left. Now she was starting to feel alive again. The brokenness of that year was still there; but she had delegated it to an area of her life that was used only to draw her into a deeper relationship with the God who had brought her out of the dark, lonely place where she had lived in the quiet of her nights. The days had always been filled with enough to keep her going. She had forced herself to do that. But the nights, before she had found the Lord, were filled with darkness and despair. The nights were when she would allow herself to feel the pain of the loss she and the girls had experienced. Her tears filled those nights and the

10

questions surfaced continuously.

Not that she understood any more today than she had back then. She didn't. None of what happened that day made any sense to her. However, she had learned through the love of the God of the Universe she could move forward. ***Philippians 3:12   Forgetting what is behind and straining toward what is ahead, I press on toward the goal to win the prize for which God has called me heavenward in Christ Jesus.*** That verse had become her lifeline. Once she had been offered Jesus, she began to find a peace that truly did surpass all understanding. It was a process, a slow journey; one Genie was sure had come out of desperation caused by the brokenness that her life had morphed into

She thought of the changes her life had taken in such a short period of time. Only God could have taken her from the valley and put her on the mountain top that quickly. She did feel like she was living on a mountain. Her girls were in good places. She loved their new home. It had been an appropriate move forward bringing more closure. The house in Georgia was filled with memories that could have captured her in the sorrows of her broken life. Their new home represented a fresh start. Plus it brought her and the girls closer into the lives of Brad and Noelle and the beautiful little girl who meant so much to all of them. Emma Rae was a joy. She literally was a ray of sunshine. Born with such a sweet disposition, she had wrapped all of them around her little finger. Especially her daddy who was so attentive to both Emma and her mommy.

Together they were building a life based on a foundation of love. Everywhere that little girl looked there was always an adult willing to cuddle and make her the center of their attention. Emma was their world. Genie shuddered to think that had things happened differently, Emma wouldn't even have existed. If God had not been in control, Noelle could have been living with the guilt so many other women live with everyday. Plus, it was through Brad and Angelina that Genie and her family became believers and had accepted Jesus Christ as their Lord and Savior. It was His love that changed their lives forever. Without understanding who He was, they could have floundered in an ocean of despair all of their lives.

Was it little more than two years since Gale had left them? In that time Genie had watched her girls develope their own personal relationship with the God who loved them. They had become amazing young women whose focus in life was to serve the God they loved completely. Genie was so proud of each one of them for the way they had learned to put God first. She had watched the sadness of their dad's leaving be replaced with the joy of accepting the loving arms of a Heavenly Father who would never leave them nor forsake them. He healed their hearts. As a family, they were so grateful for Angelina, Brad and Eyan Conroy's ability to love. Because of their desire to be obedient to the Lord and their willingness to share God's love they had captured Genie's whole family in a net of loving kindness. They graciously shared the love of Jesus and nothing in the Smith family would ever be the same again.

Especially in Noelle's life. Rape is such an ugly circumstance, one that brings with it controversy from both sides. However, her beautiful granddaughter came out of that night and Emma Rae couldn't possibly be loved more. Three families' lives were changed from that horrible moment. Only God could have taken what the devil meant for evil and turned it into something as beautiful as Emma Rae Conroy. Genie could not imagine what life would have looked like if Noelle had been able to fulfill her plan to abort this amazing little girl. What if God's hand hadn't been directing Noelle's life that night? To think she had traveled days across the United States only to end up in Angelina's arms.

Emma, at 18 months, had become the most precious baby ever in the eyes of their two families. Genie would never be able to thank Angelina or God enough for what was accomplished. He truly is an amazing God. A God big enough to watch out for us even in the tiniest details. The Bible tells us He has every one of the hairs on our heads counted. He hears us when we cry and He holds those tears in His hands. We are that important to Him. Genie would never stop praising Him. His grace and mercy endures forever. It was His grace that saved her broken family. It was His mercy, His blessing through an act of divine love, that sent His Son to the cross for her and her girls. As the almighty God, He made a decision to be loving and show His mercy on us as sinners through the death of His Son, Jesus, on the cross. But the victory came on the third day when death could not hold Him and the stone was rolled away.

Yes...Genie's family's lives were changed by the God who holds the universe.

13

Chapter Two

I Corinthians 13

2. If I have the gift of prophecy and can fathom all mysteries and all knowledge, and if I have a faith that can move mountains, but have not love, I am nothing.

THE CROWD OF YOUTH LOOKED LIKE A SEA WAVE as they swayed from side to side. They were loving the benefit concert that had been organized for the local children's hospital. Eyan had played an integral part of making sure today happened. He had such a heart for the youth. It was one of the reasons Nissa loved him. From the very beginning she had seen his heart. It seemed to be attached to the front of his chest instead of buried inside.

On top of being in charge of the Activities Committee for the youth in their church, Eyan also coached their high school baseball team, taught a Sunday School class before church and played drums with their youth worship team.

Nissa volunteered on all of the same groups Eyan worked with. Not just because she wanted to be close to him; however, it certainly was a perk. She shared that same passion for the youth. It made it easy to work side by side with him.

She especially loved working with the softball team. She had always played in school until her senior year when she had made the decision to keep her time available for visits to see Noelle. Now working with the church team filled the need that she had been left with. Her mind wandered back to last week's game.

"Miss Nissa," called the young man who had from the very beginning found a special spot in her heart. "Can you help me?"

Nissa moved to the other side of the dugout and asked, "What is it Gredin?" She smiled at the young man whose look showed he was frustrated.

"The strap on this stupid...Oh, sorry Miss Nissa... On this shin guard won't stay strapped. I'm going to need to be on the field at any moment." He finished.

"Here, let me see if I can help you."

Nissa knelt down and attempted to untwist the mangled strap which wouldn't keep Gredin's leg safe as he squatted down to catch the balls thrown by Javan, the young pitcher who had just joined the team this season.

"Hurry Miss Nissa. There's two outs. I need to be ready to go." Nissa could still hear the panic in his voice.

Seeing the problem, Nissa had thrown up a prayer. "Okay God! Give us an idea quickly. Please?" Instantly she knew what she needed to do.

"Hold on Gredin, I'll be right back." Rushing over to the equipment box, Nissa had grabbed a roll of medical tape and returned to her young catcher. "We'll have this fixed in a jiffy." Taping the shield round and round his leg, she said, "Now don't let this game go into overtime or we'll have to cut this off and then rewrap it." Just as she had finished, their second baseman, Gavin, hit a single sending Zeke, the player on third base, heading for home. The score at the plate happened just before the opponents center fielder threw the ball to first in an attempt for an out. The umpire yelled SAFE and Gabe stood up dusting off his pants with a big smile on his face. Up to the plate stepped the best hitter, he was called "The Tornado" because he was so fast. Gideon let the first pitch go by. STRIKE the umpire had yelled. He seemed calm and comfortable. Second pitch...Gideon pulled back and let it go. The ball went high, high, higher and then began its descent. It was going to be close, either a home run or an out. All eyes were on the ball. Gideon had taken off on a run just in case. Good thing he did

16

because the ball looked like it was dropping right into the mitt of the other team's player..but it didn't. It bounced off his mitt and Gideon had rounded first and headed to second. The right fielder threw the ball to the second baseman. Their short stop hurried over to cover second just in case.

Gideon was going hard. The ball was over thrown and he headed to third. Their short stop played it well. He snatched up the ball and threw to third. Gideon never looked back. He threw his head back and pumped his arms. There was Eyan at third motioning for him to slide. Down he went with the ball gaining momentum. SAFE. The crowd went wild.

Judah was up to bat. He was the calm in the storm. He kept their team's head in perspective. He stepped up to bat and smiled at the pitcher as if to say, "Okay...I'm ready." Don't be deceived; he was a hot head when you made him mad and he could use that temper to his advantage.

"Strike one!"

Nissa had watched as he stepped back from the plate, shook his shoulders and looked like he was just in need of a little stretch. Swinging the bat he moved back into position. Again, he tipped his head and waited. The pitcher sent another ball, this time high, over the plate.

"Ball one!" Judah had waited so patiently.

Then the wind up, as Judah had eyed the ball and swung. Contact. The ball flew to center field. Gideon scored. The ball was dropped and Judah was on base.

The next batter hit the ball directly to the short stop and ended the inning. The scores put our team ahead by two.

"Now get out there and win this game." Nissa had laughed with Gredin.

As Nissa had watched the young catcher run out on the field, she had been surprised when Eyan walked up to her and patted the top of her head. "Quick thinking Peanut. I couldn't have done it better myself." Her heart had skipped a few beats. Even then she questioned the Lord, *Why is it always like that Lord? I feel such a connection and he treats me like a child.*

God's answer to her had been calming, **Be still my child. Love is patient.**

Nissa always felt such peace when she would feel God's loving spirit. It still amazed her to know the God who was big enough to cause the earth to spin, cared enough to answer her questions. It made her feel loved and gave her a point of center for her world.

He answer to God had been surrender. *God, I will be patient and when I marry Eyan, he will be worth the wait.* She knew in her heart she would wait as long as it took for him to realize he loved her.

While she had been wandering off on a bunny trail with her God, a couple of the youth's girls had come up and stood by her. Looking mischievous, Nissa had asked the girls what they were up to.

"Oh...nothing Miss Nissa." Callie and Quinn had answered.

As she stood by the girls, Nissa had taken that moment to study Eyan's movements; the determined way he stood, so stoic and in control. She had watched as he calmly sent signals to his pitcher and catcher. Eyan's boys were two runs ahead in the top of the ninth. The opposing team's first batter had popped out on the second pitch. Their second batter was looking at a three and two pitch. Eyan tipped his hat and tapped his elbow. His pitcher nodded in understanding. There went the pitch and Nissa could still hear the sound of the crack.

18

It was that moment, you know the one, right after the bat connected with the ball and all seemed quiet and still. All eyes had watched to see the ball go higher and higher riding on the fringe. Would it straighten out or go foul? Was it catchable? Was this the moment everyone had been anxiously waiting to see? Would the game end or continue? The first baseman ran and positioned himself under the ball which had hung in space. Then it slowly began its descent. The second baseman had come over to cover first base. Down...Down the ball glided through the air. With his mitt ready, the young man had reached up to catch the ball when it clipped the tip of his mitt and bounced across the field. His moment for greatness had passed for the time being and he heard Coach Eyan's commanding voice say, "Grab the ball and throw it to first."

Nissa's body had gone through the motions with the young player. She had watched as he quickly scooped up the ball and threw it as his coach had said. It had been a perfect throw and had just beaten the runner to the plate. The second out. They only needed one more.

The third batter stepped up to the plate. Nissa could remember feeling bad for the pressure that was on the young man. His trip to the plate was going to determine if the game was alive or if it had come to the end.

The batter took a swing and missed. Strike one.

Lord, please let him at least hit the ball. But... Then Lord could one of our guys catch it. Thank you! Nissa had giggled at her request sent up to her Father.

Javan threw the pitch and the batter took a great cut at the ball. With all of his might he let that ball feel the power of his swing. The ball soared through the air

19

and dropped right into the mitt of their center fielder. Third out and the game came to an end.

The calm, controlled demeanor of Coach Eyan went right out of the window. He had run onto the field and all of his players were jumping on him as chaos broke out. You would have thought it was the World Series. She had loved watching as he shared their excitement.

Then he gathered himself and sent them single file over to acknowledge the great effort of the other team. There he was calm and stoic again, shaking hands with the opposite team's players and giving them high fives, telling their coaches what a great game it had been and what awesome sportsmanship their players had exhibited. Encouraging and supportive. That was Eyan. That was the man she loved. He was the one who could be completely in control when the time called for it; yet as excited as a little boy at Christmas when given the opportunity. Yes...That was the man she was going to marry...As soon as he realized how much he cared for her. She was standing on this verse from the Lord:

PSALM 20:4
May He give the desire of your heart and
make all your plans succeed.

It had been at that moment Nissa had watched the two girls as they headed onto the field with the water bucket. As they handed it over to some of the guys on the field, Nissa laughed as Eyan was drenched from the falling water. Even after the surprise attack, his excitement had continued.

* * * * * * * * * * * * * * *

Eyan loved watching the youth. There was such

20

a vibrancy to everything they did. Their love for life always amazed him. For as long as he could remember he had this desire in him to work with the youth. He found them to be so moldable. Most young children hadn't had enough world experiences to have their joy stolen from them. Still concerned with building forts and chasing butterflies, they believed the world was good. Eyan realized that as some people grew older they began to be cynical and bitter. They weren't born into this world angry and depressed. He realized children were taught those characteristics. It seemed to depend on their own circumstances, the environment they lived in and the people they lived with, whether they would hang onto the joy of childhood.

Some children lived in such desperate realities they seemed to develop a hard shell around their hearts for protection. As they grew older the shell became harder and harder. It was for those children Eyan's heart cried.

I could have been one of those kids. My dad was taken from me at such an early age and I was left fatherless. Yet, the memories of the time spent with dad were such good memories. I had been blessed with a wonderful mother and a loving home. Because of that, I survived. My life continued to be full of love and my needs were always met. If anything, my dad's dying brought me and my brother closer and created a circle of love that was just smaller. Our mother made sure the circle was only broken for a short period of time. She gave time to grieve. Then she closed the broken hole and completed the circle by replacing our dad with God. She made sure we understood the close relationship God wanted us to have with Him. I could always feel God's presence. My mother had set the example by talking *to God with us. She had taken all of our problems or concerns to Him. She included God in our praises when things were right and always made sure we did too. We grew up understanding our need to depend on Him. I could still hear her cautioning us, "Men will always let you down, not necessarily because they wanted to, just because they live in a fallen world. But...God will never let you down. His direction will always be for your good and His word says, **Never will I leave you; Never will I forsake you.***

So even when our Dad had died, we didn't blame God. We were allowed time to grieve and then we were encouraged to go about the normalcy of life. Our circle was still four. Mom, Brad, myself and God. Our dad was still there with us everyday. We talked about him. We considered how he would have answered us when there were questions; but, ultimately, we learned to go to our Heavenly Father for the final answer.

Yes, they were some of the lucky ones. Since Eyan had begun to work with the youth, he had found not everyone was that fortunate. Too many young men and women had been left alone to figure out life, even when their parents were in the home. They had been raised by TV and video games. Their homes had never felt like a safe place. Drugs, alcohol and a life completely opposite from what God had intended family to look like, had been far too often their example. Many were raised by single parents who loved them, yet struggled with time elements trying to do it all. So many just existed. They lived from day to day where it felt like no one cared.

So Eyan found those kids; or they found him. Like a magnet Eyan literally felt the pull towards them. He knew there was a passion that burned deep inside of them. That passion might be buried. They might not even know it existed. But Eyan knew. He knew God created them to love Him with all of their hearts. So Eyan dug until he found that fertile ground. Once he earned the right to speak into their lives, he started tilling until the ground was ready for the seed to be planted. Then boom...The emptiness they had been carrying was filled with the love of the Heavenly Father. The BIG... BIG...God they had been looking for their whole lives and just didn't know it.

Those kids, were the survivors. They were often deep thinkers. So, for Eyan, it was like peeling an onion. Layer by Layer they stripped away the pain and suffering; removed the burdens carried; freed them of the load that weighed them down. Underneath all of that was this amazing kid that had experienced so much in life and understood so much at an early age. Because of their deep thinking skills, they grasped the love of God easier than someone who had been privileged to experience His love all of their lives. Youth from troubled homes too often had not been told about a God who loved them and wanted nothing but the best for them. They didn't understand they have been given the ability to choose a life of love that could feel and look like joy. Too often they hadn't even considered happiness could be a part of their future. Life had beat them up and Eyan tried to light a spark that gave them hope again.

Eyan loved nothing more than watching as the desperation in them came alive to embrace the idea that they could find a better way. They didn't have to be stuck in the challenges of their past. Their future would be bright and new because God had that plan for them.

Eyan wanted to find them before the world beat them up so bad their hope for a better future was gone. So he looked. Everywhere he went he saw them. He saw them come from all over. Not necessarily from what the world called "bad homes". He had learned that "bad" doesn't always look like "bad". Sometimes "good" was "bad". Because of evil, things have become so twisted.

Eyan's wished people would stop trying to define lives? They were not called to be labelers. Of course that would be Eyan's own word. Their job had been clearly spelled out. We were called to love...Everyone! In fact it was so important to God He made it a commandment when He said that we were to love. He filled the Bible full of those commandments.

John 13:34
A new commandment I give unto you, that you love one another.

John 15:12
This is my commandment, that you love one another, as I have loved you.

I John 4:21
He who loves God loves his brother also.

When Eyan was young he had seen this poem that was written by Ruth Bell Graham. She was the wife of the Evangelist Billy Graham.

HIS BROTHER'S BROTHER
"AM I my brother's keeper?"
No. He was his brother's brother.
Zoos have keepers.
Bees have keepers.
Prisons have keepers.
Only families have brothers.

That poem had stuck with him his whole life. It was never far from his thoughts. It went with him everywhere. You could say it had become his mantra. It was important to him to be his "brother's brother" and he discovered there was a world of family out there in need. So he watched and asked God to send him to places where Eyan would find the broken and those who needed love. He listened for the moments when God would say, *"There Eyan... Over there. He needs you. He's alone. He walks by himself even in a crowd. Go and show him who I am."* Then Eyan would go.

He found himself working with the young men more than the young girls. It was easier for him to relate. However, since Nissa had moved to Hadley, Indiana, Eyan found out that she shared his passion to work with the youth and they had begun to team up. At youth events, Eyan worked with the young men and Nissa would make herself available for the girls. He had to admit they were a pretty powerful team. He liked the way she gently made her way into the girls' circles, especially those who came from broken homes. She could understand their pain and fears. It was a clear example of God taking something that satan had intended for bad and making it good.

If Nissa hadn't walked down the path of separation with her family, she wouldn't have been as effective with the girls whose lives had been tipped upside down. Because of what she had lived through, she could be compassionate and understanding. Plus, she hugged easily. Girls like to be hugged and comforted. Eyan had always struggled with that part of comforting the girls. As a young man, he had to be very careful not to step over a line of appropriateness. Girls needed that physical touch from a daddy. So many of them had no loving daddy in their homes and they were desperate. It was real easy to see when that need wasn't being met by a father. Too many times Eyan had seen those girls go looking for that affection in the arms of young men who weren't trying to meet anyone's needs but their own. So having Nissa working with him had certainly helped in that area. Even though her hugs weren't the same as a daddy's would have been, she could still hug. She was a great listener and girls loved to talk. They were usually very good about pouring out their feelings. Plus, she was a great example for these girls to follow. After walking through Noelle's journey, Nissa had, with Noelle's permission, been able to share the other side of the story. She could share with the girls a story of bad choices that showed them where it could lead. Because of God's goodness, she could literally show them how God could take what satan intended for evil and change it to good. In Noelle's story they could see the actual change.

Nissa stood on this scripture. She believed it was the foundation ground for battle preparation:

Ephesians 6:12-17

For our struggle is not against flesh and blood, but against the rulers, against the authorities, against the powers of this dark world and against the spiritual forces of evil in the heavenly realms.

Therefore, put on the full armor of God, so that when the day of evil comes, you may be able to stand your ground, and after you have done everything, to stand.

Stand firm then, with the belt of truth buckled around your waist, with the breastplate of righteousness in place, and with your feet fitted with the readiness that comes from the gospel of peace.

In addition to all this, take up the shield of faith, with which you can extinguish all the flaming arrows of the evil one. Take the helmet of salvation and the sword of the Spirit, which is the word of God.

Her message to the youth, especially the girls had always been this, "Prepare for battle. Don't let satan find you unaware." She always stressed, "We live in a world of evil where satan always looks for ways to trip us up. He wants to destroy our lives." She wanted them to understand they could determine to stand on the Word of God. They could equip themselves to beat the devil. They could put on the armor of God. They could prepare to be aggressive in the battle. They could be armed with an offensive weapon. "Determine to take control of the battle which will rage against you." She told them, "Decide today, through God, you will be victorious. Remember...God will never leave you or forsake you. You don't fight alone, He will be by your side through the battle."

She would delve into the nitty-gritty where Eyan had never felt comfortable. "Then stand...A girl on her back is never a good thing. Don't look for love from someone else. Love God first and yourself second. Fill your life up with the knowledge of God and when the time comes and you are prepared to be a helpmate, then God will send the person that He created for you. That person will love and respect you because he will understand the special gift God gave to him through you. Get ready to experience a relationship that can only come through sharing the love of the Lord. Don't look to unequally yoke yourself with someone who doesn't know the Lord. That can only bring you pain, suffering and division. Wait on the Lord. Follow His direction and not your own. When we wait for His perfect timing, we find He has only the best for us; but it's when we become totally absorbed in asserting our own wants and needs we lose the ability to follow and serve Him. Don't become your own worst enemy. Satan will use you to destroy you if you let him. Love God, love yourself and love others through Him."

I love the way the girls always listened so carefully to what Nissa has to say. She speaks with passion and humor. She makes hard areas to travel seem easy and comfortable and the girls just seem to understand.

Yes God, Eyan would think, *Nissa was a good addition to the youth team. Thanks for sending her our way.*

Chapter Three

I CORINTHIANS 13

3. If I give all I possess to the poor and surrender my body to the flames, but have not love, I gain nothing

NOELLE AFFECTIONATELY STROKED BABY EMMA'S soft hair as she slowly breathed air in and then out. She marveled at the perfect creation that lay sleeping so angelically on the bed beside her. Noelle couldn't imagine a day without her sweet explorations and curiosity. Watching her grow and develop was a blessing beyond words for her and Brad.

To think it had only been a year and a half ago. That night had sealed Noelle's already changing life. She had not even had time to accept that the daddy who had always been her protector had left her and her family. Without even an opportunity to plead her case he was gone. Nothing remained except the hand written letter that turned their world upside down. Then off to college with all of the brokenness tucked deep inside, she began creating a life for herself that included parties and drinking. The noise of that world dulled the hurt that was always present. Or so she thought, until the night of the fraternity party when she was drugged and date raped. That night a total stranger violated all she had left. She had not escaped from the pain of that when she found out she was carrying her violator's baby.

Noelle's only thought from that moment on was to run away to protect her family. She had to find a way to get rid of the "mass of cells" that had taken residence inside of her. The pregnancy clinic had told her she could have an abortion because it wasn't really a baby yet. No one had to know. Just like that her problem would be gone. She was desperate and full of anger and rage. Making a choice to take care of her problem herself, she had run away. She didn't even care where, as long as there was a clinic that could take this invader out of her body.

Now lying here with the perfection of that "mass of cells", she couldn't help but thank God continually for loving her enough to protect her from herself. She thought of the millions of women who believed the lie and now lived with the reality of that lost life. Noelle threw up a quick prayer asking God to put someone in their lives to help them understand He had healing in His love for them. She wanted those broken lives to know that only through His love could they find true peace and forgiveness.

The crazy part of this story was He directed her even when she didn't understand about His direction. She didn't know He loved her that much. But He did, and she was thankful everyday for the life that she had. Watching Emma grow and seeing the wonder in her, Noelle could not imagine a day without her or the love of the man who followed God's direction for his life.

Brad Conroy, the extraordinary man she would spend the rest of her life with, the man who was the most amazing father to their daughter. Brad was the true definition of God's love. His love empowered her as they built an intimate relationship with each other, while serving others. Because they shared God's genuine love, neither of them were looking to have their own needs met. That kind of love can only begin with a foundation on Jesus Christ.

Noelle had once heard it described by a wise southern pastor who said, "When we are saved, God plants His love there and as we grow and mature our love grows, we have to learn to express it. With His love, we are a fountain full of love and He wants our fountain to overflow. We all start selfish and then as we grow into

Him, the love starts to flow. For the love to grow, we have to be attached to the source. The only true, genuine love is born of God."

Brad was the best at genuine love; he exhibited the unselfish, sacrificial giving of himself daily. He expected nothing back and he wasn't looking for anything for himself. He learned that from his mother. Angelina loved to serve others. She put them above herself. It had just come natural for this family to think of someone else first.

Noelle's heart filled with an overflowing of love every time she thought of them and what they have done for her and her family. They were lost and beyond sad. It wasn't until the Conroys offered them Jesus they began to see hope again. Noelle began to see that God satisfies the hungers and desires of our heart, everyone of them. He even changed her thinking. She used to think love originated in the brain. Now she knows it starts in the heart. Her love thoughts come from her heart.

She thought about the time when her family was going through the loss of her father. That was such a dark time for each of them. People were cruel. Everyday was especially hard for her and her sisters. The very kids they thought were their friends were so quick to turn their backs on them. Noelle, Nissa and Anaya felt alone and broken. They felt like everyone was talking about them when they couldn't possibly understand what had happened to their family. She could still remember the feelings of separation and anger. There were so many emotions she couldn't process at that time because of the lack of knowledge of the Heavenly Father and His love. When she found the Conroy family, they represented the look of God's genuine love. They built her self-worth and taught her through God she could feel complete again.

33

She learned that God's love, real love, allowed her to be kind when misjudged and enabled her to forgive those who had wronged her...Including her earthly father.

Now, here she was, married to the most wonderful man who loved her with all of his being. Everyday was a new adventure for Brad, Noelle and little Miss Emma Rae.

Thank you Father for Your love that surpasses all understanding. And for Your promise to never leave me or desert me. You are always faithful to complete all of Your promises and I am truly blessed.

Snuggling closer to the little one beside her Noelle's eyes slowly drifted shut and she enjoyed these moments that she knew would be over in a blink of an eye.

****

Coming from the barn, Brad had entered the room and the vision before him had taken his breath away. There on the bed, cuddled together and wrapped in the arms of love, had laid his wife and child, as they slept ever so peacefully. Brad still could feel his chest tighten and the joy that had flowed through him couldn't be put into words. Blessed. That's all...Just blessed.

He had quietly moved over next to the woman who shared his life and his bed. Her arm had been gently draped over Emma in a protective manner. There was no place he would rather be than laying next to them.

He thought back over the last couple of years. Back in time to the day when God dropped a scared and sad little woman child into his life. Even now he still remembered those protective feelings that had welled up inside of him that day; feelings he hadn't been able to define and hadn't understood. As he stood over her now, those same feelings began all over again. He would lay down his life for her; fight an army to keep her safe. Then looking at Emma, his Emma, he marveled at how it could be possible, as even stronger feelings took hold of his heart. This was his family; the family God had given him. He felt the strong responsibility that had been placed on his shoulders not only to see to their every day needs; but to be their spiritual leader. To lead them in Godly ways and encourage them in the Lord. Brad had done what seemed natural to him...He prayed.

Father, I am just a man, a mere mortal, called to do a heavy task. Though I know You never ask us to feel burdened; yet, the job seems to important to fail. Help me to do what You have called me to do. Help me to be a great husband and father. Help me to teach them You and to be obedient to fill them with the vastness of Your word.

He carefully lowered himself onto the bed turning as he moved and Noelle's eyes had opened. She smiled as she saw him coming.

"Shhhhhh." He had signaled with his finger pressed against his lips.

As she nodded her head, she had given him a smile letting him know she was glad to see him. As he cuddled closer, he remembered the fresh scent smell of her hair as it tickled his nose. He had buried his face into the soft curve of her neck and nuzzled her possessively. This was the woman God had created just for him and he marveled everyday at the joy of his life.

For this flash in time, they had laid quietly, softly, enjoying their moment of intimacy. They rested while Emma napped, knowing that when she woke the energy she exuded would require all of their attention.

Noelle, had been content for this moment as she relaxed between the two bodies that made up her world. The world that God had built.

Chapter Four

I CORINTHIANS 13

4. Love is patient, love is kind.

It does not envy,

it does not boast, it is not proud.

DAYS HAD GONE BY SINCE MICHAEL'S TRIP TO THE adult care facility where his aunt lived. However, his aunt was not what haunted his thoughts. *What do I do about the man in the end room?*

The question was always there. Night and day he revisited his options. There was a constant tug of what direction he should take. Nothing of what he had seen that night made sense. Michael had called the facility several days after he saw Gale lying in the bed helpless with tubes hooked to machines.

"Tender Care Adult Home", the voice on the other end of the phone had answered.

Michael paused unsure of what to say next. Nothing he had practiced seemed right. "Yes...I'm calling about your resident in Room 126. It's the suite on the end of the north hallway. Gale...Gale Smith. I'm wondering if I could speak with him?"

Silence filled the space between them.

Breaking that awkward moment the voice answered, "May I ask who is calling?"

"Oh...Is he not taking calls?"

"Well...Yes...I mean..."

The voice trailed off unsure about how to answer Michael's questions. "If this is an inconvenient time, I could call back at his convenience."

"Perhaps that would be better. In fact why don't I have you call back tomorrow and talk with our director. She'll be of more assistance than I have been. Call any time between 8:00 a.m. and 5:00 p.m. Ask to talk with Becky. Thank you and have a good evening."

She practically hung up on him. It was clear

she didn't want to be responsible for giving away any information. Everything about the conversation was uncomfortable, the tone of her voice, her unsure manner, the very way she abruptly hung up without giving Michael a chance to question her any further. All of this, added together with what Michael had seen that night, left this sick feeling in the pit of his stomach. Tomorrow he would call back. Hopefully he would get the answers he so desperately needed. Then he'd have to make more decisions.

His mind had been running through all of the scenarios he could think of. Car accident? Attack? Nervous break down?

It had never made sense. There were no answers. What could have caused the man he knew to do what he did? Why would he leave his wife and daughters whom he certainly seemed to adore? Now this. There had to be answers that would allow Michael a way to explain what he had seen. Once he had answers, then he would decide what to do with his new-found information.

Tomorrow wouldn't get here soon enough.

****

Gale heard the knock on the door. The disease had left him his hearing...So far. He tried to raise a hand that flailed wildly in the air as he attempted to signal, "Come in."

Through the doorway walked a big man, tall in stature and personality, in a bright aqua shirt with a wild tie picking up the color of the shirt. Smiling, Pastor Dan walked over to the bed, grabbed a chair and sat down. "May I?"

The man in the bed blinked, "Yes."

40

Reaching over Pastor Dan grabbed the trembling hand and enfolded it in the monstrous patties that finished off the span of his long arms. "Good to see you Gale. I missed our visits last week. Remember I told you I had to leave town to visit a newborn niece who didn't enter this world at the top of her game."

Gale thought of those three moments when his own girls were born and the joy they brought into his life. He motioned with his eyebrows a question of concern to the man who had become a close friend.

Dan answered, "She's holding her own for the moment. However, she could use a lot of extra prayers. She got a little anxious and jumped the gun. Should have stayed and cooked a little longer. Wasn't quite ready. She's very tiny. Use some of your praying time for her. I would appreciate that my friend and I am sure her parents would also. Her name is Avery. Quite a pretty baby and a strong little fighter. Amazing what God can do in a short time. She was born at 26 weeks. Her lungs were not quite ready. She's in a good hospital; but you and I both know that prayers are her best line of defense. Her mother, Else, is my niece; my brother's daughter. The family is pretty distraught. It has been a scary time for them. They went from the excitement of a first grandchild to the unknown of the future."

Standing he walked to a white board that was on the wall across from Gale's bed. Taking a piece of chalk Pastor wrote on the board. "I will add their names to your prayer list so you can remember them when you're praying. It's always a comfort for me to know I have a warrior joining me in prayer. Our list is getting quite lengthy. Let's review."

Pastor Dan went over each name and gave Gale updates. He was sad to remove two of the people from

41

the list. "Gale, Aaron is at peace. He went home to be with his Lord last week surrounded by the people who loved him. We prayed him right into heaven and out of his pain. He left us while I was gone; but I talked with the family as soon as I returned and they were very thankful for all of our prayers. It was a comfortable passing. Eighty-six years is a ripe old age. He was ready."

"And here is good news...The young lady who was here rehabilitating from the car accident has been released and is now at home continuing her recovery. I'm thankful we could be of service to her and her family."

Dan continued to give updates on the list of names without faces for Gale. Pastor understood the need for everyone to be useful. It was especially important for someone in Gale's condition. His mind was sharp as a tack; while his body failed him miserably.

"I can't stress again the importance of the prayer job that you and I do together. God says where two or more are gathered, there He will be also. When we join our prayers together, they become so much more effective." Turning to face his friend in the bed he said, "Thank you for partnering with me in this role. It really does make a difference."

Gale moved his eyes and signaled with a smile that he was glad to be able to help and would certainly pray for little Avery. He attempted to nod his head to let his friend know he was sorry for him and his family.

Pastor marveled at the ability Gale had to express himself with his eyes. The eye movements were so minute, yet could say so much.

Pastor Dan remembered the times at the beginning of their relationship when he wouldn't have been able to say those words to Gale without being ready to go to war himself. When he first met Gale, he was scared, frustrated; but mostly he was angry. There wasn't a thought for God unless it was in bitterness. Gale was still able to use his vocal cords to talk. He would say, "If there was a God, I wouldn't be in this place. If there was a God, why would he do this to me? No...Don't give me that God talk...I don't want to hear it."

Pastor had been patient. Day after day he would stop by and have conversation with Gale that always ended the same way. Pastor Dan, before leaving would say, "Gale, are you ready to talk to me about God?"

Gale would say, "Leave that God talk at the door."

Laughing, Pastor would leave answering on his way out, "Now you know I can't do that. I'll be back."

And he did come back day after day. Always a story to tell with a twist about the God that Pastor Dan loved so much. Gale listened out of politeness...And boredom.

It was very lonely living in the small quarters that now encompassed his world. Oh, he had trips down the hall to therapy and for a while he had gone to the social room where many of his fellow residents ate everyday. The crowd hadn't been very lively. Most of them 80 or older. He hadn't fit in.

As he began to lose control over the parts that made him who he was, he stopped going. The staff tried to encourage him in the beginning to get out and surround himself with others. Soon even they gave up as he lost the ability to talk and couldn't control his flailing appendages. He was sure it just became easier for them. Add the fact that they probably felt sorry for him. Why not? He did.

Pastor Dan had been there for all of the emotional changes that were happening to Gale. As this ridiculous

43

disease quickly moved to capture all that it could, the two men moved closer together.

Pastor Dan knew from what Gale had shared with him that his life had looked so much different. Gale had been a man in control of his situation; living a life of influence. Gale had shared a few pictures of his past life with Dan. There had been a beautiful wife, three adoring daughters; he had the world in his grasp. Success, love, money...He had it all. Until one day when it all came crashing down by the words of a doctor, "You have ALS, Amyotrophic Lateral Sclerosis, Lou Gehrig's Disease. It's a disease of the nerve cells in the brain and spinal cord that control voluntary muscle movement. It's a motor neuron disease."

It was a moment in time that Gale couldn't change. As much as he tried to forget what he had been told the signs began to surface. It became harder and harder for him to hide them from Genie. Gale reached a point where he had to have more information. That day in the doctor's office, he had refused to hear anything past his diagnosis.

"Don't tell me that Doc. I don't believe you. No one in my family has ever had anything like this and I won't either. You must be wrong. I refuse for you to be right." He left that day and was never going back there again.

A year later he returned to the same doctor and said, "Okay, tell me more about this ALS."

This was what he heard. The disease frequently began in your hands, feet or limbs. It then spread to other parts of your body. As the disease advanced, the muscles would become progressively weaker until they were paralyzed. It eventually affected chewing, swallowing, speaking and breathing.

44

Early signs may be difficulty lifting the front part of your feet and toes. There may be weakness in your legs, feet and toes. Hand weakness or clumsiness. Slurring of speech or trouble swallowing. There may be muscle cramps and twitching in the arms, shoulders, and tongue. As the disease progressed, there was usually a need for a feeding tube directly in the stomach. Choking was a common complication. Loss of weight and aspiration could become problems. Pneumonia, lung failure, loss of speech. Caring for yourself would become difficult. Eventually there would be a need for assistance with breathing from machines; usually beginning just at night and progressing to constant mechanical ventilation.

Gale stopped the doctor, "Is there any good news? Can you give me any hope?"

"I'm afraid not."

"And the prognosis is?" Gale needed to know what he was facing.

"People lose the ability to function and care for themselves. Death often occurs within three to five years from diagnosis. One in four patients survive for more than five years."

"So let me make sure I've got this. I am going to become an invalid, requiring constant care and then I'm going to die. There is nothing that can be done to stop any of this from happening. I'm going to die."

"That's correct." The doctor gave a few minutes of processing time and then said, "I'm sorry."

Gale left that day realizing his future was not one he would want for his worst enemy and especially not the family he loved so much. From that day he began to work on a plan. He realized he was already a year down. Time was not going to be his friend. He found an attorney and began putting his financial life in order so

Genie and the girls would be taken care of and not have to want for anything.

The hardest part of his plan was finding a way to walk out of their lives so they would not come looking for him. It had to be clean. He realized it would hurt them; but watching him die a crazy death had to be worse for them. So he did what he felt was right. After another year of organization and loving them as much as he could, he realized the time had come. If he was going to leave it had to be soon. The symptoms were advancing and if he didn't leave, Genie was going to see there was a problem.

He devised his plan to write a letter explaining he had found another woman that he couldn't live without. He left them with the attorney's information and told them that everything would be taken care of through him. There were divorce papers he had already signed. The house was theirs and they would receive money monthly. All contact would go through the attorney. And then he was gone.

After hearing his story, Pastor Dan assured Gale he had made a wrong decision. If his family loved him as much as he said, they had some rights in this story too. One day he told him, "Gale their rights go right up to the very end of your life."

"No Pastor. I'm at peace with my decisions."

"Yes you are...But are they?"

"What do you mean?"

"Did you leave them a way to find any peace in their life after you closed the door?"

"I don't understand."

"Exactly. And neither do they. You left them with no way to find closure. Think about it. You may have opened a whole new Pandora's box. They may be

46

stuck with feelings they're going to have to live with for the rest of their lives."

Pastor Dan had never made any leeway towards changing Gale's mind about contacting his family. This was his life now. He had resolved himself to living in this facility until he died. His prayer now was that it would happen quickly.

So far the disease was advancing as predicted. The doctors weren't sure why his trembling had become so violent. The one thing they were sure about, it wouldn't last. He would lose that too. They assured him he would see the day when nothing would move. His limbs would quit working all together. His muscles, that once were strong enough to swing a golf club, throw his girls into the air as they giggled with glee, or gently caress the woman whom he adored, would desert him.

Now he found humor in the thought that he embraced the trembling. At least it was something. *What would it be like when nothing moved any more?* That same thought ran through his mind daily.

The last six months had seen the addition of a tracheotomy. His breathing tube attached to that and the ventilator helped bring him life sustaining air. But those eyes said so much in a twitch or blink. Pastor Dan often thought about all of the people he knew who could blabber on and on and never say anything. Here was a man who couldn't say a word with his mouth, yet could portray sentences with his eyes. He liked to think of it as a gift. Often he would say, "Gale, don't forget to thank God for the gift of your eyes. Not everyone can do what you do."

One day Pastor Dan said to him, "I've often heard it preached the eyes are the window to the soul. Yours are able to reach into someone's else's soul. God knew

47

they were exactly what you were going to need."

Pastor Dan was thankful they were past the anger and had moved into a very comfortable relationship where he would freely talk to Gale about the Lord who loved him so much that He had laid down His life for him. That same God was with him everyday...Even the hard days.

While he was gone, Pastor Dan had made a decision. The times he had attempted to talk to Gale about his past and his family, Gale had shut down and made it clear he wasn't going to have that conversation. Pastor Dan wouldn't live with that; however, he didn't know how to maneuver around it. He made a decision and had already began to put it into practice. Today he was going to share it with Gale. He wasn't sure how it was going to go over. What he did know was that there was family somewhere and they had the right to know how Gale was. Though Pastor Dan would not break the confidence they shared, he knew someone who *"is able to do immeasurably more than all we ask or imagine, according to His power that is at work within us."* Knowing this, Dan decided to go to work. Everyday he began to pray fervently asking God to make a way to reunite Gale and his family. His request was for sooner than later. Though none of us know how long we have, Dan was watching this man lose more all the time. Pastor Dan knew Gale's time was running out.

"Gale...I made a decision while I was gone and I've already put it into actions. It involves you and I'm not sure how happy you're going to be with me. But I'm sure it's the right thing. If God doesn't agree with me, then I guess nothing will change. If He does, then I'm praying your life changes immediately."

Gale's eyes said he wasn't sure about what

Dan was doing. In fact they hardened just a bit with skepticism.

Pastor Dan pressed on. "While I was traveling in the car, God and I had discussion about the fact that you are here by yourself."

Instantly Gale's eyes narrowed and he glared. At least Pastor Dan knew he was glaring at him, an example of just how truly expressive those eyes could be.

"I've asked God to reunite you with your family; whoever and wherever they are."

Gale's arms began to flair.

"Now calm down buddy. Don't be mad at me. If God wants to send your family, He'll make a way for all of you. He'll make it work out. If it isn't a good idea, then He won't. It's just that simple. Besides...It's out of both of our hands. The prayers have been thrown out there. Now it's up to God."

Pastor Dan didn't say anything else for a while. He just let it soak in. He had known going into this conversation just how angry Gale was going to be. He also knew, dying alone is a terrible way to go. But for a Christian, walking into the arms of Jesus with those you love surrounding you, can be a beautiful, healing moment. As the house pastor, Dan knew he had to do something or he wouldn't be able to live with himself. He had been at bedsides of those who were escorted to the gate and into the arms of their loving Savior and those who went alone. He didn't want that to be the way he remembered Gale.

He said, "This may be a selfish decision on my part and if it is then God will deal with the situation correctly; but I care enough about you that I don't want you to face death by yourself. There...That's the truth. I care about you!"

49

What could Gale say to Pastor's finish. Besides what was going to happen now. Time was running out and he had covered all of his bases. He certainly didn't want to be mad at the only friend he had left.

Gale gave Dan a look that surrendered but left no doubt that this conversation was over.

Pastor Dan took the hint and for the rest of their visit they talked about Dan's trip away and the things he saw while he was gone.

In Pastor Dan's mind though, he prayed as hard as he had ever prayed for his friend.

****

Michael, called back the next day and asked to talk to Becky, the Director of the facility.

"Whom shall I say is calling?" He was asked.

"Just tell her I am calling in reference to Gale Smith."

Silence fell over their conversation for seconds. "One moment please." Michael again felt the unease of yesterday's conversation. *Something was not kosher,* he thought to himself.

Michael waited for such a long time he began to wonder if they had disconnected his call. Then he heard, "Good afternoon, this is Becky Laird. I am the Director of Tender Care Adult Home. A message was relayed to me that you are looking for information about someone. Is that correct Mr. Dunn?"

Vague...Very vague. Michael thought, *the mystery continues.* "Yes, my name is Michael Dunn. I am a friend of Gale Smith and I'm interested in helping him in anyway I can. I'm just trying to find out what that help would look like."

"Mr. Dunn, I'm afraid I'm not going to be able to assist you. It's our policy not to divulge any information about our clients here at the home."

"Look...I am the Dean of Students at the University so I am well aware of the violation of privacy. I was also close enough to the situation with Mr. Smith and his family that I feel an obligation to rectify a very wrong situation. I simply would like to proceed in a way that would be beneficial to Gale and not cause him more distress. If you can't help me, then I certainly understand your position. Just know I'm still going to move forward." He paused giving her time to process all he had just said.

"Mr. Dunn, why don't I transfer your call to our resident Pastor. Perhaps Pastor Dan can assist you in a more appropriate way."

"I would appreciate that very much. And... Thank you. Michael hadn't intended to pull the "I'm a very important person" card; but desperate situations required desperate moves. Right now he was willing to do whatever it took.

As he waited he thought to himself, *now what?*

The phone rang three times as Michael waited on pins and needles. He knew he was about to open up a huge sore. He also knew he had no choice.

"Pastor Dan here. How can I serve you?"

Here we go. "Good afternoon. My name is Michael Dunn, I'm the Dean of Students at the university and also a long time friend of a resident in your facility."

Pastor was used to getting calls like these. Family and friends often called and asked him to check in on some family member who was a new patient here at the home. Or maybe someone was going to celebrate a birthday and family was looking for information and assistance. He was always more than willing to do just that. In fact it was his job, which he loved very much.

"Hi Michael. What's the name of your friend?" Pastor Dan grabbed a sticky note so he would have a visual reminder.

"Gale Smith."

Silence. Michael knew he had just changed the game.

"Excuse me? Could you repeat the name one more time?"

"Certainly...Gale Smith."

"Praise God for answered prayers."

"I'm sorry. What do you mean?"

"God has just used you to answer my prayers. I'm so thankful we're going to have this opportunity to talk before you see Gale. You see, I started praying God would reunite this man with his family wherever they may be. You, Michael, will be the vessel God is going to use to make that happen. I, for one, am very thankful for your call today." He paused for a moment and taking a deep breath he continued. "As Gale's pastor, you understand I can't divulge any personal information. However, I certainly can listen to anything you would like to tell me that would help this situation. That is, if you're in agreement that reuniting his family is a good thing and you're on board with that plan.

"Let me tell you what I know. Maybe then we can make sense of this situation for both of us."

"Perfect."

"I was a long time friend of both Gale and his lovely wife, Genie. Together they had three beautiful daughters and a great life. Then, over two years ago, Gale left a letter telling them he had found a new love and he couldn't live without her. He told them he was

52

leaving and he left them set up financially. Everything was handled through an attorney. They never saw Gale again. They were never given the opportunity to have discussion with him. He closed the door tight."

"The timing certainly seems right. I have known Gale for about two years. Am I to assume that you know where he is now?"

"My aunt is a resident at your facility. I was there to visit her when I got turned around and found myself at the opposite end of the hall. She's at the other end of the hallway. I saw him lying in his bed. Needless to say...I was shocked beyond belief. I left that night without saying anything to anyone. I needed some processing time. Now I'm trying to decide how to proceed in the best manner for everyone involved."

"I see. Michael, are you in contact with his family still? Would they want to know about his situation if there was a way?"

"Genie came to work for me as my Administrative Assistant after Gale left. I know them very well and I can assure you they would want to know. They would not want him here by himself. However, knowing Gale, I'm also assuming he left to protect them from what's coming."

There was a pause in the conversation.

Michael continued, "Am I to assume you are not going to divulge any personal information to me; even though I'm trying to help?"

"You are correct. You, of all people, understand the laws of personal information."

"From what I saw, I'm going to assume he is dying."

"You may assume whatever you'd like Michael. I'm sorry you found your friend in such a way. It must

53

have been very difficult for you. As it will be for his wife and daughters. Knowing Gale as I now do, this is going to be very difficult for him also."

"How do I proceed."

"Well just a few days ago I had a conversation with him. I told him I was asking God to intervene and bring him and his family together again. He wasn't very happy with me. I just told him it was in God's hands to do as He pleased. Now Gale will just have to accept it pleased God to use you. However, I would like to be with you when you see him. I'm assuming you do plan to come to see him?" Pastor Dan asked the question realizing Michael hadn't said anything about coming again.

"Yes. I plan on coming. I also plan on contacting Genie and letting her know what I've discovered. I believe she has a right to know."

"Will you do this for me? Will you ask her to wait until you have the whole story. I can't give that to you. We'll have to let Gale give permission for you to know. I want to protect his privacy as much as I can without leaving him alone in his time of trial. Does she live in this area?"

"No. She and the girls have moved to Indiana. This will come as quite a shock for her also. And...Yes, I do understand about Gale's privacy. I will tell exactly what has happened up to this point and I will let her know I will call her after I have visited tomorrow. Will that work with your schedule? I could be there around 5:00 p.m."

"Yes...That would be perfect. I will anticipate your visit. Michael, I will also be praying for the right words for you to use as you tell Mrs. Smith. God bless you for your call. Good day."

Michael sat looking at the phone after he had hung up. He was going to wait for that prayer to find its way to God. He was in need of some divine assistance with the next conversation he was about to have. He anticipated there would be no pleasure in opening this door for Genie and the girls.

Chapter Five

I CORINTHIANS 13

5. It is not rude, it is not self-seeking, it is not easily angered, it keeps no record of wrongs.

MICHAEL PLAYED OVER AND OVER THE conversation he just had with Genie. There had been no easy way to say what he had to say. How do you tell someone who had been through what she and the girls had that the man they loved hadn't left them for another life as they had been told. He left them so he could die alone.

He knew exactly what Gale was thinking. He was trying to protect them from what was coming. He didn't want them to have to take care of him and watch him slip away. He was being noble.

Who was Michael to tell him what he had done wasn't the right thing. Michael didn't know what he would have done had he been placed in the same situation.

His mind played over and over what he would say to Gale. Nothing seemed to be appropriate.

Michael was glad he had already called Genie. Now, no mater what Gale said, Genie knew and it couldn't be taken back.

Michael had tried to be gentle, if there was a gentle way to say what had to be said. At first Genie had been so excited to hear from him. They had only talked a few times since she had moved away. He had intended to stay in closer contact, but life had slipped away. And now here he was.

In his mind he replayed his conversation with Genie. "I'm afraid I have some news to share with you. I'm not sure how you're going to feel about it. I came face to face with a truth I couldn't keep from you."

"Michael, you're being very mysterious. My

goodness, you're bordering on frightening me."

"I'm sorry Genie. I just don't know how to say this. I've practiced it every way I can imagine and nothing seems right."

"Please...Just say it."

"Okay...I was at the adult home to visit my aunt. She's a resident there. I thought I was headed in the right direction. But I had made a wrong turn. Maybe in God's eyes it was the right turn. I hope so. I hope He is leading this."

"Michael...Please?"

"Right. I was in the wrong hallway and it brought me to the room at the opposite end of the building. I looked into the room and there, in the bed, was...was a...was...I'm so sorry Genie...It was Gale."

A lifetime passed in the silence...

"Gale?"

"Yes."

"In an adult care facility?"

"Yes."

"Why? How?"

"He apparently has a debilitating condition."

"What do you mean?" The shock in her voice was heart breaking for him.

"I think he's dying."

"What?" Now she was crying.

"I don't know much yet. He doesn't know I know. I've talked with the resident Pastor. Pastor Dan was as helpful as he could be without violating Gale's privacy. However, he's been asking God to intervene and help connect Gale back with his family."

"I don't understand."

"I know...This must be so much for you to absorb. I'm headed there right now. I'll be going to see him with

58

Pastor Dan. I get the feeling He doesn't think I'm going to be well received. I'll call you as soon as I leave the home. In the mean time, why don't you pray. Prayer has been what started all of this. Let's continue to let God lead. Genie, again I am so sorry. This isn't the way I would have wanted to give you this kind of information."

"No...Don't be sorry. I wouldn't have ever known if you hadn't called. Thank you so much. I will pray and I will be waiting desperately for your call. Thank you again. I am grateful. God be with you."

"Thank you Genie. This has been hard for me. I can't imagine what you're thinking."

"Honestly, Michael, I'm not even sure what I'm thinking yet. We'll know more soon. Right?"

"Yes, as soon as I can call I will."

Michael had felt a sense of relief having finished the conversation with Genie. Now if he only knew what waited ahead for him. He couldn't help but wonder... Would he be welcomed?"

****

Genie sat down as she stared at the phone. Never in a million years would she have anticipated a conversation like the one she and Michael just had.

A part of her wanted to think it was just a prank. She had known Michael far too long to even harbor a thought like that. No, coming from Michael she knew everything he had just said was true.

What did it mean? The man whom she had loved, who had broken her heart and let her think he didn't love her any more was dying. Genie didn't want to believe he had staged all of this to protect her and the girls from his death. Was his death going to be that horrendous they would need to be protected from it. Wasn't death just a part of living. Isn't that what they said in the wedding vows, 'until death do them part'. Not this. Not separation and then death all alone.

Genie did the only thing she knew to do, she began to pray.

Father, what are the words I should say at a time like this. Be with us. Be with Michael. Be with Gale. Be with our girls. We need You. Only You can make sense of a situation like this. Help us all to practice the traits that are Yours. Help us to love as You love. Help us to forgive as You forgive. Give us compassion and helps us to think of others instead of ourselves. Father, You have carried me in times of storm. Please keep me focused on You. Help me to walk on the water and not be afraid. Keep my eyes focused on You and not on the waves. Don't let them upset my footing. Help me not to falter. I trust You. AMEN.

Oh...And Father, be with Gale and help him to be receptive to Michael. Let him know we would want to be with him. Remove any prideful spirit in him that would keep us at a distance. Remove any shame he may be feeling about the decisions he made. Let him feel my love. Help him to know I have never stopped loving him. I'm asking for a softened heart towards us. Reunite our family...For whatever time we have left. AMEN.

Genie sat in silence. Her mind was too confused to think.

Be still and know that I am God.

Her spirit heard His voice and was thankful for His assurance. Only He could make everything right. She was going to trust Him.

Genie thought back to the day Emma came home from the hospital. She remembered the flowers that were delivered to Noelle with the note signed from her dad. He knew she had the baby. He sent her words of love. He must have been following them all of this time. But how? Then she realized...It doesn't really matter. What mattered was he loved them and had spent this time all alone dealing with whatever it was that was taking his life. He had already missed so many moments he would have loved being a part of. Then the questions came. *How many more moments would he miss? How long do they have to show him their love?* Genie knew what her answer would be. She loved him from the beginning and she would love him to the end.

What about the girls? They had been able to forgive him for the pain he put them through. How would she tell them this? So many thoughts were raging through her mind. This was the father they had worked at forgiving. Now they would find out he had loved them all along and his leaving had been to protect them.

Oh Father...This is going to be so hard.

Nothing is impossible for those who love the Lord. Be strong and courageous. My promises are forever...They are yes and amen.

****

Michael arrived at the home more than an hour early. He wanted to spend some time with his aunt before he met with Pastor Dan. After all, he hadn't seen her the day he had stumbled into the reality that Gale was at the home. His mother was still pushing for him to visit. He couldn't tell her what had happened the night he had gone.

After a nice visit with Aunt Denise, the time had come. Here he was knocking on Pastor Dan's door. He could feel the perspiration under his shirt.

"Come in." He heard from the other side of the door. Turning the knob, he pushed the door forward knowing there would be no going back.

The room was very orderly. It smelled of something earthy, which matched the man who sat behind the large mahogany desk. Pastor Dan stood and came with an extended hand. Michael noticed a firm grip, very welcoming. What you couldn't miss was a large smile, almost impish in nature. He was sure he was looking at a man who could be a real jokester.

"Good evening Mr. Dunn. I was anxious to see what a vessel of God was going to look like today." Pastor Dan was pumping his hand with enthusiasm. It had a calming rhythm.

"Please call me Michael. To be honest with you I'm feeling very unsure and anxious. I'm not sure how to respond under the circumstances. There are a lot of emotions surging through me right now."

"Maybe we can talk for a moment and I can help you sort them out." Motioning towards the chairs in front of his desk they both sat down. With Pastor Dan facing him, Michael felt even more anxious.

"I don't even know where to start. This has all knocked me for a loop." Michael offered.

Pastor nodded as if he totally understood, "Why don't you start by telling me a little about your relationship with the man at the end of the hallway."

"Well...We were friends, good friends, golfing buddies. We shared dreams and ambitions. Our families found ourselves together often at business engagements and community service. We ran in the same circles of friends and acquaintances. His wife and mine organized many events and fund raisers together. Genie's a wonderful woman and after he left his family, she was devastated. They were the most unlikely couple to end up like this...Whatever this is. Genie had always been a stay at home wife and mother. When Gale left she applied for a job as my administrative assistant. I snatched her up without hesitation and she didn't let me down. Then over a year ago, she sold the home Gale had left her and the girls to a professor who came from Indiana University. She bought the professor's home in Indiana and moved there for a fresh start. From what she said, she never had any answers about what went wrong. It left her heart broken; yet, she did what she had to do to make things as easy for the girls as she could. As I alluded to, she's an amazing woman and she deserved to be treated better than this."

"What do you think this looks like?"

"I'm not sure. My mind has replayed the picture of that night over and over again. I can only assume something happened to Gale that brought him to this situation." Michael shook his head.

"As you know Michael, I can't share his personal information with you. I do hope when the two of you meet again, he will do that. What I would like you to know is that I began praying God would somehow reunite him with his family. You are, I believe, the answer to that prayer. I can also ask you to prepare yourself...He may not respond the way you would like. By that I mean he may not be welcoming. I beg of you to be patient. He needs you. Whether he's willing to admit it or not.

He continued, "Michael, are you a praying man?"

"Yes Pastor, I'm a believer. I've been talking to God a lot these last few days."

"Then would it be all right if we were to pray together for God to go before us as we go to meet your friend?" Pastor used the word "friend" to remind Michael of their past.

"Yes...Certainly." Michael bowed his head.

Pastor Dan started to pray.

Heavenly Father, we come to You with thankful hearts that You have answered my prayers so quickly. I thank You for Michael, this friend of Gale's who has been thrust into such a sad situation. As we go to visit with Gale, Father we ask You go before us and prepare the way. Prepare Gale's heart to be accepting of the man who comes with compassion and concern. Give Michael the ability to understand and Gale the ability to physically explain. Father, Your ways are not our ways. Help us to understand when the path seems so tumultuous. We trust You to meet all of the needs of those involved and we pray for Genie and her girls and ask You be with them as they wait for You to move. To You be the glory. AMEN.

"Amen." Michael echoed.

"Are you ready?" Pastor asked as he stood.

"As ready as I will ever be." Michael responded as the two men headed for the door.

****

Gale had already been through his evening routines. He liked to start early. It was always more rushed as the night moved closer to shift change. He required so much assistance. It was just easier on him if he got a jump start on his protocol. Although it did leave him with a lot of time to be laying on his back in bed. The evening staff would come in and turn him part way through the night. Bed sores were always a problem for someone in his condition.

Tonight he was uneasy and he knew why. Pastor

Dan hadn't been by to see him during the day. He always tried to stop in even if it was just for a few minutes. Ever since he had told him how he was praying, he had been nervous God would jump on board with Pastor's prayers and everything he had done so far to protect Genie and the girls would be over. It had always been his plan since day one of this horrendous diagnosis to see they didn't have to watch him slowly die. Accepting the inevitable had been hard enough for him, it would be worse if he had to watch them watching him. No...He didn't want God to answer Pastor Dan's prayers.

So as he lay in bed, he was praying just as fervently God would not interfere with his plan and He would just take him home quickly.

He heard the knock on the door and turning he saw Pastor Dan.

Pastor stopped and with a smile on his face he said, "Well...I want you to know I'm quite pleased with myself. God is still answering my prayers. He must think I had a pretty good idea because He answered it quickly."

Turning Pastor Dan motioned for someone to enter the room.

Gale froze.

Michael took a few steps, paused long enough to see the reaction on Gale's face, then continued straight to the bed. Bending down, he took Gale's hand into his own and shook it as if they were long lost friends who had been separated because of circumstances beyond their control. "Gale, I'm so glad to see you. I hope you feel the same way."

Gale stared at his friend for a moment in time. Then they started. Gale's betraying tears were streaming down his face. The emotion of this moment was too much for him to contain. Michael laid his head onto the chest moving up and down assisted by the machine that made sure he continued to breathe. As his tears wet the hospital gown that Gale wore, the two men silently opened their hearts to each other and healing began for both of them. Now they could get past all of the hurt, confusion and pain and allow God to take them to a moment of acceptance and renewal. Even though Gale had asked God to keep this meeting from happening, secretly he was so relieved not to be in this circumstance alone. The relief of having someone to share this with was surprising to him. He hadn't acknowledged how hard it had been to carry this burden by himself until now. Now there was Michael.

"Gale...I have so many questions. I don't know where to start. First, I guess I should ask if it's all right with you if I ask them?"

Michael blinked his eyes in response to his friend's question.

Pastor Dan spoke, "Gale, perhaps I could be of some assistance until your friend figures out your secret code. Would that be okay with you?"

Gale blinked again. Pastor walked over and taking a couple tissues, he wiped the tears that were still sliding down his friends cheeks. "Okay." Looking at Michael, Pastor Dan said, "What questions can I help you with?"

Michael hesitated only for a moment before asking, "What happened?"

Pastor, being so careful not to overstep the welcoming they had received from Gale, looked to him before answering. Gale again blinked giving permission. Pastor nodded back then facing Michael he said, "As I know it" and looking back at Gale he said, "correct me if I'm wrong, Gale was diagnosed with Amyotrophic Lateral Sclerosis, ALS, or you may be more familiar with it as Lou Gehrig's Disease." Pastor Dan paused to give Michael time to absorb what he had just been told.

Michael shook his head acknowledging he was at least aware of the disease.

"I believe Gale came to live at this facility shortly after his symptoms began to advance to a point where he needed assistance."

Facing Gale, Pastor Dan continued, "I think I have been a part of your life for about 18 months. Is that correct Gale?" Pastor was making sure Gale was an active part of this conversation.

Gale blinked two times for yes again.

Michael was watching their interaction. If Pastor Dan could communicate with Gale, he could too.

"You left to protect Genie and the girls...Didn't you?"

Gale blinked yes to Michael.

Michael nodded his head as if that very statement brought everything into a more clear picture.

"Obviously your symptoms advanced quickly."

Gale again blinked twice.

"You know I'm here to stay right?" Michael nodded. I want you to know I've already told Genie I've seen you. She's at home waiting for a call."

Gale's machine seemed to take a deeper breath; the tears welling up in his eyes again.

"Gale, she has to be told. She needs answers. In trying to protect her, you caused her so much pain. She needs to understand. You left her with too many questions."

Michael could see Gale was becoming noticeably more agitated. Reaching over he again took his friend's hand and said, "I promise you, I'll be here with you and Genie. We'll do this together. I'll be strong for both of you. You can count on me. To the very end my friend."

Michael wasn't sure if that was going to be enough to change his friend's mind. He gave him time to accept all that had just been said and then he added, "Gale...I understand what we're looking at. You're facing your final chapter of life on this earth. We've been friends long enough that you should understand I won't let you walk it by yourself. Genie will need to be with you too. I know what you were trying to do; but don't rob her of the time she has left with you. She loves you. She has always loved you. She will continue to love you. Let her close this chapter with you."

Pastor Dan thought that was the most beautiful plea in a situation like this he had ever heard. He waited to see how Gale was going to respond. Ultimately...It was his decision. Regardless of what Pastor Dan thought he should do, it would be his job to support whatever decision Gale made. He knew he had already tread as close to the line as he could. He was just thankful God was willing to answer his prayers for unity.

Michael waited, knowing he was pleading the case not only for himself and Gale, but for Genie and the girls.

Gale closed his eyelids for a moment in time. When he opened them, he blinked slowly surrendering to the love of his friend and thankful someone was going to come along beside him. Even though he felt like he had done the noble thing, this body, this prison that held his spirit, was a very lonely place to be. He had to admit he was glad to have someone tell him he would not have to be alone.

Chapter Six

I CORINTHIANS 13

6. Love does not delight in evil but rejoices with the truth.

GENIE SAT AT HOME BY THE PHONE WAITING FOR Michael's call. He had promised he would call yet tonight as soon as he left Gale. She was thankful the girls had plans for the night and wouldn't be home until later. As she watched, the second hand on the clock seemed to be at a stand still. She was sure the hands hadn't moved since she had entered the living room as she eagerly waited for the ringing. Standing, sitting, pacing round and round the room, Genie felt like she was about to jump out of her skin.

Gale was in an assisted living home. The thought played in her head. She couldn't imagine why. Had there been some kind of accident? Was he recovering from something? Michael had been very vague. Try as hard as she might, he wouldn't give her any more information that just that. He was in this facility. *What could that mean.* There were not that many options for a vibrant man of 50. The options she could think of were not very good ones.

What would knowing this information change anyway? He had been diligent to remain lost to her and the girls. There had been no tracks to follow; no leads to direct them to him. He hadn't wanted them to find him. He hadn't wanted them in his life. His actions had spoke that message loud and clear.

But now what? What would it mean for her? So what if she knew he was in an adult care living facility? That didn't change their circumstances...Did it?

Genie could feel the old wounds come bubbling up to the surface. She could feel the tears of frustration begin to fall onto her cheeks.

She laid her head into her hands and began to let the tears roll. *Why God? Why would You bring him back into the forefront now when we have begun to rebuild our lives? It hurts so badly. I barely survived the first time he was gone from me. Father...I don't understand. Why?*

My daughter, put your trust in Me. I am faithful to keep my promises. My word tells you that 'weeping may endure for a night, but joy cometh in the morning'. I would not lead you where I wasn't going to go with you. I tell you that 'there is a time to weep' and I also tell you that 'there is a time to laugh'. I promise I 'shall wipe away all tears from your eyes'. Do you trust Me that much?

Yes Father, I trust You. It's just so hard to consider that the pain of yesterday could return.

Yesterday you were a different person. Today you know the truth. Today you will understand. Trust Me daughter, trust Me.

Genie continued to converse with the One who held her tears in his hands. She could feel the peace descend on her soul. She was making a definite decision to trust Him. Because of how much He loved her, she didn't have another option.

The ringing of the phone startled her out of her apprehensive moment. She grabbed for it.

"Hello?"

Michael was still trying to understand Gale's situation. Gale was dying and he had already come to terms with the angel of death. Because of Pastor Dan's prayers, Michael had been brought into Gale's life. But what did God want him to do now that he was here?

That really was the question he needed to answer. *What did God want from him?* Whatever it was, he had to wonder, *am I strong enough to do what God wants?* Could he stand by and watch his friend die? Michael wasn't sure.

Then there were the girls. *What was he going to tell Genie in just a few minutes when he made the call.* Michael would not be surprised by her strength. He knew Genie's character. She would be waiting and he also knew she would be flying down here as soon as he gave her the news.

What would be easier to accept? Would she have been better off if he had kept this new knowledge to himself. Or did she need to have the information to make things right between them?

Then he played out the scenario. *What did the story look like between Gale and Genie now? Would she be able to understand that his motives, though they were misdirected, were put into play to protect her and girls?*

Michael continued to ponder all of the ways he could have this conversation. None of it seemed appropriate. How was he going to tell her the man she loved, and Michael was still sure she did, was laying in a bed hooked up to a machine helping him to breathe? How do you tell someone you care about something so awful?

He didn't know...But...He was going to find out as he slowly pushed her name from his "favorites list" on the phone in front of him.

$$* * * * * * * * * * * * * * * *$$

"Michael, is that you?" She continued to ask with no reply coming from the other end.

73

Then as she heard the clearing of his throat he answered, "Genie, it's me. I'm sorry. I wish there was a better way to say this to you...There just isn't."

"Michael...Just tell me."

"Gale is living in the care facility I told you about. However, he's dying..."

"What?"

"Yes. It's as I told you. He has a disease called ALS or Lou Gehrig's Disease. It has a short life span once it has been diagnosed. I hate to tell you he's in the final stages. I wouldn't think he has more than a few months, if that."

"Is that why he went away?"

"Yes...Yes it is...He was trying to protect you and the girls. This is by far a very debilitating disease. ALS can take your muscle movement. Your every move is dependent on someone else."

"Is that what has happened to him? What muscles are affected?"

Michael continued cautiously. This wasn't a conversation that should be happening over the phone. "It appears to me they are all affected."

"What do you mean all?"

"He's bed ridden. He requires someone to do everything for him including turn him and reposition his legs and arms. Genie his body is wasting away. He is skin and bones."

The silence that came through the phone was paralyzing in itself. "Genie...Are you okay?"

"Yes. Thank you Michael. I know this must be very difficult for you."

"I wish I was giving you this information in person. It certainly doesn't seem right for you to be by yourself as you're finding this out."

"I'm all right. Is there more I need to know? Can I call him? Is there someone who can take a phone to him and hold it up to his ear?"

"Well...Actually...There is more you need to know."

"Okay...I'm waiting." She answered with a vibrato in her voice.

"You can't call him Genie. ALS also can affect the vocal cords and breathing. I'm afraid all of this has happened to Gale. He can't move his muscles, or at least he has very little control over his limbs. They tremor quite badly, almost like Parkinson's. He doesn't seem to be able to manage them. They appear to be in movement most of the time. However, he's on a machine that somehow assists in his breathing. He has a tracheotomy. His vocal cords are affected. He isn't able to talk. He communicates by blinking with his eyes. He actually is quite good at using his eyes to communicate his feelings. I wasn't sure how I was going to understand; but I did. His ears do seem to be working well. He understood everything I said."

"His eyes were always so expressive." Genie thought about the man who had been her rock. "Oh Michael." He could hear her softly cry.

"I know. I think we have to focus on the little things. We need to celebrate what we have."

She continued to cry. Not for her loss. She was crying for Gale's loss and the fact that he had been going through this all by himself. *Or was he?* She didn't really know. Although Michael hadn't mentioned another woman.

Genie had to know. She had to ask the question, even though she may not like the answer. "Has his girlfriend stood by him through all of this?"

"Genie, there was no other woman. There never was another woman. He just concocted that story so he could convince you. He made the whole thing up after he found out about the ALS so you and the girls wouldn't have to watch him go through this horrendous death. He has done all of this on his own to protect you girls...His girls."

Genie didn't know whether she was happy or sad. He hadn't left her for another woman. He must still love her. However, he'd been struggling through this process of loss alone. Grieving the loss of his...His what? She needed to know the whole story. So she asked, "Are you sure he's going to die?"

There it was, out in the open now and he would have to tell her the truth. "Yes Genie. He is dying and it appears to be progressing quickly. From what I read on the internet, after I saw him, the information appears to be very accurate. Everything is shutting down. He is going to die...My guess is soon."

"Michael, I have to go to him. Will he let me?"

"Yes, I think so. He wasn't on board with it in the beginning. In fact he pleaded with me in his own way. Let's just say he was receptive when I said he needed to let you walk this path with him so you can finish the story. He surrendered. I'm sure he will now be receptive to your coming. I believe he will be looking forward to you being there with him. He seems very lonely. It is very sad Genie. It broke my heart. I want you to understand so you can prepare yourself. I don't want you to be as shocked as I was."

"I'm so sorry Michael. I know that you loved him too."

"I did...I do. It just is difficult seeing him lying there so alone and dependent. He was such a vivacious man. His energy level could match anyone I knew. Now he's so...Broken. I wish there was something I could do. Only his spirit is still evident. That's probably why he's still living."

Genie was taking in everything Michael was saying. She didn't want to miss a word; yet there had been so much information to absorb. What she did know was that Gale needed her and she was going to get there as quickly as she could.

"Michael, I don't know how I could ever thank you. You've been a true friend; to Gale and myself. I'm going to go now. I need to start making arrangements. I'm going to get a flight out as quickly as I can talk with the girls. I'm going to assume they're going to want to come also. We have a distance to close up between us in more ways than one."

"I understand. If there's anything else I can do, please call me. If you girls want a place to stay, our place is always open to you."

"Thank you Michael. I know you mean that. I'll be in touch."

"I plan to go see him again. Maybe even tomorrow depending on when you're getting here. I just don't want him to lay there anticipating this meeting by himself."

"If you see him before I get there, will you please let him know I'm coming as quickly as I can. Let him know...Well...Let him know I love him."

"I will Genie."

"Thank you again and good night Michael."

✳✳✳✳✳✳✳✳✳✳✳✳✳✳✳✳

Genie sat waiting for the girls to come home. She felt the burden pressing her down. Movement wasn't possible. Even the tears she could feel didn't seem to be able to fall. Shock. Yes, that had to be it. She must be in shock.

How had this happened? How had what seemed to be a perfect life, fallen so far away from perfect? She was trying to understand. She really was; but none of it made any sense to her.

Gale left her for another woman. Only now she had found out there never was another woman. Instead she found out he had a disease, an incurable disease. This time he really was going to leave her. He was going to die. She would have to grieve him all over again.

And then there were the girls. She had to think about them. They had forgiven him when they thought he had abandoned them. What would they think now? Would they be able to understand? Would this just open up their hearts so they would break all over again?

Father, how do we do this?

My daughter trust Me to walk with you through every day. I will never leave you or forsake you. Have I not called you to have compassion for every man. Did I not tell you to feed those who are hungry? Did I not tell you to give drink to those who are thirsty? Did I not tell you to see a stranger and take him in; to clothe the naked? I called you to visit the sick. Inasmuch as you have done these things unto one of the least of my children, you have done it unto me. Comfort the feebleminded, support the weak, be patient toward all men. Love as family. You are all my family; connected through Christ and His love for all of you. Remember My Spirit dwells in you and the fruit of that Spirit is love, joy, peace, long suffering, gentleness, goodness, faith, meekness, temperance. I have given you a job to do. I have equipped you to do it. I will walk with you and the girls. You will fight a good fight; you will finish the course; you will keep the faith. And in the end, I will hold you and say well done good and faithful servant.

Okay Father. I will do what You are asking of me. Please help me to go in the direction You want. Help me not to get ahead of You. And give me the words to explain this to the girls. Thank you Father for Your constant comfort. AMEN.

****

Noelle couldn't imagine what her mother would be calling a family meeting for at 8:00 p.m. She knew this, it wouldn't be happening if it wasn't important. As she and Brad hurried to the car, she was thankful Angelina was home and able to stay with Emma. It was almost her bed time and Noelle didn't know how long this meeting was going to last.

Brad asked, "Did she give you any idea what this was about?"

"No clue. She apologized for calling so late; but said she really needed to talk to all of us and it would be easier if she only had to go through it once."

"That doesn't sound like your mother at all."

"I know...Brad, you don't think Mom is sick or something do you? I just couldn't stand it if..."

"Hush. We aren't even going to speak that. We're not going to borrow trouble. I'm sure everything is going to be fine. Let's not play the guessing game. She'll tell us when we get there." Brad reached over and taking her hand in his, tenderly brushed a kiss across her fingers.

Noelle took a deep breath and smiled back at

the man who always seemed to be able to center her universe. "Thanks Honey."

"It'll be fine." He said as they were pulling into the driveway of her mother's home.

****

Anaya opened the door before giving them a chance to ring the doorbell. "Thank goodness you got here fast. Mom wouldn't tell us anything until everyone was here."

Brad wrapped his strong arms around Anaya's tiny shoulders and said as he kissed the top of her head, "Deep breaths Honey. Everything is going to be all right. We're all together. Whatever is happening we'll weather it as one."

"Thanks Brad." She said as she grabbed a quick hug for strength. "I do feel better knowing you're here with us."

"I'm not going anywhere."

They walked into the living room where Noelle's mother and Nissa were setting. Noelle walked up to her mother and looked at her closely before giving her a hug. "You okay?"

"Yes Honey. I'm fine. This isn't about me."

Noelle looked at her sisters; but their faces expressed that they did not know what was going on either.

"Why don't we all sit down and I'll try to explain why I've asked you all to come together."

Doing as their mother asked, they all found a spot quickly. Noelle mentally registered the apple/cinnamon candle that was burning and the soft music coming out of the stereo. Other than the tension in the room, it seemed like any other time.

Genie, not wanting to drag this out for them, went straight to the story "I don't really know the best way to tell this story, so I am just going to tell it the way it happened to me. I received a phone call from Michael Dunn last night. He had been to an adult care facility to visit his aunt. While he was there he noticed another resident."

Genie paused as if she didn't know how to continue.

"Who could he have possibly seen that would cause you such a struggle?" Nissa asked.

"Mom?" Anaya and Noelle said at the same time.

Brad knew before she continued what Genie was about to say. In a quick moment he played out several scenarios. None of them made sense except this one. Reaching over he took Noelle's hand.

Genie coughed as if needing to clear her throat.

Brad said soothingly, "It's okay Genie. I think I understand. Why don't you just let it go. We'll work through this together."

Genie looked at her son-in-law with love in her eyes as if to say 'thank you". But try as hard as she did, she couldn't say the words. There seemed to be something blocking them from coming out.

"Could I ask you a question? Would that help? Brad offered with a strength that was so common for him.

Genie nodded her head yes as the tears slowly slid from her eyes.

He continued, "Are you trying to tell us that the person Mr. Dunn saw at the home was your husband, the girl's father?"

"What?" Came from all the girls at the same time. They gave their mother a look saying they thought that was ridiculous.

However, the look on her face sent them for a spin. As she grasped her hands in her lap, looking down she nodded. Brad had guessed correctly.

"Yes. The man Michael saw in the facility was your father. He didn't stop to check on him the first night. He was so taken by surprise that he just left. He called and talked with a resident pastor and made arrangements to meet with your father. The pastor went with him."

"Why didn't he just talk to Dad the first night?" Nissa asked.

"It seems he was taken by surprise by the condition your father was in." Genie continued before they could ask another question. "You see your dad is in a terrible situation. He has a disease. ALS. Lou Gehrig's Disease."

"Oh my gosh. Do you know what that is?" Nissa apparently understood the severity of the situation.

"Yes. It's a debilitating disease. There is no cure. The outcome is a death sentence. Apparently your dad is already on a machine to help him breathe. It has progressed quickly."

"Is this his punishment for leaving us?" Anaya asked.

"Anaya, God is a God of love and forgiveness. He isn't someone who zaps people who sin with a disease. If that were the case we would all have diseases. We are all sinners and there is no degree to sin." Brad interjected.

"Brad is right, Anaya." Genie offered her youngest daughter a smile hoping to give her some degree of comfort. "In fact, Michael found out there never was

82

another woman. Your dad used that as an excuse to leave us. He did so to protect us from what was coming with the disease. He didn't want us to have to watch him die such a horrendous death. I'm sure, he thought he was choosing an easier way for us. If he walked out of our lives, we wouldn't have to watch as this disease took his life."

"Mom...You are saying dad is dying soon?"

"I don't know all of the particulars yet. I'll know more tomorrow. I'm getting a flight out as quickly as I can. I'll go there and see for myself. I need to see what I can do to help him through this. I can only imagine how lonely this has been for him. After all, it can't be easy for a man of his fortitude to surrender everything; to be helpless and not even be able to take care of his personal needs. Remember while we were struggling with him leaving us, he was struggling with the knowledge we thought he didn't love us any more. The truth is, he loved us so much he was willing to live the last of his days alone to protect us." Genie finished with tears running down her face.

"Oh Mom." All of the girls were circling around her as they cried for the loss they had experienced and the time they had missed with their dad.

Anaya was the first to say it, "I want to go with you."

"Me too." Nissa agreed.

Brad looked at Noelle and nodded to her as she said, "I think we should all go."

"Oh, Girls. I don't know. This is going to be so very hard. Are you sure you want to see him like this?"

"Mom...We've believed a lie for a long time. It's time we help him adjust to the future and whatever it holds. Don't try to protect us now so we lose even more time with him." Nissa interjected.

Noelle smoothed her mom's hair back and wiped the tears as they fell from her eyes. "Mom...Whatever happens we can do this because we have each other. Remember those were the words you told me not that long ago when I was scared and on the run. As long as we are together, we can face anything. Well...Dad has been facing this totally alone. Now we have to open up our circle and let him come back. We need to finish this journey with him. You can't protect us. He tried to do that. It didn't work. We were just as broken. We didn't heal until we let Jesus come into our hearts and put us back together again."

"Mom...We don't even know if he knows Jesus." Nissa said.

"We have to let him know we've forgiven him even before we found out all of this." Anaya said.

"Okay. If you're sure, then I'll start making arrangements for four tickets."

Noelle sent a signal to the man who seemed to know what she was thinking before she said it. His reply was, "You had better check to see if Baby Girl needs a ticket. I'm thinking he would love to meet his only granddaughter. If anybody can make him smile it would be Emma Rae."

Squeezing his hand, Noelle lovingly thanked the man she adored.

Chapter Seven

I CORINTHIANS 13

7. It always protects, always trusts, always hopes, always perseveres.

As the plane began to pick up speed, Genie laid her head back on the head rest. Here they were gliding through the air effortlessly as if they didn't have a concern in the world; however untrue that was. She hadn't slept well last night as so many thoughts continued to run through her mind. Will Gale welcome their intrusion into his plan? After all, he had gone to great lengths to keep them out. Here they were coming without him asking them to come. She wasn't sure she could handle rejection from him a second time. Even though her head said it hadn't been rejection; for over two years it had certainly seemed that way. It felt that way. Now, literally overnight, she had come face to face with the reality he was dying and even in the planning of his death, he had been thinking about her and the girls. Though that may be the truth, it was having a hard time sinking into her soul; the part of her that had experienced the pain of loss.

Genie looked across the aisle where Noelle and Nissa were entertaining baby Emma. What a delight she was. Thinking back to the time in their lives when Noelle had run while contemplating having an abortion, Genie could hardly believe that would even be possible. The joy they each experienced through that little girl's life, left Genie in disbelief that anything could have been bad enough to consider the ugliness of taking her life. She had been a part of them from the minute they knew she existed. The family loved her before meeting her.

As she thought about Noelle and that time of her life, it occurred to Genie, her daughter had the same mind set as her father. Troubling times brought them both to a decision to put away their own feelings and focus on the rest of the family. Their desire to protect the family they loved was so strong they were willing to do whatever it took; even at their own expense. Noelle, more so than the rest of them, would probably understand her dad's decisions. Thinking back in time when Noelle was young, more than once Genie would remember saying, "You really are your father's daughter. You even think like him." The reality of that was again meeting her at a close and personal level. Noelle and her father were really such strong people.

Strength. That was what they were all going to need to get through this. Including Gale. Genie began to think about strength. *Where does my strength come from?* Immediately Bible verses began to come to her:

Nehemiah 8:10 The joy of the Lord is your strength.

Psalm 28:7 The Lord is my strength and my shield.

Proverbs 24:5 A wise man is strong.

Isaiah 30:15 In quietness and in confidence shall be your strength.

2 Corinthians 12:9 My strength is made perfect in weakness.

2 Corinthians 12:10 When I am weak, then I am strong.

These verses were the ones on which Genie needed to focus. They were not new to her. When she first became a Christian she had done a study on strength. It had helped her to learn to stand on His unfailing grace and to depend on Him. Now here she was again. She knew she couldn't do this with her own strength. She had already been assured her God would fight for her. All she had to do was keep her eyes focused on the source of her strength. God would do the rest. On those words of assurance, Genie closed her eyes and fell asleep, catching up on the lost rest from last night.

★★★★★★★★★★★★★★★★

Anaya reached over and gently gave Genie a little shake. "Wake up Mom. We're getting ready to land."

Genie opened her eyes taking a moment to realize where she was. "Goodness! I must have dozed off. How did I sleep through the whole flight?" She asked.

"You must have needed it. Sleep is a good thing. My guess is none of us slept very well last night. At some point in the trip, I fell asleep too. When I woke up I looked over and saw all three of them were sleeping too." She nodded over to Noelle, Nissa and Baby Emma, who were now busily preparing to land.

Genie reached over and taking her baby's hand in hers gave a loving squeeze. "I really am glad you all wanted to come. This is going to be hard enough. Without all of you, it would have been impossible. Thank you!"

"There isn't anywhere else we would be at a time like this. We just have to come to grips with where we have been so we can move forward. Together...That's how we'll get through. Together. I just hope Dad understands or will let us teach it to him." Genie could see that hesitancy was also weighing on Anaya. If she were to make a guess, they probably were all thinking the same thoughts. If they had learned anything during the last few years, it was they were stronger together with God as their foundation. Alone they were broken. Alone was a lonely place to be.

The plane began to descend. This was Genie's

least favorite part of flying. The going up and the coming down always gave her just a moment of hesitancy.

Anaya, recognizing her trepidation, decided now would be a good time to distract her, "Mom...While you were sleeping we decided maybe it would be best if we went to the hotel. It might be easier on you and Dad if you had some time alone. We were just thinking maybe you would like that. But if you want us to go with you, we will. Whatever you think."

"Actually...I've been thinking the same thing and I just didn't know if you girls would understand. I know this is your time with your dad also. I certainly don't want to take that away from you. It's just, we don't really know what to expect or how he's going to handle all of us coming."

"It will be fine with us to wait until you think the time is right."

"Thank you girls for understanding." Genie was touched again by the maturity her girls exhibited.

Taking her mother's hand Anaya squeezed, "It's okay Mom. We've got God on our side and if Dad doesn't know Him...He will before we leave."

Genie nodded as she smiled at Anaya. "Absolutely Honey. Absolutely."

****

It had taken a while to gather all of their luggage. Especially with Emma. For a little thing, she sure required a lot of stuff to travel.

Now the girls were settling into the hotel rooms they had reserved, two rooms with a connecting door. Genie didn't care anything about the accommodations. All she could think about was getting to Gale, finding out what they were dealing with and letting him know they cared.

She had found a hotel in the same town as the home. Michael had been very helpful. He was very sincere in his offer for them to stay at his home. However, Genie felt like it would be better for all of them to have some privacy. After all, they didn't really know what this trip was going to look like. Plus, she thought Emma would handle the trip better if she wasn't in a strange home with people she didn't know.

For the time being, the girls were going to settle in and let Emma take a nap. Before Genie left, the girls asked if they could all pray together. The time they spent talking with the Father calmed Genie's nerves. She felt better prepared to see Gale. She really could feel the strength that only the Lord could give. *Thank You God for Your faithfulness.*

Michael had suggested it might be helpful on her first visit to go with Pastor Dan. He explained she would have to get used to his form of communication. "Pastor Dan is very good at interpreting what Gale is trying to say. It made the visit easier until I became familiar with his eye signals. If you'd like, I'll make arrangements for the two of you to meet in his office. What time do you think you'll be there?"

They agreed on a time, and that time was now. Genie took a deep breath as she knocked on his office door.

"Come in."

Opening the door, Genie walked into the office of the man who had been spending time with her husband. Immediately he was up from behind his desk and greeting her with a warm hug. "I'm so sorry Mrs. Smith. I know this must come as such a shock to you. I wish I could

91

give you news to make all of this better. I can't. There is no easy way to do what you are about to do. However, I can tell you I've already been in to see Gale and he knows you're coming."

Genie was comforted by the understanding of the towering man in front of her. "Thank you for all you have done. I can't say thank you enough. I'm struggling with Gale being by himself through all of this. We, my girls and I, appreciate all you've done to help him."

"Please, call me Pastor Dan and know it has been my pleasure. Gale is a wonderful man. I wish I had known him before the disease took it's toll. I don't know if Michael told you; but I began praying and asking God to use someone to reunite your family. I'm just thankful He answered my prayers so quickly."

He continued, "Do you have any questions or concerns I could address before we go to his room?"

"Just one...Is he okay with us coming?"

"I can reassure you he is eagerly waiting for you. You just said us. Are there more of you here?"

"All three of our daughters and our grand daughter are at the hotel waiting. They thought it might be easier for him, and myself, if I came alone first."

"Very wise daughters you have. Come on. You've come a long way and I'm sure you're anxious to see Gale. Let me take you there. I'm at your disposal. If you would like to be alone that's perfectly okay with me. However, I can also stay for awhile if you think that would be helpful."

"Thank you...I would like you to stay and help us through these first awkward moments. Michael told me you know the whole story about our separation."

"Yes I do. What Gale did was very noble of him to protect you that way and at the same time ridiculously

92

unwise. I'm sure there were many painful nights for all of you. Please know he shared those nights also. I can tell you this, he loves you all very much."

Opening the door he said, "Shall we?"

"Yes...Please...I want to see my husband."

****

Thinking back Genie wasn't sure how she could ever describe what she had seen as she entered the room. The only man she had ever loved lying helpless in that bed. The pain of their separation fell away as she looked at his frail body. The energetic man who had been her life, was lying there with a machine helping him breathe. He was so very still; except for the constant, erratic movement of one arm and hand.

He turned to look at her as she entered the room. The look on his face said it all. **He...Loves...Me!** Genie walked up to his bed and taking his face in her hands, she leaned down and tenderly kissed his cheek. She let her lips linger there just feeling the warmth of him. He smelled like her Gale. She sat down on the bed beside him and stared into his eyes of love. Words were not necessary. She laid her cheek next to his cheek and time slipped away. His tears mingled with hers. Neither one of them wanted this moment to end. They had waited far too long for it to happen. They had loved each other since college. They had loved each other through the birth and raising of their children. And now...They would love each other through death. One thing was certain, Genie would make sure they would live every moment until that time in love.

Genie didn't know how long they laid there. Pastor Dan had stepped out of the room and was waiting just outside. He recognized their need for privacy as they reconnected their lives into one. It wasn't until he heard Genie speaking that he finally reentered the room silently.

Looking into the same eyes she had pledged her love so many years ago she said, "I don't want to do this with you. It certainly isn't what we planned and dreamed about for so...so many nights. But understand this, I would rather do this with you for whatever time we have left than do without you for one more day. I have loved you since we were college sweethearts and I will love you 'till death do us part'. Do you understand me? Together we can get through whatever comes our way. We were united into one body. We joined ourselves together. We are together now and I will not leave you. As long as there is breath in either one of us, by ourself we are not complete. We will cherish every precious moment God gives us. I will hang onto you for as long as I can and be thankful for whatever life we share. Do you understand me? I'm here for our life."

Gale looked with tenderness into the eyes that had always held him mesmerized. This woman was strength and had always been. He needed her strength. Why had he ever doubted she could do this? In fact, she would do this better than he would.

Blinking his eyes twice, he told her all she needed to know. He was glad she was here. There weren't words he could have said that would have let her know any better than the look of love that was shining through his eyes.

"I know." Was all she said.

He used what little control he had over his facial muscles to try to smile at her. It was difficult and the look came off crooked.

Genie ran her fingers over his lips. His smile looked perfect to her. She tenderly stroked his cheeks, not being able to get enough of the feel of him. It had been too long and her fingers were desperate for the touch of him.

"Hum, hum...," Pastor cleared his throat to let them know he was still there.

Genie turned and smiled. She nodded for him to come and join them.

Looking at Gale, Pastor said, "I could say I was sorry God answered my prayers and I could ask her to go; however, that was the most beautiful moment I have ever experienced. You should just tell me 'thank you' and we'll call it good."

Gale blinked twice.

Pastor knew what he was saying was more than thank you. He was saying what words could not convey. He walked over to the other side of the bed from Genie and taking Gale's hand in his he said, "You are welcome my friend. You are welcome."

"Now what can I do for the two of you? I know you have some catching up to do and I certainly don't want to get in the way of that. If you need me to help with any of this, I certainly can. Or I can just leave you alone. It seems very clear to me Genie isn't going to need any instruction on communicating with you. She probably reads your mind before you think it."

Genie took the lead, "Thank you Pastor. The girls and I can't thank you enough for your prayers. We are so glad to be here."

Genie immediately noticed the change in Gale's eye expressions.

"What is it my sweet?" She ran her fingers through his hair. Something she had always done when they lay in bed in the quiet of their moments sharing precious time together. Now she realized just how precious that time had been.

He again signaled with his eyes.

Genie thought back for a moment and realized what he was asking. "We?"

He blinked twice.

"Yes my love. The girls are here with me. Emma, our precious little granddaughter, is here also. They insisted on not missing a moment with you. Though they were thoughtful enough to allow us this time together first. When you're ready, they'll come over from the hotel. We're only about ten minutes away."

Genie could sense the unsure emotion he was feeling.

She began to calm him, "Gale, they are very excited to be with you again. I can tell you this, when you left there was a lot of anger in them. In all of us. We didn't understand. Because of that anger, Noelle ended up in a terrible situation. Out of that came a relationship with God that none of us had ever anticipated. Emma Rae also came out of that time in Noelle's life. Do you know what I am talking about?"

He blinked once letting her know he didn't understand completely.

"We can discuss that later. For right now what is important is that through Christ, we began to heal. Part of our healing came through praying for you. As we prayed for you, we were able to forgive and began to put our lives together again. It was only through His love for us were we able to understand what made no sense. He showed us He was in control and all we had to do was love Him. Gale, what I am trying to say is, we forgave you a long time ago. Even before we knew all of this.

We forgave you and asked God to find you wherever you were. We asked Him to put someone in your life to show you the love of the Lord. We were able to look past the ugly part of our separation and return to being thankful for the beauty of the relationships we shared with you.

Gale's eyes were filling with tears again.

"Shhhh...Shhhh. It's going to be all right now. This is just another step in the plan He's working out."

Gale blinked twice.

"Honey...Do you know the Lord? Have you found Him in this journey you've been on?"

Gale looked at his dear friend, Pastor Dan, and blinked his eyes twice.

"It was like pulling teeth; but we got him into eternity kicking and screaming." Pastor laughed.

Gale blinked multiple times.

Laughing he continued, "Okay...It wasn't quite that bad. But you have to admit I'm pretty funny."

Gale blinked only once.

"What? Fine. At least I appreciate my sense of humor."

Genie seized the moment, "Thank you Pastor. Nothing is more important than a personal relationship with our Savior." Raising Gale's hand to her lips and kissing it gently, then holding it to her heart she said, "If there was only one thing I could change in our past, it would be a shared love of the Lord as a family. We spent too many years away wandering in the desert. We worked so hard putting our life in the box that we created, little did we know without Him, there was no life."

Gale blinked twice.

"Now we have it all. He gave it to us through His blood on the cross. *We can do all things through Christ who strengthens us. Amen?*"

Two blinks and a hardy AMEN came from the men who were sharing the moment.

"And with that...I'm off. It's easy for me to see you're going to be just fine." Reaching across the bed and grasping Genie's hand, Pastor said, "Genie, if you need me for anything, you know where to find me. It has been my pleasure. I look forward to sharing more time together."

Again, taking his friend's hand in his he continued, "Gale, you are a lucky man. Your wife is beautiful both on the outside and inside. I leave you in good hands. Let her love you. She needs it as much as you do. Now... Hurry and call those girls over here. My guess is they are on pins and needles waiting for that phone to ring. I can feel the love already and I haven't even met them. Good-night my friend and God bless you all."

On that note, he turned and walked out of the room leaving them alone again.

"Oh my precious husband."

Gale blinked once and again that confused look crossed his face.

Genie focused on what she had just said. "Husband?"

He blinked twice.

"Yes Gale. You are my husband. I never signed the divorce papers. It never felt right. I tucked them away thinking there was no need for me to sign something I never wanted anyway. I never heard from you about not signing them so I just left things as they were. Now I understand why." Smiling she teased him. "So...Whether you like it or not...I'm still your wife and you are still the love of my life."

Gale blinked twice and she again laid her lips against his face and nuzzled ever so gently.

He closed his eyes in bliss and together they lay as he rested in the comfort and knowledge that he was loved.

****

Anticipation...Trepidation...Nervousness..Fear of the unknown...Anxiousness...All were words explaining the feelings that were coursing through the girls as they were on their way to the facility their dad called his home. They had been ready when the call came.

"Girls, it's time. Your dad is very eager to see all of you. Anytime you're ready is fine." Genie continued. "It's going to be all right. We're all going to be fine. God is with all of us." She hoped they would understand what she was saying, "We can do this. We are strong. Your father knows the Lord also."

As they entered the facility, they were silent. It was as if they were entering a shrine. Their legs were like dead weight. All of them felt like they were moving in slow motion. Could this really be happening. Were they about to find their father in a state that no one could really prepare for?

"May I help you?" The receptionist at the facility asked.

"We're looking for our father, Gale Smith." They were given directions and their trek continued. "Down the hall, turn left, follow it to the end room. You'll find your father in the end suite." The receptionist had answered.

And so they did. With a soft tap, they slowly opened the door. There in the bed, as they entered the room, was a shadow of the man who had been their strength, the man they adored, the man who had left them with no explanation, laying helpless.

"Daddy." Noelle was the first to speak. With tears running down her cheeks, she walked quickly to the other side of the bed. Handing a sleeping Emma to her mother, she leaned over the bed, laid her head on her father's chest and sobbed.

Anaya and Nissa came to stand across from their mother who allowed them the time they needed to cry and wash away all of the pain and brokenness the separation had caused. The three girls surrounded their dad with love. As Genie watched, she thanked God they had found His peace. In this moment of reunion, as different as the future looked, they were all together... Loving...Crying...Healing.

The tears flowed equally for all. The pain of separation was gone. A new life was beginning. This wasn't the life any of them would have chosen. Yet it was the life that was to be.

Anaya was the first to break the silence. "Daddy, we understand why you did what you did. We don't agree with it; but, we know you thought you were protecting us. Now you have to let all that be in the past. We have to be a family again. We have to be together. We can't find you and lose you all over again, it would hurt too much. We love you. Do you understand what we are saying? We want to be with you. We want to help you. We can do this together. God will be our strength."

"Daddy, we are stronger than you give us credit for. We are survivors." Nissa added.

"Hear what we're saying. Whatever it takes, wherever we have to go, no matter what the circumstances to come, we'll face them together...United." Noelle had dried her tears and was stroking his face. "We need you in our lives no matter what that length of time looks like.

There's not one of us in this room who is guaranteed another minute on this earth. This is a second chance for all of us. You have to agree with us so we can be together again."

Gale blinked twice.

Genie interpreted. "Girls, your dad communicates very well with his eyes. One blink means no. He can make that look very stern." She smiled at him with love. "Two blinks means yes. He can show you love with that look. If you see a look of confusion, then you just have to rethink whatever it was you just said and clarify."

Nissa took his hand, "This can be fun, kind of like charades."

They all looked at her as if she had just said the most ridiculous thing, then realized that under the circumstances, it was perfect.

"I'm thinking of one word..." Nissa said as she traced a heart over the top of her chest.

"LOVE!" They all yelled together.

Gale looked at his girls and understood how blessed he was. *Thank you God for protecting me from myself and loving me enough to correct my mistakes.*

At that moment a little whimper was heard from Grandma's arms.

Noelle motioned for Genie to give Emma to her. As she positioned her daughter so her father could see her she said, "Daddy, this is Emma Rae Conroy. She is an amazing, beautiful spirit and you'll live on through her. She is another part of your legacy."

Gale blinked twice through the tears as they slid down his face. This seemed to be that kind of a day for him. He was okay with that. No matter what happened from this point on, this day would be perfect.

As Emma reached toward the man in the

bed, Noelle placed her gently onto the bed beside her grandfather. Fearlessly, as if she knew what he needed, she snuggled into his side and fell quickly back to sleep.

Through the innocence of a child the decision was made, they were a family again.

Chapter Eight

I CORINTHIANS 13

8. *Love never fails. But where there are prophecies, they will cease; where there are tongues, they will be stilled; where there is knowledge, it will pass away.*

BRAD HAD NEVER BEEN SEPARATED FROM HIS GIRLS since he and Noelle were married. He had never slept alone since that night. He didn't like it. As he lay tossing and turning, the night dragged on. Around 2:00 a.m. he had opened their bedroom window in hopes that the sounds of the night time would lull him off to sleep. Tomorrow was going to be a long day if sleep didn't come soon.

Noelle had called after the plane had touched down and they were settled in the hotel. She had asked him to pray that the meeting between her mom and dad would go well and God would be in the midst of their time together. He did so, cherishing the time of listening to her voice. It was a relief Emma had traveled well. He had been on planes when young children had not. It was no fun for those who shared the ride; or for the parents who were trying to diligently keep a crying child happy. Brad had been concerned for both Noelle and Emma. However, he was encouraged that the experience had been a good one for both of his loves.

"Of course she was good. I had a talk with her before you left. I threatened her with a spanking if she didn't behave well. I explained her behavior would reflect on my parenting skills. I reminded her we didn't want anyone thinking I'm anything but an awesome dad. She's totally obedient."

"Right. And when have I ever seen you spanked that little girl. She has you totally wrapped around her finger. You jump if she says jump. I should spank you." Noelle laughed as they bantered back and forth about the little girl they both adored.

Brad loved to hear his wife laugh. His mind ventured back when he first saw her and the sorrow that defined who she was at that moment in time. He never wanted to see her that sad again. It broke his heart to think of her as anything but joyful. Yet he could hear the hesitancy in Noelle's voice. "Are you okay?" he asked.

"I'm missing you. I'm unsure about how we'll be received. After all, Dad went to great lengths to separate himself from us. That could say so many things."

"It could say he loved you more than words could express; or more than life itself, his life. As misguided as it was, it could have been a very protective father emotion. If he didn't know the Lord, it would be easy to listen to the voice of satan. He's a master at division. His plan certainly wouldn't be to have anything good come from a bad situation."

"My head tells me you're right. My heart is afraid it could be broken again. We don't really know what his mind is like. Just because he was good when Mr. Dunn was there, doesn't mean we will be welcomed."

"You know what I think?"

"What?"

"I think you are over thinking all of this. Let your mind rest. Begin to prepare yourself to do the God thing...LOVE! He'll take care of the rest."

"You're such a smarty pants. You know what?"

"What?"

"Someday some lucky lady is going to have the best husband in the whole world. She's going to spend the rest of her life in the arms of an amazing man. Oh wait...that's already happened and I'm the lucky lady.

Brad continued their game, "You think so, huh?"

Yes...and speaking of arms, I know a pair that are

missing you right now. They are desperate to be wrapped around that strong man body of yours."

"Boy howdy! Talk like that will get me on a plane and headed to you right now."

"Come on. Show me what you got."

"Don't temp me little girl. And don't get me wrong. I think you are right where you need to be. But letting you go took some real willpower. So don't start with that sassy talk. I can't even begin to tell you how much I'm missing the two of you and you've only been gone part of one day.

"Oh Brad...I love you so much."

"I love you too, Honey."

"I'll call you as soon as I can after we see Dad. Mom is there right now. We thought it best if she had this time with him before we all go."

"I think you girls are very wise women. I also think this is going to be a great time of healing."

"Thanks Babe. Talk to you later?"

"You bet! I'll be praying. Tell the other girls I'm praying for them too. Love you."

"Love you."

And with that the voice that was in his thoughts always was gone. Brad did just as he said he would, he prayed unceasingly throughout the day and night. Literally, as the night dragged on he continued to pray. He played over in his mind the call from Noelle after she had seen her dad.

"Oh Brad...It's the saddest picture I've ever seen. That moment when we walked into the room was like my mind took a flash shot and now I close my eyes and see it over and over. There he laid, so helpless. He isn't even able to move his arms or legs. Although his arms flail around uncontrollably and sometimes his legs just

107

tremor or kick. He can't speak. He's lost all control of his muscles. He has to be turned to prevent bed sores. Someone has to make everything happen for him that has to happen."

"I'm sorry Noelle. I'm sure it was very difficult for you to see your father in that shape."

"If you would have know him before, you could understand better. He was strong and in my eyes he was bigger than life. He could swing me up into his arms as if I was a feather, even when I was older. The three of us girls could wrestle with him at the same time and never get the better of him. He loved to golf. We took long walks around our neighborhood. Sometimes he would run and we would ride our bikes and he would still keep up with us. Now he can only communicate with us by blinking his eyes."

As Noelle began to cry, he allowed the time. He knew it was important she be allowed a time for tears. As he spoke words of comfort, his mind went to God's word. He grabbed his Bible and found what he was looking for.

At the right time he said, "Noelle, can I read *Ecclesiastes 3:1-8?*"

"Yes. Please."

There is a time for everything, and a season for every activity under heaven:
> *a time to be born and a time to die,*
> *a time to plant and a time to uproot,*
> *a time to kill and a time to heal,*
> *a time to tear down and a time to build,*
> *a time to weep and a time to laugh,*
> *a time to mourn and a time to dance,*
> *a time to scatter stones and a time to gather them,*

108

a time to embrace and a time to refrain,
a time to search and a time to give up,
a time to keep and a time to throw away,
a time to tear and a time to mend,
a time to be silent and a time to speak,
a time to love and a time to hate,
a time for war and a time for peace.

"Noelle, Honey, this is a season. I don't know what God has in store for all of you; but I know this, whenever we walk through the fire, He is always there. He uses the fire to purify us. It can be painful; but, when we come out the other side, if we allow His work to be done in us, we will be strengthened. God will have burned away our impurities. Let's look for the opportunities through this to grow. Let's be a light in the darkness. What about your father? Does he know the Lord?"

"Oh yes! They have a resident pastor who has been spending time with him daily. You remember Mr. Dunn telling us he talked with him, he led my dad to the Lord. I'm very thankful for that."

"See. God will always make a way to grab another one out of the grasp of satan. How is your mom holding up?"

"Amazing. Would we expect anything else from her? Watching the two of them together is like there was never a break in their relationship. It just shows me how much she loved him. You know, she is a beautiful woman and I'm sure during this time of separation she's had men who have shown an interest in her. I just realized she hasn't even accepted an offer of a dinner out. I didn't know until today that she is still married to my dad. She never signed the divorce papers."

"Really..."

"Nope." Noelle repeated her mom's words, "She said. 'It just didn't feel right'." My dad knows now too. They are still man and wife. There is such a bond between them. Mom can usually read his mind before he needs to communicate."

"Is she already sleeping? It's been a hard couple of days for her."

"I don't know. She wouldn't leave my dad. When we left, she had crawled up onto the bed and snuggled in with him. He wasn't objecting."

"So I take it he is accepting of all of you being there?"

"Absolutely. I did what you suggested. When we went into the room, I immediately let him know we loved him. Anaya and Nissa too. He knew we were there for the long haul. He knew we were going to be by his side. We all cried. I didn't feel like they were tears of regret or pity. I felt like they were tears that were washing away all of the pain. It was kind of like a fresh spring rain. Everything is clean and new again. That's what it felt like. We were clean and new relationships were starting."

"That's beautiful Noelle. I wish I could have witnessed it. I'm sure God was pleased."

"It felt good."

"What about our little Emma? Was she the star of the show?"

"Brad, you wouldn't believe what she did. She had just fallen asleep in the car on the ride over. When we got there and entered the room she was still sleeping. She woke up as we were greeting Dad. I had positioned her so he could see her. She snuggled into his side and fell back to sleep. She finished her nap with Grandpa's love cuddling next to her. It was beautiful. Certainly that moment sealed the deal. He was totally smitten. Couldn't have sent us away had he wanted to. Which he didn't. Plus the entire time she slept by his side, his arms didn't jump once."

"Now that's God at work."

"Boom!"

"Noelle, I'm so happy for all of you. But I miss you so much I can't hardly stand it. This big old bed of ours is so uninviting without you in it. I don't know how I'm going to sleep tonight."

"Well...Grab my nightie and snuggle it. Close your eyes and pretend I'm there with you. You could even spray some of my cologne on it. Then it would smell like me."

"It's not you. Nothing can replace you."

"That's so sweet. I'm the luckiest girl ever."

"We are blessed. Now I want you to get some sleep. I assume you're going back to the home tomorrow. Do you guys have any idea what happens next"

"Well...Nissa, Anaya and I know what we want to happen. We just haven't had an opportunity to talk to Mom yet. We aren't sure what she's thinking. Maybe tomorrow we can get some time alone with her."

"Do you want to tell me what you're planning?"

"We want to bring Dad to Indiana."

"Can he make a trip that far?"

"We don't know all of the specifics. I'm sure it would have to be a medical transport of some kind. It doesn't matter. We can't leave him here. Mom isn't going to leave him. At home we could take care of him ourselves. I don't know how much longer we'll have him with us. It isn't good Brad. So we want to have every day we can. We can't all stay here. Home is the only way to make that happen. He needs to come home."

"I understand. Let's just pray God will open all of the right doors to make that happen. He is big enough to do all of that."

"You're right. I love you."

"I love you too. Now give my little one a kiss for me and tuck yourself in. Morning will be here before you know it."

On that note they had said good night and Brad hoped Noelle was getting more sleep than he was.

****

Genie woke up. The light peaking through the blinds seemed strange to her. She started to stretch and realized she couldn't. Something was against her. Then she remembered...

Looking up she saw him looking at her. She smiled, "Good morning".

Gale blinked twice.

He began to tear up. The effort it took for him to shake his head was apparent.

Genie reached up and tenderly caressed his face. The morning stubble tickled her fingers and she remembered how much she had loved the feel of him first thing in the morning. "It's all right. We are going to be fine."

He seemed agitated.

"What Darling? Do you need something? What can I do?"

He blinked once.

"Are you trying to tell me something?"

He blinked twice.

Genie was silent for a minute as she tried to put herself into his position. She looked at him and asked hesitantly, "Are you trying to say you are sorry?"

He blinked twice.

She smiled. "Shhhh...Shhhh. I know. It's forgiven. Let's not spend what time we have together living in regret. We can't change the past. We can only live in the present. The past is gone and forgotten. Today is what we focus on. I love you and I know you love me. That's all that matters. Okay?"

He blinked twice.

She giggled like a little girl, "Do you want to tell me you love me?"

Two excited blinks.

"How about we create our own language? When you want to say 'I love you' just blink three times. Then I will know what that means."

Gale blinked twice. Then very slowly he... Blinked...Blinked...Blinked.

Genie nuzzled his cheek and said, "Those are the sweetest words you have ever said to me."

They stayed that way awhile longer and then morning routine took precedence. Genie could sense Gale was uncomfortable having her there while the nurses were buzzing around doing what had to be done. Though it didn't bother her, she didn't want him to be put into a situation that made him regret having her there. Leaning down by his ear she whispered, "If it's okay with you, I'm going to take a few minutes to slip out and freshen up. I promise I won't be gone long."

He blinked twice.

She kissed his cheek and walked out of the room.

She thought she was headed to the bathroom. Instead her feet turned, as if on their own volition. She found herself knocking on Pastor Dan's door.

"Come in." She heard as she turned the knob.

"Ahhh. Genie. I wondered when I would see you. Sit. Talk. Cry. I know this has been hard for you."

"I thought I was prepared. I wasn't. I had no idea." The tears began to fall. She could feel them hitting her hands which were folded in her lap. Tears that came harder and harder from some place deep down inside.

"I'm sorry."

Pastor Dan came and positioned himself on the corner of his desk. She thankfully accepted the box of tissues he offered.

"I didn't mean for this to happen."

"Nonsense. I would have expected nothing less. In fact, I would have been concerned if this didn't happen. I refer to this as one of those shakable moments in life. Those moments which rock you to your very being. Right to your core."

"My heart is breaking for him."

"You cover it very well. The love you have for him shines through all of the sadness. I would also suggest that your heart is breaking for yourself also."

"I don't want him to feel I pity him. I want him to know just how much I love him."

"Let me tell you something. This sucks. It really does. And guess what?"

"What?"

"He knows that it sucks. It sucks for him too."

"But I don't want him to think it affects the way I feel about him. He has enough to deal with."

"Genie, his body is failing him. His mind is as sharp as it ever was. He knows how terrible this is for him and he knows how terrible it is for you. Don't pretend to protect him. That puts you both in the same roles you have already played, only reversed. You can't protect

114

him from what is happening. You can walk through it with him. You can love him. You can try to make life as comfortable for him as possible. But you can't change the facts and the facts are that this sucks. He knows it and you know it."

"Right! It does." She started to cry harder.

Pastor just let her cry.

"I've been told you're a remarkably strong woman. I can certainly see that. Don't try to be too strong. It won't help Gale and it won't help you."

Genie used the moment to release all of the pent up emotions she'd been experiencing since yesterday. Taking a deep breath and blowing her nose, she looked straight into the eyes of this man and said, "I need you to help me take him home. I want to bring him to Indiana. How do I go about making that happen?"

$$*****************$$

The door was closed to their dad's room when they got there. Knocking and hearing no one answer, they pushed the door open slowly.

There he was sitting in a chair. Straps were holding him tightly and a machine was working his legs up and down as they bent at his knees. He blinked quickly as if to say, "Come in".

Emma broke free of her mom's hand and ran in her toddler way to his side. There was a stool beside his bed and she pulled it over so she could sit right by his chair. Noelle could see how much he wanted to hold her. Just to be able to reach down and swing her up onto his lap. Those days were over and the two of them were working it all out. She was just going to have to change her way of thinking. Emma was okay with loving him just the way he was. Not perfect. They were all going to have to become comfortable too. There really was something about the innocence of a child.

The rest of the party entered the room and went over to give him a kiss.

Nissa said, "Where's Mom? We thought maybe we could go and have some breakfast together."

Anaya immediately realized that questions were very uncomfortable for him unless they required yes or no answers. So she rephrased it, "Is she getting cleaned up?"

Gale blinked twice.

She continued, "Has she had breakfast yet?"

He blinked once.

Noelle pulled up a chair and the other two plopped themselves on his bed. "When she gets back, we'll go get breakfast. Emma had a banana from the continental breakfast bar so she can wait for a little while."

Just then Genie entered the room looking fresh. No one could detect she had herself a good cry. "Morning everyone. Hi Baby Girl." She walked over to Emma and kissed the top of her head as she sat intently watching Gale's legs move up and down to the rhythm of the machine. She was fascinated.

Noelle jumped in, "We haven't had breakfast yet. Want to join us?"

Genie looked to Gale as if to say, "Would that be okay?"

Gale blinked twice quickly.

She gave him a kiss and said, "We won't be long. We'll just go some place close by."

He blinked twice again.

Grabbing her purse she headed to the door and the girls followed.

116

Nissa said, "We'll be right back Dad."

He blinked again.

"Come on Emma. Let's go get something to eat."

Emma stood up from the stool and patted her grandpa's leg good-bye.

Gale blinked at her too.

As anxious as the girls were to have a conversation with their mother, they allowed her a few minutes to unwind. The waitress had brought their waffles which were smothered in a fruit topping. Genie was savoring her one cup of coffee she indulged herself with every morning.

"Girls...I have something I want to tell you."

They looked at each other then settled their gazes on Noelle. "Good. We have something we want to talk to you about also. Why don't you go first."

Genie didn't know how to say this except to jump right in. "I'm going to make plans to bring your father home to Indiana with us." She said it very firmly because she wanted the girls to know she wasn't going to tolerate any negative discussion.

Smiling Noelle said, "Well good. That makes our conversation with you easier. We want him to come home with us too."

"You do?" She seemed surprised.

Nissa said, "Well of course Mom. Where else should he be but with us."

Genie chuckled, "I guess I should have known you would feel that way. Let me tell you what I did this morning. I went to Pastor Dan and told him what I, excuse me, we, want to do and asked him to help us with

117

the arrangements."

"What did he say?"

"Well, he asked me a question."

"And..." Anaya prompted?"

"He asked me what your father wanted to do."

"You told him he wants to come with us, right?"

"I couldn't actually say that since we haven't asked him. We haven't talked about the future yet. This was not something I had even thought about until it just came out of my mouth while I was talking with Pastor Dan this morning. I just knew I couldn't leave him here...Alone."

"We feel the same way Mom. He can't be by himself." Anaya said with tears starting to slide down her face.

Genie patted Anaya's hand. "I was waiting to talk with you before I moved forward with your dad. I wanted to make sure he saw we were in agreement. Girls, this will be difficult. I'm sure we'll have some nursing help; but the main responsibility will fall on us. Do you understand what that means?"

All three of them said, "Yes!"

Nissa continued, "Mom, Dad belongs with us. We don't know how long we have to spend with him. We certainly don't want him to be by himself when God says it's time." Then she started to cry.

Genie reached across the booth and took hold of Nissa's hand. It's okay. I've been very strong in front of your dad. But this morning when I went to talk to Pastor, I couldn't make the tears stop. You know what he said?"

"What?"

"He said he would expect it of us. Plus he said... And I quote, 'It sucks!' He said we know it and so does your dad."

118

Noelle added, "So we cry. But we'll laugh too. There will be good days and there will be bad. You said it to dad yourself, together we can get through anything. That has become our family motto. He needs to come home."

"I agree. Let's make it happen." Nissa voiced her opinion.

"How?" Anaya asked.

"Well...This will be a process. We'll have to coordinate several steps. We'll have to get the house set up properly. I'm thinking the master suite on the first floor can be adapted quite easily. Pastor Dan suggested we talk with hospice on this end and have them contact hospice on our end. We'll have to fly him there with a medical helicopter. This is going to take a few days. So...I think you should all go home and help by getting the house in order. Once you're there, I can let you know what we're going to need and you can get it in place."

"How long do you think you'll be? I mean, how much time to do you think we have? What I mean is... How much time do we have with him?" Anaya asked through a teary voice.

"I don't know. I haven't had the nerve to ask that question. I'm not sure if they would have the answer anyway. After all...God knows our beginning and our end. It doesn't say anywhere I've read He told anyone else that day. What I do know is it won't be enough time regardless of the day."

"You're right. So we move ahead as if we have forever. Because that is what we have. His forever." Noelle interjected.

"So true Honey. Our first step will be to talk to your dad when we get back. Agreed?"

"Agreed!" They all answered.

119

"Ahhged!" Baby Emma shouted.

****

Kissing his forehead Genie said, "We're back. Did you miss us?"

Gale, who was still sitting in the chair, minus the therapy machine now, blinked twice

"Gale, it's a beautiful day outside. Let's load up and go sit in the sun. Do you ever get to go outside?"

He blinked once.

"Why not? Is it possible?" Genie asked.

Two blinks.

"Do you have a wheelchair?" She continued.

Two blinks.

"Good." Noelle said. "I'll go and get a nurse to help us. A walk will be wonderful for you Dad. You always loved to be outside." She exited the room.

Nissa and Anaya got excited about taking him outside. "You did always loved the outside Daddy. I have such sweet memories of all of us outside." Anaya said as she gave him a big squeeze. She covered the sadness that crept through her as she felt his bones through the clothes he was wearing.

Emma, who beginning to understand they were talking about going "auwside", was excited to be a part of that for sure. She marched around the room clapping making everyone laugh.

Noelle came back with a chair and a nurse in tow. She was almost as excited about this adventure as his family was. "I wish we had more time to take every resident outside. The fresh air would be so good for all of their spirits. But you know...Too little staff to make all the extras happen. Mr. Smith, you are going to have such a good time. Now girls, let me show you how to help him transition from place to place."

So with a quick lesson in transferring and learning to guard all of the tubes and cords, the girls were sure they had it under control. Off they went with all of his machines attached to his chair. Genie was holding one of his trembling hands and Nissa holding the other as Anaya maneuvered the chair. Noelle, with Emma giggling away, trailed along enjoying the scene that played out in front of them.

"Emma...This is a good day!" Noelle smiled at her daughter.

Chapter Nine

I CORINTHIANS 13

9. For we know in part and we

prophesy in part,

B RAD FOUND EYAN SITTING AT THE KITCHEN TABLE having breakfast.

"Where's Mom?" He asked.

"She had to leave early for the restaurant. Some large brunch meeting today; she had extra stuff to prepare."

"Gotcha."

"I might say you look terrible." Eyan offered to his older brother. "What's up. Can't sleep without your baby by your side?"

"Laugh if you want; but I kind of like cuddling with that girl. I slept alone a lot of years. Now that I have a choice...I choose her."

"I hear ya. They do tend to get under your skin. You get used to them and then when they're gone, things just don't seem the same."

He had Brad's attention now. "Want to tell me where that came from. It sure doesn't sound like my brother."

Eyan laughed. "It's just that Nissa is always around. She helps me with the youth and she's really good at it. They relate to her. She has a sweet spirit; yet she can appreciate my crazy ways. She isn't demanding or up tight like all of the other girls I've tried to date. She loves and serves my God and is willing to share my visions. She's excited about mission work and isn't afraid to get dirty. She's loyal and caring. She loves her mom...And my mom."

"Hey? Are you describing a woman or a pet?"

"You know what I mean. I just have never given a relationship much thought. Like you, I just figured when the time was right God would just make it happen. I really hadn't thought about using any of my energy to work on something like that."

"Well, maybe that has to be your first question to yourself. Are you willing to work on a relationship? Because they're a lot of work. Now don't get me wrong. The right person certainly makes the work a lot easier. Are you going to put this person's needs above your own? There's a surrendering that has to take place on both sides."

"I get all of that. I'm not new to relationships in general. I just haven't been willing to give all of myself to another girl before."

"With Noelle I knew I don't want to be with anyone else. She's never far from my thoughts. Then there is that lump in the pit of my stomach when I think about her."

"Exactly. I've got that feeling."

"Eyan, does Nissa suspect you feel this way?"

"You mean like...Have I said anything to her? Not a word. Honestly, I didn't really know myself until she left. She's just always here. She's at the church. She's at the fund raisers. She's always willing to help. I don't have to ask, she's just wherever I am..."

The look on his face was priceless. "You don't think she feels the same way do you?"

"Boy...For such a smart guy you are really dense." Brad laughed.

"You think she likes me?"

"You think!" Brad answered.

"Wow...What do I do next?"

"I think you had better pray about this for a little bit. This revelation is too new for you to move ahead yet. You wouldn't want to do something that would damage the friendship you already have. Ask God to reveal to you if this is the woman He created for you. He'll let you know."

"Yay...That's a good idea. I'll pray about it. I'll start right now." Eyan jumped off the bar stool and headed for the door with a smile on his face that was almost silly. As he started out the door he stopped and yelled back, "Hey...You pray too. Okay?"

"You got it. I'll pray too."

"Thanks." He laughed. "It's going to be a great day; a really great day."

On his way out the door his brother answered back, "Yup...It's a really great day." Smiling at the direction God had just turned his brother's life, Brad did as asked, He prayed.

****

Her phone rang. They had stopped near a table in a nice little park in the courtyard of the home. The area was really very quaint. There were flowers in bloom waving in the slight breeze that brushed against their faces as sunlight kisses touched their skin. It was a beautiful day. A day to be savored.

The persistent ringing of the phone, while Nissa looked frantically in all of her pockets, broke the quiet of their moment. "I'm sorry." She apologized as, finding the phone she quickly stepped away to answer. "Hello?" She was confused by the name identifying the caller.

Eyan answered eagerly, "Good morning!"

"Eyan?"

He laughed, "Yup...It's me."

"Really? Is something wrong?" Nissa just could not believe he had called her.

125

"Does something have to be wrong for me to call you?"

"Uh...Yes. I would think so."

"Well...Nothing is wrong. You seem so surprised?" He was beginning to feel a little uncomfortable.

"I am surprised."

"Why?"

"How long have we known each other? In all that time have you ever called me? You've had other people call me to give me messages from you; or you have left me written notes asking for my assistance with something. But...To pick up the phone and dial my number...That has never happened. Ever."

"Well, I have a phone you know."

"Yes I do know. In fact, I've called you before when I needed information or an answer to a question. You've never seemed to be someone to just chat on the phone."

More and more it was becoming apparent to Eyan that Nissa was totally shocked. This was no act. She really couldn't fathom why he would be calling. As he thought about what she was saying, he realized she was right. He had never called her before, not even when he needed something from her. No wonder this seemed so out of character for him.

"Did you need something?"

"Nope."

Not just the distance; but, an uncomfortable silence sat between them.

"Oh...I see."

A long pause ensured.

"Eyan?"

"Yes?"

"Ummm...You called me. Did you want to talk?"

"Well...Sure...Um......I just wanted you to know..."

Then nothing. He didn't finish the sentence.

"Go on." She coaxed.

"Well...You see...I just wanted to say..."

Silence...

"Eyan, I'm listening. You can say whatever you want to say to me."

"Gees, why is this so hard?"

"I'm not sure."

"Well...I just wanted to say... I think I miss you."

Nissa caught her breath as she thought about how to respond. He had said 'think', like maybe he wasn't sure if he missed her. She decided to take the casual approach. "That's nice, very nice. It's nice to be missed."

"Good." He seemed relieved. "In fact, I think I may call you again. For no reason...Just because I want to. Just so you know...I want to...I do want to."

He sounded as if he was attempting to convince himself. "Great. I'd like that. You can call me any time."

"Okay. I will. Well then, have a good time and I hope everything is going well."

"It is. Thank you for asking."

"All right then. I'll talk to you later."

"Okay. And Eyan?"

"Yes?"

"Thank you for calling."

"You're welcome. Good-bye Nissa."

"Good-bye Eyan."

Nissa couldn't help but smile as the call disconnected.

She was on her way back over to the group when

her phone rang again. Answering with a smile on her face she said, "Yes."

"Hey. I just wanted to say that I guess I'm really bad at this; but, I promise I'll get better."

"You did fine. Thanks for calling back."

"Okay...Bye!"

"Good-bye Eyan."

As she joined her family she could see the questions on their faces.

Anaya said, "You look pretty happy."

"I am."

Anaya continued, "Are you going to tell us who put that smile on your face?"

"Eyan."

"Eyan?" Noelle's shocked looked said it all.

"Yup...Eyan."

"Seriously? What did he want?" Noelle couldn't contain her confusion.

"Nothing."

"Then why did he call?"

"Because!"

"Because why?" Anaya jumped into the sister conversation.

"Because he's just figuring it out."

"Figuring what out?" Noelle still had no clue what was going on.

"Figuring out what I've known for a long time."

"Which is?" Anaya was enjoying the cat and mouse conversation as much as Nissa was.

"That he loves me."

"WHAT???" They both shouted.

"I said he loves me."

Noelle asked, "Did he say that?"

"Not yet. He barely got through the call as it was.

It'll take him some time to get to the point of saying those words. But I'm patient. I've been patient this long and I'll be patient as long as it takes. You mark my words... He loves me."

Gale loved watching and hearing the exchange between his girls. He had missed them so much. The thought of losing them again was almost more than he could bare. What other option did he have? How could he allow them to watch what was coming down the road for him? He didn't even know how much time he had; but he did know they had lives. They had done exactly what he had hoped for...They had gone forward. He would have to say good-bye and let them go back to their homes.

Genie was watching Gale enjoy the girls. She could sense how happy he was being a part of what was going on around him. She decided now was the time to broach him about coming home with them. Reaching over and taking hold of his hand she waited for him to focus on what she was about to say. "Gale...I talked to Pastor Dan about something today. When I asked for his help, he asked me what you wanted. Then when the girls and I went to breakfast, they had already discussed the same with each other. The four of us are in total agreement. We need to know how you would feel about it."

He blinked twice as he waited for her to continue.

"Gale, I can't...we can't...lose you again. I don't know what the future holds and neither do you..Only God can direct those paths. It's our job to stay focused on Him and Him alone. We can't make our decisions based on what the doctors believe. We have to be true to who He created us to be and remember He has a plan for our lives. I'm just thankful we're together again and we've been given a chance to put our family back together."

Gale wasn't sure where this was going; but he did know he couldn't let them be saddled with the burden he had become. He began to blink quickly. It was clear he had become agitated. How was he going to make them understand what death was going to look like for him?

"Listen...Please hear us out?"

He closed his eyes and she heard him take a deep breath through the machine. When he opened his eyes she continued. By this time the girls had realized the conversation was happening; they joined Genie and their dad.

Genie looked him straight in the eyes, hoping to reach him in the depth of his soul. "We want you to come to Indiana with us. We want to stay together as a family. We need you in our lives for as long as we can have you. You need us. I know you thought this was the only option. We understand you were protecting us the way that you thought best. You were wrong. We're all sure of it. We can be strong enough; whatever it takes. Just don't leave us again. We can't do that. We can't."

Gale closed his eyes. Genie could see there was a single tear falling down his cheek. Noelle reached up and wiped it away. She said, "It's okay to cry. We all cry for the sorrow we're facing. We just have to cry together Dad. Don't make us cry by ourselves."

Nissa, stroked her dad's hand, as she began to plead her case. "Dad, I'm falling in love. Brad's brother is falling in love with me. I need you to be a part of that. I need you to meet him and give me your approval. I want to know there was a relationship between you two. I want to be able to tell my children their grandpa loved their father. Those are important things for a girl. You've been gone too long and I've missed too much."

130

"Daddy...Let us love you? Please love us? Anaya rested her head against his shoulder.

The tears fell ever so slowly from his eyes. What could he say? How could he make them understand what they were asking was complicated? His life was difficult. No...His life was ridiculously hard.

Genie said, "Let me try to read your mind. You are worried about us and the difficulties we'll face with you. You don't want us to have to see the hardships you live with. You want us to remember you strong and healthy. Correct?"

Gale blinked twice and then closed his eyes again.

She continued, "So let me tell you that if Michael hadn't found you, we would have lived out a lie. We had to work at not being angry with you. Anger causes bitterness and resentment. Only through Jesus Christ were we able to find a way to forgive you. You allowed us to think poorly of you. That couldn't really be the legacy you wanted to leave behind. You were way to good a man to be remembered as an adulterous man who left his family to fend for themselves."

"Daddy," Noelle reached out, "We know where this is all headed. We understand this will be difficult. It's because of the wonderful husband and father we remember that we're wanting, no needing, you to come home with us. We won't forget. Regardless of your decision, we'll now remember you as the loving man who put us first; who was willing to lay down his own needs to protect his family from the sadness of his life. We just wanted to have the same opportunity. We wanted to be able to show you we're willing to make those same sacrifices. That's what family does. And no matter what...We are family. We love you."

Genie continued, "Gale, believe me when I say... We harbor no false impressions...We know what we're facing...We know you're going to die. Isn't that the same spot we're all in? No one is promised tomorrow. What if you were to lose one of us today? We could leave here and have a car accident."

Gale blinked quickly.

"I'm just trying to show you we have to live every day as if it's our last; we don't know that it isn't. If that was God's plan, wouldn't you want to savor every moment you could?"

Gale slowly blinked twice.

"We feel the same way. We want every day that's available to us. We want to feel you. We want to smell you. We want you to watch us. And if that's all we have, we want every minute. Please...Please don't take that away from us again." Genie ended with the tears slowly falling down her cheeks.

Noelle decided to pull out the big guns. "Daddy, look at Emma running and playing in the grass. It doesn't take much for her to enjoy her day. She makes the most of her situations. She blesses us every day and every day is more knowledge and growth for her. Every day she spends with you is one more chance for her to remember who her grandpa was. We can tell her about you; but you can show her the most important element. You can show her love."

Nissa jumped in, "You see Dad, we remember you differently; because we were lucky enough to have those days with you. But regardless of the way your body has let you down, we know you love us. We can feel the love you have for us. So can Emma. She can feel your love. Don't deprive her of you."

The girls had him surrounded. They were

embracing him with their love. He could feel the protective shield they were building around him. It was too strong to fight. He didn't want to fight. He wanted to surrender to their love. He had been slowly dying alone for too long. If he had to die, he wanted to be loved till the end.

Gale looked at Genie and with tears in his eyes he blinked slowly twice.

Genie kissed his hand and said, "Thank you."

He blinked twice several times.

She responded with "You're welcome."

✷✷✷✷✷✷✷✷✷✷✷✷✷✷✷✷

Pastor Dan found them enjoying the sunshine and warmth of the day. "So there you are. This looks great. Looks like you've found a great place surrounded by those who love you, my friend."

Everyone greeted him enthusiastically.

Genie was so excited to see him, "We have great news. We are ready to move ahead with the plans to get us all back to Indiana."

Pastor squeezed Gale's shoulder, "That's great... Just great. I'm so happy for you. You're making the right decision. If I were in your shoes, I would want to be around those who love me. You, my friend, are loved."

Gale blinked twice.

"Lucky man. Regardless of the situation. Lucky man." Pastor was visibly touched.

"So what is our first move? Where do we start? We talked about it and I'm going to send the girls back home. They can be our connection at home. Gale and I will follow when everything is in place. I'm hoping it all

133

happens quickly."

"I don't know about 'quickly'; however, we'll do our best to get the ball moving. I think our best bet would be to contact the Wings of Hope Hospice here. I don't know for sure, I've never been involved in something like this. I'm thinking maybe they could coordinate everything with the Hospice in your area. Maybe together they can move through all of the specifics quicker."

"I think that's a great idea. In fact, I'll call Angelina and ask her if she could make a few phone calls for us. Once we have the information, then I should be able to make the arrangements from here. If you could connect me with Hospice here, I'll go right now and get the ball rolling. The girls can stay with Gale while I see about scheduling an appointment to talk with them.

Gale began to blink quickly.

Genie immediately stopped and included him. "I'm sorry. I didn't mean to bulldoze over the top of you."

He blinked no, hoping to let her know that wasn't it.

She thought through the words she had just said, "Do you want me to meet with Hospice?"

Two blinks.

"Do you want to be there when that meeting happens?"

One blink.

She continued to search for the right question. Pastor Dan loved watching her master her way through their new way of communicating.

"The girls. Do you want the girls to stay with you?"

He blinked several times.

Genie smiled sweetly at him, rubbing his hand

she giggled, "Be patient with me. I'll get it. I promise. I was always pretty good at reading your mind."

He blinked twice in agreement.

Thinking for a moment a light bulb went on, "Gale are you tired?" Looking at her watch she said, "We have been out here for over two hours. Would you like to rest?"

He blinked twice.

"Bingo!" Anaya yelled.

"Okay", Genie said. "Let's get you back to your room and while you rest, we can all work on some of the arrangements. Maybe you girls should prepare to head back home?"

Noelle was the first to speak, "I think we should stay until you have met with Hospice and we have a definite plan set in place. Then we can start for home and get things in place on that end."

Nissa and Anaya agreed.

"Okay...First things first...Let's get you settled." Genie leaned over and kissed the top of his head.

So, off they went with Emma spinning around and around the chair as they rolled into the building. She was oblivious to anything except the beauty around her and a family full of love.

****

Gale couldn't believe how efficiently the girls had gotten him back in bed. The nurse came in just as they were finishing. She applauded them. "That was impressive. I've had trained CNA's who couldn't do it any better."

"Thank you. We'll only get better." Nissa said as she patted her dad's arm.

135

"Gale what a lovely family you have. I hope they can stay for a while."

"They hope not." Pastor Dan offered. "They're getting ready to take him to Indiana to live with them. Lucky man our friend Gale." He said as he rubbed Gale's leg.

"Well...If that isn't the best news I've had all week. Everyone will be so pleased to hear it. Can I spread that around? Not every day we see something positive happening here. Bless you all. Bless you."

"Yes. Please feel free to spread the news. Maybe someone would have some suggestions to help us accomplish this as quickly as possible." Genie could only hope.

"Well if anyone can help you, Pastor Dan can... He is a wealth of information. We believe he's the smartest man we all know. He's always jumping in and saving us here...Literally too". They all laughed at her little play on words as she exited the room.

Pastor yelled after her, "I'll make sure your bonus is in this week's pay check."

She gave him a thumbs up as she closed the door.

As Gale settled in for his rest, Genie's mind was already putting together a list of steps. "Girls, while your dad rests, why don't I take you over to the hotel and you can let Emma have her lunch and a nap. Plus, that will give you time to make arrangements for a flight home."

"Pastor, can you connect me with the nearest Hospice agency. I want to call and see about an appointment with them yet this afternoon."

"Gale, you rest. We're headed home as quickly as I can make it happen." Genie smiled as she jumped into her take charge personality.

Pastor laughed on his way out, "Gale you had

better do what she says. You're going to need all of the energy you can find. This wife of yours is going to get us all on a plan of action that's going to move quick. In fact, move over. I may need to rest a little first too."

"No rest for you Pastor. You have a job to do."

Gale blinked twice and then his eyes closed as if they were too heavy for him to keep open any longer.

Each of the girls kissed him tenderly and Emma did the same. "We'll meet you in the car Mom." Noelle said giving Genie time to say good-bye to their dad.

Closing the door behind them, Genie walked over to the bed and looked lovingly at the man already asleep. "Don't worry my sweet, I'll see you get home. God will give us time." With that she kissed him and was off to plan what would be his last trip of any distance.

****

Genie was anxious about the meeting with Hospice. It was vital to her family she make them understand the importance of this move. She reminded herself that God was with them. He had already made a way for Hospice to see her immediately. In fact she was on her way there right now. Relieved the meeting was happening yet this afternoon, she played out in her head all the reasons she would give them for the necessity of a speedy transport.

It was a short drive to their office and had taken her less than 10 minutes. As she was pulling into the parking lot, she realized she was crying. How long had the tears been falling? She wasn't sure. What she was sure of was she had to pull herself together. She had to be strong. Talking to herself she began to chastise, *Stop this! Now is no time to fall apart. Gale's reconciliation*

137

with our family depends on you. You have to make this happen in a timely matter.

Then she heard His voice, ***Daughter...Why do you do this to yourself? Have I not made your path clear and walked along with you? Do not burden yourself. Be obedient. Do not be a Martha. Still yourself and be a Mary. Sit in my presence and listen to what I have to say. I will make a way. My way is not your way. It may seem impossible now; but with Me all things are possible."***

Genie instantly began to relax. She could actually feel His peace flow through her and bring her to a point of calm. She began to pray.

Father, thank you for being omnipotent or without limit; for knowing what I need before I know. I will try to remember to depend on You. If I should look away for a moment, please be my ever present help in time of need. I need You. We all need You. I love You God. AMEN.

Sitting for a moment and resting in the assurance of His love for her, Genie's mind took her to the story of Mary and Martha in the gospels. Jesus and his disciples had come to a village where the two sisters lived with their brother Lazarus. They were known for their hospitality and love for Jesus and His disciples. On this particular day, when Jesus arrived, Mary wanted to sit at the feet of Jesus and listen to what he had to say. Martha was concerned about all of the preparations that needed to be made and she went to Jesus to complain that Mary was not helping.

Genie remembered her thoughts the last time she had read this in Luke. Even as Jesus was correcting Martha it was personal and endearing. He used her name twice as He said, ***"Martha, Martha. You are worried and upset about many things, but only one thing is***

138

needed. Mary has chosen what is better, and it will not be taken away from her."

To Genie it had come as a reminder not to get caught up in the busyness of the world and forget what we need is to sit at His feet. We need to read His word and feel His love. He wants to be personal with us. Our relationship with Him is more important than anything else the world thinks it needs from us.

Genie knew she was going to be facing a mountain. The path she had already chosen would be a hard challenge. She also knew the girls would be walking that road with her. Their strength would have to come from the Lord. It was going to be crucial they stay connected to Him.

On her way into the meeting with Hospice she was reciting:

Psalm 121:7-8
The Lord will keep you from all harm. He will watch over your life;
The Lord will watch over your coming and going both now and forevermore.

Thank God that He is a faithful God who is bound to keep His promises. She had a renewed peace about her as she entered the building. She was persuaded all was going to work out for the good.

After getting off the phone with Noelle, Brad was already anxious for tomorrow to come. He had missed his wife and baby girl so much. More than he could have ever imagined before they left. His heart was torn; he knew the sorrow that Noelle was facing. All too well, he knew what it felt like to lose a parent you love. He also understood this would be yet a more complex situation for her family. The fact they had lost so much precious time with their husband and father, would leave them desperate to capture all of the time they could together. He didn't know much about ALS; however, from what Noelle had already told him, he didn't see how they could have much time left. He also was concerned about the ugliness that this death would mean for Genie and her girls. Not that death is ever pretty. It's just that this didn't seem to be something that was going to allow for a peaceful passing. His heart was breaking for the women who had come to mean so much to him and his family; these women who had become family.

Noelle had told him of their plan to bring him home and he had been praying all afternoon for Genie as she was making arrangements. His prayer was that it would be a smooth, safe transport, without complications; or as few complications as someone in this man's condition would allow.

He began to ponder the relationship he would have with 'this man'. After all, Gale was his father-in-law. And though their time together was apparently going to be short, he wanted it to be meaningful. Brad thought about what he would want Gale to know about him. In the end it came down to only two things that really seemed important for him to understand. One...He loved Noelle and Emma. Two...He would do whatever it took to keep them safe and happy. Isn't that what Gale had thought he was doing when he chose to leave them. He was trying to protect them because he loved them and he thought leaving was the best way to keep them away from the sorrow that was coming. Whether right or wrong, this was a man who was motivated by love.

Not forgetting that Gale made his choice knowing

what he was going to be facing alone; Brad couldn't help but have respect for the man who was coming to live out his final days. Isn't that what every man wants from the people he loves? He wants to know he is respected and he wants to be loved. Brad was determined to make sure Noelle's father understood he respected him for the strength he had shown in the decisions he made. Gale would be able to rest knowing Brad would make sure all of his girls were safe and loved. When he married Noelle, he also accepted the responsibility of Genie, Anaya and Nissa. However, after the conversation he had with Eyan yesterday, he didn't anticipate he was the only Conroy boy who was going to make sure the girls were in good hands. Yes sir...He knew that look; the one he saw in Eyan's eyes. He knew his brother was still figuring it out. He also knew with God's help, it would all become clear in the right time.

It was pretty funny watching the pain Eyan was going through trying to make sense of his changing emotions. What just seemed to come natural for Brad, wasn't as comfortable for Eyan. The very idea of a relationship with Nissa seemed to leave him struggling. Brad chuckled as he thought to himself *this should be fun.*

✳✳✳✳✳✳✳✳✳✳✳✳✳✳✳✳

Three hours later, Genie was on her way back to the hotel to pick up the girls. The plans had already been worked out. The hospice agency had been so helpful. She even had conversation with the agency at home that would be working with them once they had arrived. No one could have been any nicer. Everyone made her feel very comfortable. It was going to be a little tricky getting the timing all worked out perfectly. They would each take care of that on their respective ends. The two agencies would coordinate travel times to make sure everything came off like clock work.

Genie's only request, which wasn't a possibility, was that they would allow her to fly with him. Because of the medical assistance he would require, that wasn't going to be an option. It was more important to have that space filled by someone who could assure Gale's travel would be comfortable and safe. They were going to make sure there were enough attendants to meet whatever needs he would have. In fact, they were going to be sending someone over to the care facility tomorrow to assess his needs and talk with Gale about any concerns he might have.

As she prepared to connect with the girls and head back to see Gale, Genie was feeling very comfortable about what had already been accomplished for the move. *Thank you God. You certainly did make a way.* She thought to herself.

Pulling into the hotel she saw the girls in front by the fountain letting Emma have some outdoor time. They spotted the rental car immediately and began to gather their stuff. Emma was a little hesitant to leave the water play until Momma told her they were going back to see Grandpa.

"See Gampa?"

"Yes Honey, see Grandpa." Momma told her as she fastened her into the car seat that would travel back with her on the plane tomorrow morning.

"Well?" Nissa was the first to ask.

"It all went really well. I'm so relieved. Hospice is well underway to making it all happen. They will be sending someone here tomorrow morning to find out what will be needed medically and to help them finish up the plans to move him on the next day." The girls all took note of the fact that their mom seemed much more relaxed than when she had left for the appointment. All of the girls had sensed her anxious spirit. Now they recognized their mom's calm way of taking charge when she had an important conference or gathering to coordinate.

"So fast?" Anaya asked. "Are they sure they can be prepared for him that quickly? Can we be ready for him at home by then?" She continued.

"They're positive. However, if something were to come up tomorrow, they still have time to change plans. As far as home, I spoke with the Hospice agency that will be serving us already. They are planning on bringing all of the equipment that will be needed in the morning on the day he arrives. If you girls can meet them there, I think we're in good shape."

All of them answered with an immediate reply of, "Sure. Absolutely. You bet!"

"Mom?"

"Yes Noelle?"

"I mean...Are you sure you're okay with this. You know...bringing Dad home to..." She trailed off not wanting to say the words.

"To die. That's what you are asking isn't it?"

"Yes." She hung her head and a tear drop fell onto her lap. "Yes...To die."

"I would give anything if this weren't happening. I worry about you all and the memory this will leave in your minds about your dad. But...I could no more allow him to stay in that home and leave this earth by himself than you could. Don't get me wrong. I cry every time I think about it, as I'm sure all of you do. God reminded me today of where our strength will come from. He will make sure we have what we need. He isn't going to bring us this far and leave us by ourselves. He will walk through this with us. Can you imagine how your Dad feels? Yesterday he thought he was here to die on his own. Now he knows how much we love him and that we are strong enough to surround him on his last journey. During one of the conversations I had with the agency nurse today, she reminded me to be open and honest about my feelings. She said we should remember Gale is having similar feelings. He didn't choose this. The disease chose him and left him with very few options. So he's feeling all of the same things we are: sad, angry, lonely, mad, frustrated. He feels all of those same emotions and it's important to voice them and acknowledge they exist. The problem for your dad is the disease has taken his ability to voice anything. So we're going to have to be his words and yet be sensitive enough to allow him dignity to speak. Pretending we're happy isn't a real feeling for this situation. Though we can be happy we have reconnected, we can't possibly be happy we're living in this nightmare. Neither is your dad. So we talk. We make sure he knows we're comfortable with him releasing all of those emotions and it isn't going to change anything if he needs to do that. There will be times when we'll need to vent also. It's okay for us to vent in a positive way. In fact they'll encourage it."

"This is hard seeing him looking so broken. Losing his voice is the hardest for me." Anaya said.

"I know. It breaks my heart too. Your dad and I used to complete each other's sentences. We were close enough we thought alike. I'm hoping we can still be that close again. I hope I can be his voice." Genie said.

There was silence in the car as they all contemplated the changes in their lives.

Then Nissa announced, "I think we can do this!" If we didn't have Jesus yet, then it would be impossible. But we do. I believe with Him we can be strong and courageous. Remember what Paul says in *2 Corinthians, My grace is sufficient for you, for my power is made perfect in weakness.* He continues to say, *For when I am weak, then I am strong.* I think what that means is we've been given an opportunity through Dad's weakness to show God's divine power. It won't be easy. We know that and so does Dad. Because he's a believer too, we can all stand on the faithfulness of God. His promise is this, *He will keep us strong to the end, so that we will be blameless on the day of our Lord Jesus Christ.* So we stand...In one accord...We stand."

Genie, so proud of her daughter said, "Nissa that was beautiful. What a great reminder to us all. If I remember that scripture correctly, he goes on to say we need to all agree with one another so that there may be no divisions among us and that we may be perfectly united in mind and thought. Is that where we are as a family? Are we united in bringing your dad home with us?"

"We are Mom. We talked about all of the options while you were gone and we agreed we want Dad to be with us. We want him to really understand we've forgiven him and that we love him very much." Anaya spoke for Nissa and Noelle.

Genie parked the car in the lot of the care facility and shut it off. Turning to face her daughters she said, "Well girls...I guess we know what our job is. We're called to love your dad into the arms of Jesus."

The sadness of the moment just reinforced the truth of what had been said. As a family, they were going to love like they had never loved him before.

****

Gale was waking up from a long nap. The morning spent outdoors had really refreshed his spirit. However, he hadn't had that much movement in a very long time and his body was letting him know it wasn't happy. Though he had no control over his legs, he knew they were in spasms. It was uncomfortable. He tried telling his body to stop in hopes his mind would trump the muscles that didn't seem to want to cooperate. He didn't want the girls to have to see this.

It was then the thought hit him. If he went with them, they would see this and more every day. It was degrading enough for him to have a nurse tending to his constant needs; but, the thought of his daughters having to take care of him as if he was a baby was wrong. Every instinct in him tried to refuse their offer; except the one that mattered...His heart. In his heart, he wanted more than anything to go with them and spend every moment he could in their love. They had been so gracious. It could have been so different. After leaving and letting them think he didn't love them anymore, they could have turned their backs. Gale knew the first year had been exceptionally hard on his family. He knew because he had followed them as closely as he could without them finding out the truth. In the beginning, while he still had movement, he had continued to put his plan into place. Yet, he watched them from afar. From the outside it looked like they had picked up the pieces and carried on. Genie had gone to work with Michael, for which Gale had been very thankful. He knew it was best for her to get out of that house and have less time on her hands. He knew she had to be questioning what had gone wrong; what had she done wrong to cause him to fall out of love with her. He knew her well enough to know she would think it had been her fault.

If there had been any other way. But there was now another way. He was going to go home with them and they would watch him die slowly. They had already seen how little of himself he resembled. The only thing his original plan had accomplished was the loss of time they couldn't get back.

Had he really done this all wrong? Why had he run from them? Was it pride? Was he so prideful he wouldn't stay if he wasn't who he thought he should be? He...Not God. God knew who he was inside and out, even back then.

Or maybe that was what this was all about? After all, during their separation they had all found a relationship with the Lord that hadn't existed before. Was that the purpose? Or did God just take a bad situation and use it for good? That was possible wasn't it? Gale was willing to acknowledge without Christ in his life he made some really bad decisions.

God...Why didn't I surrender years ago? Why did I have to always be in charge? In the end, none of that other stuff mattered. I'm still here lying in a bed, unable to move, waiting for someone to tend to my needs.

These were the questions that had plagued him for so long. He played them over and over in his mind until the fatigue of trying to find the answers made him weary.

Pastor Dan said to him one day after reading the questioning through his eyes, "Stop it. Stop searching for answers to all of the hard questions. Sometimes bad stuff just happens to good people. God does not cause sickness and disease. Satan is the mastermind behind all of the garbage in our lives. Remember his mission...

He comes to kill, steal and destroy. God can use what satan intended for evil for good. God always has a good plan for our lives. He wouldn't have created us with a plan and made that plan bad. *Jeremiah 29:11-14 "For I know the plans I have for you" declares the Lord, "plans to prosper you and not to harm you, plans to give you hope and a future. Then you will call upon me and come and pray to me, and I will listen to you. You will seek me and find me when you seek me with all your heart. I will be found by you," declares the Lord, "and will bring you back from captivity."* He is a loving God. Don't fret. Just trust."

Gale often reviewed Pastor's words. Lying all day allowed too much time for a mind to wander and he had to make a conscientious choice to think on good things. So he spent his time thinking on his family and the times they had together. If he didn't, the bad thoughts would try to resurface from the depths of his mind where they seemed to have taken up residence.

Today was no different. He had made himself mind weary on top of his physical fatigue. He was going to choose to say...*ENOUGH!* It was time to stop trying to figure everything out. He wasn't in any shape to be a control freak any more. Now he was going to let God be in control. Gale had given his creator free reign and it wasn't in him to take it back.

So there he lay just waiting in anticipation for Genie and the girls to return. He was going to choose to be happy and enjoy what time they were going to have. Especially his little Emma. He would give almost anything if he could take her into his arms and swing her in the air ending with a huge hug. Or even to sit quietly in a chair and read to her, what joy that would bring!

But, like Paul, he had a thorn to bear. He hadn't

asked for it and for whatever reason, God was not healing it. Not that Gale was going to stop asking. He asked God everyday to take this away and make him whole again. Yet...It continued. Was he to assume this was for God's glory? He didn't have the answers and thinking too deep gave him a headache. So he was accepting of his situation...On most days.

He heard the knock on the door as it slowly opened. Little Emma was the first one in. Running without a care in the world she came bounding for the bed when Noelle caught her up into a big swing in the air. Giggling they came straight to the bed where Emma leaned forward and planted a wet, juicy kiss on Gale's forehead. He blinked quickly hoping they could see how glad he was they were back.

"Hi Dad." Noelle said kissing him next.

Genie made her way around the bed to the other side and taking his hand in hers, she kissed it several times.

He blinked slowly three times.

"I love you too." She said as she nuzzled his hand against her cheek.

Nissa and Anaya gave them their moment before they also lovingly kissed their dad.

No one was oblivious to the fact that the tremors were worse than before.

"Did you have a good rest?" Genie asked.

He blinked twice.

"Good. We have lots to fill you in on. If you're comfortable, we'll start with the girls and their plans. Before we do, is there anything we can do to help with the tremors?"

One blink.

"Okay...Then let's move ahead." Genie made a

decision not to make a big deal out of the uncontrolled movements that she knew were making Gale more uncomfortable. She also knew he would be concerned about all of them watching this happen. But these were going to be a part of their lives and they were going to have to deal with them...Like it or not. So she just continued as if they weren't happening and the girls followed her lead. She had made a decision to be strong enough for all of them. Right now was as good as any time to start.

The evening was filled with a quick fill in of all the plans. Gale found out the girls would be leaving in the morning. Genie would be taking them to the airport. While she was gone, Hospice would be making a visit to assess all Gale was going to need to make the trip comfortably and to make sure the house would have everything set up when he arrived.

He was a little agitated when he found out Genie could not travel with him. However he calmed as she quickly explained he would need several attendants and there would simply not be enough room for her. Genie made sure he understood how important she felt it was he have every possible attendant available to help him make the trip as comfortable as possible. She explained she would leave early in the morning, a few hours before him and she would be waiting at the airport when he landed. An ambulance would be waiting with assistance and someone would be there to pick her up and they would follow him to the house.

"I know this is going to be a difficult day for you. The two agencies that we are working with have assured me they will do everything in their power to make this as comfortable for you as can be."

She continued, "Once we get home, there will be

nurses around the clock for the first couple of days to help us become comfortable. We want to make sure we understand all we need to do."

"Dad, don't worry...We'll be the best caregivers you've ever had." Anaya said as she rubbed his feet through the socks he wore.

"Right! You wait and see. We're going to be the best medicine you have." Nissa laughed.

Blinking twice, they knew he agreed.

They all enjoyed their time together; but Emma was getting sleepy and they had an early morning flight tomorrow. Genie suggested they say good-night to their father and she would run them back to the hotel.

Knowing this was going to be hard for them, Nissa tried to lighten the moment. Taking his face into her hands, with the excitement of a little girl giggle she said, "Listen, in two days we're starting a new adventure together. We'll be in our own home, we'll have more time and we'll be more comfortable. I promise you when you get there, everything will be ready. Don't worry about a thing. You just get there! Hear me?"

Gale blinked twice into the eyes of a loving daughter.

"We're all going to be okay. Got it?"

He blinked again and she tenderly kissed his cheek and stepped back.

Anaya smoothed his hair after kissing his forehead. Leaning close to his ear she said, "Don't worry. I know that I'm your favorite."

Gale blinked multiple times letting her know he got the joke.

The room was silent for a moment and then they all began to question her and laugh, "What?" she answered innocently.

"Love you Daddy."

He blinked his love back to her.

Noelle held Emma up and said, "Tell Grandpa you will see him in two days."

"Two!" She said holding up three fingers. "One, two. Go!" Her attempt brought giggles from everyone.

She kissed her Grandpa and patted his cheek.

Noelle handed her off to Nissa and leaning forward, whispered into her dad's ear, "Don't worry... It can be our secret...I will let Anaya think she is your favorite. You and I know you love me the most." And she quickly kissed him farewell.

They all knew he was wanting to laugh as his eyes blinked quickly over and over.

Genie, giving him a loving kiss said, "I'll be back as soon as I grab a quick shower."

Gale tried to blink to her she didn't have to come back. She knew instantly what all the blinking was about. She laughed, "You can't get rid of me that quick. I can't get enough of you. I intend to cuddle up in that bed right beside you tonight...Unless you object."

Gale blinked a big "OKAY".

"Good. Then I'll see you in just a little bit. You rest until I get back. I won't be long."

On that note they waved as they all walked out of the door and headed to the hotel leaving their dad and husband anxious for more.

****

Brad was laying in bed reading his daily devotional thinking about tomorrow when he would go to the airport and pick up his girls. He couldn't wait. His arms felt empty not having them there to hold. Had it only been a short part of his life they had shared? It felt like they had always been a part of him. They had become an extension of his being. Now without them, he felt lonely and incomplete as if a part of him was missing.

Those thoughts brought him to his mother. He wondered, *Is that how she's felt all of these years without dad, the man who completed her? Is that why she's never considered another man? Is it impossible to replace that spot in your life when you have been connected on that intimate level?* Brad wasn't just thinking about being man and wife. It was more than that. When you've found that person who's the other half of you, there is this connection and you just know they were created for you. He thought of swans. They mate for life and when something happens to one of them, the other just continues through to the end of their life. They finish their life cycle. It just isn't the same ever again. *Is that how Mom has felt all of these years?*

A knock on the door brought him back from that distant place of pondering.

"Come in."

The door slowly opened and there was the lady who had held his thought so recently.

"Are you up for some company?" His mom asked.

"Absolutely. I was just thinking about you." He laughed.

She came in and positioned herself in the rocker that Brad had given Noelle on the day of their wedding. "Thinking about me? Why?"

"I was just sitting here feeling sad and lonely, wishing Noelle and Emma were back. I miss them so much and they have been gone only a couple of days."

153

"And you were wondering how I have done it all of these years?"

"How have you, Mom? I know that you've missed Dad miserably. Yet, you've gone on and made a life for Eyan and me."

"And myself. I've made a life for myself. Don't think there weren't times when I wanted to crawl into bed and pull the covers up over my head. On those days I would have a good cry and tell him how much I missed him. Then I would go on with my day." She shrugged. "It wasn't like I had a choice. God saw fit to take us at separate times. He left me in charge of you two and I wasn't going to let your dad down by doing it wrong. I had an obligation to his memory to be the best parent I could be. I was only going to get one shot at raising you guys to be responsible, respectable young men. The kind of men who people would want to be around. I wanted you to be men of honor, the best men God had created you to be. I couldn't fail. The price would have been too great." She finished with a smile.

"Thanks Mom."

"For what?" She asked.

"Thanks for caring that much. Thanks for sacrificing your wants and needs to see that ours were met. I hope we didn't let you down?"

"Oh Brad...You and Eyan couldn't have met my expectations any better. You're the best sons a mom could ever have and your dad would be so very proud of you."

"I love you Mom."

"I love you too."

A knock on the door broke the moment between them.

"Come on in Eyan."

"How did you know?" Eyan asked as he opened the door.

"Who else would be joining this little party at this time of the night?" Brad answered with a laugh.

"So what's going on up here?"

"Nothing...Mom just came to cheer me up because I'm missing my girls."

"I know what you mean."

"What does that mean?" Angelina asked her second son.

"Well...I guess that absence does make the heart grow fonder. With Nissa gone, I've been figuring out a few things. Like...I really like that girl and I didn't even know it."

"Like?" Brad asked.

"No. I've been hit hard. That girl is totally under my skin. I've been asking God if this is what love feels like?"

"Oh Eyan, that's wonderful. I'm so happy for you. Are you serious enough to do something about it?" His mother asked.

"I already did. I called and sort of let her know. It was a terrible phone conversation. I butchered everything I was trying to say to her. I ended up having to call her back and apologize because I did it so badly. I promised her I would get better at that kind of thing." He chuckled. "I guess I've been so caught up in my life and ministry work, I had begun to take her for granted. She was just so easy to include in all I did and planned. She was just there. Then when she wasn't...well...I missed her. All of the sudden I realized I wanted her to be there. I didn't just need her...I wanted her."

"And does she share those same feelings?" Angelina remembered the night she was with Genie and

155

the girls when Nissa announced she was going to marry Eyan someday.

"I don't really know. This is all so new to me. It literally developed overnight on the phone. We really haven't had time to explore our feelings."

"Well, have you talked with her more than your botched up call?" Brad asked.

"For sure. I find I want to call her every time I have a thought. I like to know what she thinks about it. Plus, it's a funny feeling; but I just like to hear her voice. Know what I mean?"

"Sure do." Brad laughed. "Noelle completes my thoughts. What I miss she catches. She comes with a female perspective where I can only think like a man. That's why God calls them 'helpmates'."

"Well she told me they are coming in tomorrow. I told her I would be at the airport to pick them up." Eyan said.

"Really...Because I told Noelle I'd be there to get them."

"Well, that's not all bad. I figured you'd want to see Noelle and Emma as quick as you could. So, I'll just take Nissa with me. That way we can talk through some of this."

Brad laughed, "I remember the first time Noelle flew back here from Atlanta. I could hardly get through the day waiting for her plane to land. I swear the clock hands didn't move that day and I was at the airport way too early."

"That's it. That's how I feel. I swear...Nothing has ever been so painful."

Angelina and Brad had a nice little chuckle at Eyan's expense.

They are so much like their dad, she thought to

herself. He fell in love with her the same way. These Conroy men don't waste any time. Once they have made up their mind, it's made up. She could already see it in Eyan. He was in love and she couldn't be happier. Nissa was a wonderful young woman and would make a great wife. Now she just had to sit back and watch it all play out. Time would tell; but she was willing to bet there was a wedding in their future.

Chapter Ten

I Corinthians 13

10. but when perfection comes, the imperfect disappears.

KNOCKING ON THE DOOR THE YOUNG WOMAN called into the room, "Mr. Smith?"

"Come in." Pastor Dan extended his hand, "I'm Pastor Dan, the resident 'jump-in-wherever-I'm-needed' guy. Mr. Smith is the handsome man in the bed. He's asked me to sit in on this meeting with you. I'm a better talker and he is a better listener. Mrs. Smith has asked us to make apologies for her absence. She's gone to take their daughters to the airport. They're flying back today to ready their home in Indiana for this little trip. Won't you have a seat?" He motioned to a chair that was already positioned by the bed."

"Well of course. Thank you." As she sat down she reached over and took hold of Gale's hand.

Gale thought to himself *she's not old enough to be in charge of making decisions about a move this complicated.*

"Mr. Smith, my name is Devon Ashton and I'm going to be your coordinator for this move. We're excited to be able to help you and your family. I want to reassure you we're going to do everything within our powers to make you as comfortable as possible. Your safety and comfort will be our number one priority. I'm sure you're going to have many questions and I'll try to answer all of them to your satisfaction. We want you to feel at ease with all that will be happening. By tomorrow morning at this time you should be getting ready for take off."

Gale looked at Pastor and blinked twice.

"Mr. Smith's vocal expression has been challenged by his situation. Although, we are all becoming very good at reading his blinks. One for no. Two for yes. And multiple blinks could mean, "what the heck are you thinking...Who put you in charge."

Gale began to blink quickly.

"Okay...Okay! It may not mean that. I do like to put my own spin on his sentences." Pastor laughed along with Devon. Everyone in the room seemed to relax including Gale.

"I see what I'm up against. Two clowns! Well okay...I'm pulling out my 'slapstick comedian' personality. I can be pretty funny myself." Devon joined in the teasing.

Gale liked her. She made a difficult situation more tolerable.

"Mr. Smith?" She paused as he made a definite one blink move."

Pastor jumped in, "I think he would like you to call him Gale." He looked at his friend, "Correct?"

Two blinks

"Then Gale it is." She answered.

Looking at Gale, she said, "I asked to be able to see your medical file so we would better be able to assist you. Is that available?"

Gale blinked twice.

Pastor reached behind and grabbed a very thick file. "Most of the information is on computer; however, they have summarized his needs on the top pages. If you need anything else, they're all more than willing to be of assistance."

"Thank you." She reached for the file and took a few minutes to peruse through the pages. "This is very helpful and appears to be very informative. I can tell from this doctor's report exactly what we're going to need. May I have a copy of this?"

160

"Absolutely. I can get that for you right now." Pastor took the report and said, "I'll be just a minute." He patted Gale's hand as he headed for the door.

"Gale, this is the first time we, as an agency, have had the opportunity to speak with you about this move alone. You seem to be very much in charge of your capacities. I just need you to confirm you are sure about making this move and that no one is coercing you. We need to verify there is no force or threat causing this relocation. Do you want to move to Indiana?" Devon paused giving Gale time to respond.

Two very distinct blinks.

"That was a yes, correct?"

Two more blinks.

"Very well. I thought so. Mrs. Smith made quite an impression on our staff yesterday. She seems to be a wonderful person and she certainly loves you very much. That was very clear. You're a very lucky man."

Gale's emotions welled up and tears slid down his cheeks as he blinked twice. He knew more than anyone how lucky he was to have his family responding to his needs after what he had done to them. They certainly knew how to exhibit God's forgiving mercy and grace. The love they had all shown him was not based on emotions or feelings. They had made a decision to be committed to him without any conditions and no matter what the circumstances. Yes...He was a lucky man. He was loved by his family and loved by God. Gale knew God was just waiting for him to finish out his purpose here on this earth. He also knew eternity with God was right around the corner. So he was going to choose to be joyful while he was allowed to be here. Gale knew joy was more than happiness. He had learned from his past life that joy was not based on financial success, good health or popularity. His joy came from believing in God, obeying His will, receiving His forgiveness and participating in fellowship with other believers. Even in his condition, he had found ways to minister to others and share the gospel. Just the sheer example of the way he handled himself while walking out this debilitating disease was a witness of the grace of God's love. He had been able to find that state of peace. He lived in the assurance of his future. Because of that, there was no fear. He lived with a sense of contentment. Peace is freedom from worry, disturbance and oppressive thoughts. Those nagging thoughts could certainly plague him. He often had to take control of his thought life. He had to make a definite effort to choose peace. When he focused on the positive, loving nature of God, he was able to relax and let God be in charge of his life.

For Gale it had been a learning process. He had to learn to have patience with a body that was betraying him. He had to learn to have a quality of restraint. Patience for him was bearing pain and problems without complaining.

Then everyday he had been given the opportunity to practice kindness. There were challenges for him daily that required assistance from so many different people. He tried to be eager to put others at ease. He practiced a sweet and attractive temperament. In doing so, he hoped people saw the love of God through him.

Goodness was easy for him. He was in a position that kept him humble and thankful for everyone's help. The staff here at the facility were certainly deserving. So he practiced a selfless desire to be open hearted and generous in the little he could do to show them his gratitude. He tried to be faithful through a firm devotion to God and loyalty to those around him. Even now, in

162

this unthinkable position, he had seen God working and acting on his behalf.

Just in the way God masterminded his reunion with his family was evidence of God's love for him.

So...It was the least he could do to practice having a humble, non-threatening character. There were those days when he found himself slipping into anger. On those days he allowed gentleness to calm his spirit. He'd learned the hard way that gentleness is not weak or passive. Even Jesus himself claimed to be 'gentle and humble in heart'.

Everyday he tried to conduct himself agreeably and practice self-control. He tried to find the harmony that came with staying inside of God's will. Self-control was doing God's will and not living for one's self.

On his wall hung a gentle reminder for him to read daily:

> *But the fruit of the Spirit is love,*
> *joy, peace, patience, kindness,*
> *goodness, faithfulness, gentleness*
> *and self-control.*
> *Against such things there is no law.*
> *Galatians 5:22,23*

Though his body was weak, his spirit was strong. Though mass was failing he had the mind of Christ.

"Gale, if you have any questions that I could answer for you, I'm more than happy to do so."

He was brought back from his mental wanderings by her question. He thought for a minute about what she had just said and then blinked twice.

"Is it about the flight?"

Two blinks.

"Would you like to know what tomorrow will look like? I can walk through that with you and maybe some of your questions will be answered."

He blinked two times again.

"Great. We will leave instructions for your staff here at the facility on the time schedule we'll be following. They will know exactly what we'll need for them to do so you're ready to go when we get here. Our staff will arrive at 8:00 a.m. and we'll be leaving at 8:30 a.m. by ambulance. There will be a doctor and a nurse who will be with you from 8:00 a.m. until we hand you over to the ambulance crew. When we land in Indianapolis, your wife will be there and will follow the ambulance to your home. At that point, another doctor and nurse will be taking over. They will make sure both you and your family are comfortable. Any instructions that need to be given will happen before they leave. The Hospice staff won't leave until they are sure your family will be able to assist in all of your needs. That first night there will be a nurse staying at your house. She'll make sure everyone is settled in after the long day. From that point on someone will stop in periodically to check in and they are always available 24 hours a day if you should need something."

She paused giving Gale time to register all she had said.

"Gale...You understand what the hospice agency's directives are don't you?"

He looked at her wondering what she was saying.

Then she continued, "We are there to help you spend the last bit of time you have on this earth in a comfortable and peaceful manner. We offer no intervention that would prolong your life. We practice comfort measures. The objective is to spend quality time loving your family and building memories. If at any point your family decided to call an ambulance or ask for medical intervention, the contract we have established with you and your family will no longer be valid."

Gale blinked twice. He understood perfectly well what would be happening. He would be reuniting with his family so they could spend what little time they had together before he died. Yes...He more than anyone understood what was happening here. He had been marching towards the end for a while. The only difference now was that he didn't have to march alone.

****

Genie found Gale sleeping when she returned from the airport. The girls were somewhere in the air as she was driving back to the facility. Her mind was in overdrive trying to think of anything and everything she would need to make the trip tomorrow and have in place at the house when Gale arrived. She had been making a list since yesterday. She gave that list to Anaya along with her credit card and said she would call first thing tomorrow morning if she thought of anything else.

Anaya looked at the list and laughed, "Mom...I think this list is nervous shopping. Dad can't use half of the things on this list."

"I know Honey. I'm just wanting everything to be as simple for us as it can be. That way our energy can be focused on your dad's needs."

Nissa stepped in saying, "Don't worry. We'll do everything just the way you're asking. We'll be ready. Hospice will help us with the room setup and anything else we may need. It's going to be okay Mom. The important stuff will happen tomorrow with the move. You and Dad need to try to rest tonight. Tomorrow will be a long day for both of you."

She kissed her girls twice more and hugged Emma extra tight before letting them board the plane. They had been each other's strength these past couple of years and that wasn't going to change. Wasn't she the one who always said together they could get through anything. Well...These next few days, or weeks, whatever God granted, would tell if that was true. *Genie just relax and let God be in charge.* She thought to herself as she drove back to the facility.

As she sat in the chair watching her husband sleep, she prayed. *Okay God, I'm going to need you more than ever. Please be with us tomorrow and let everything go smoothly. Let there be no glitches. Keep all of his life-sustaining equipment working properly, let him be comfortable and relaxed. Help him not to worry and please give me an extra measure of peace. I want to depend on You; but I keep taking the problem back. I have to fight the urge to be in control instead of letting You lead. I just want everything to be okay so badly. There is so much of this that isn't in my hands and I'm being asked to trust people I don't even know. But God, I know You know them and I trust You. I'm asking that You put the right people in the places they need to be; from the pilot to the medical staff. I know You wouldn't have brought us this far to cause us more grief. You are a faithful God and we are Your servants. Help us to be strong and courageous as we walk through tomorrow and the coming days, weeks and months, if that is Your will. We love You God. AMEN.*

Just as Genie finished her prayer, she heard a soft knock on the door. She rose from her chair and went to see who it was. On the other side stood Michael and his wife. Genie was excited to see them. She stepped out into the hall and explained Gale was resting. "Let's go out to the garden. It's such a lovely afternoon. I'll catch you up with our plans. So much has happened since we talked last."

Genie talked with her friends and answered as many of their questions as she could. After almost an hour, she suggested he should be awake and they could have a nice visit. Leaving the peace of the garden with the beautiful flowers and birds flying in and out, the three of them headed in so Michael could say good-bye to his friend.

Before entering the room Genie turned to Michael and said, "I can't thank you enough for what you have done for our family. By uniting us, we've been given a second chance. We know our time is only fleeting; but it's already been a healing time. We'll spend every minute we have loving each other and thanking God for the time He has given back to us, the time you gave back to us. I'll always be eternally grateful to you." She stepped forward and hugged him and his wife before wiped her tears, took a deep breath and opened the door.

Gale was sitting in his chair. He must have woke up while they were gone and his assistant told him he had more visitors. It was at their suggestion he agreed to the chair even though he was still so tired out from his time outside yesterday.

"Gale, you have company." She said as she stepped aside and allowed them to enter the room.

Michael entered as if nothing had ever changed between them. Walking straight to the chair, he took hold of Gale's hand and patted it lovingly. "Hello my friend. It is good to see you again."

Gale blinked multiple times letting Michael and his wife know he was happy to see them."

"Genie has been telling us about your big day

167

tomorrow. We're very excited for you. We'll also be praying everything will go smoothly."

Gale looked at Genie. She walked over to him. He continued to blink quickly.

Genie smiled at her husband as she smoothed his hair, "Are you wanting to tell Michael something?"

Gale blinked twice.

"My guess is you want him to know how grateful you are. Is that it?"

Gale blinked twice.

"Me too. I wanted him to understand how very thankful we are for his loyalty to our family. I told him we'll always be grateful that he connected our family again." She laughed, "We truly are on the same wave length."

Gale blinked three times...Slowly.

"I love you too." Genie returned her love knowing that was his signal.

Michael and his wife felt like they were watching the dance of two 'mourning' doves as they played out their love for each other.

"Well, I'm glad to see the two of you have picked up right where you left off. There always was something exceptional between the two of you. I'm thankful I was in the right place at the right time."

Genie put her arm around Gale's shoulders and gently rubbed his arm. "Tomorrow will be a long day for Gale. We'll both be happy when we're home and everything is in place. However, the two Hospice agencies we've been working with have been wonderful. They really made it so easy for us to consider this move."

"You can rest assured our family will be praying for all of you tomorrow and through the following days. Is there anything we could help with?" Michael offered to his friend.

Gale blinked once letting him know all was well.

Genie added, "We certainly will appreciate your prayers. I know both of us will relax when the move is over."

Michael rose from the chair he had been sitting in; walking over to Gale he took his hand and tenderly shook it. "It has been my pleasure to call you friend. I'll keep you in my prayers and check on you often. Enjoy everyday God gives you with this beautiful lady of yours and love those girls. You're a lucky man to have found love like this. I love you my friend."

Gale blinked twice.

Michael and his wife stayed only a little while longer knowing that Gale would need all of the rest he could get for the big day tomorrow. Michael looked back and waved as he closed the door behind him.

Gale looked at Genie with tears dropping down his cheeks.

"I know my love. I know." She said as she held on to him as if to keep the enemy away for as long as she could. They both knew that the day of final good-byes was coming. On that day she would not be able to hang on. They just hoped to have enough time...Even though they both knew there would never be enough.

Morning came all too quickly even though the night seemed so long for them both. Neither one of them slept very well. Their minds continued to run full speed ahead. Sometime around 3:00 a.m. Genie told Gale they needed to pray for peace. She began praying as they lay in bed snuggled up together.

Father, we are desperate for You and Your peace that surpasses all understanding. We are anxious about this trip. We continue to trust in You; however our human

169

*nature is to worry. Remove those wearisome thoughts
from our mind and calm our spirits. Let us relax to the
point that we can get some rest for the long day ahead
of us. Quiet the thoughts that continue to run through
our minds. Let our Spirits take the lead and help us to
surrender all to You. We love you God. We thank you
for Your faithfulness, for your grace and for your mercy.
Remove satan from our presence. He is not invited to be
a part of our lives. He is not welcome. He can no longer
wreak havoc with our conscious minds. We are Yours.
And we rest in the assurance You have only good for us
and no evil can touch us while You are in charge of our
lives. Your word tells us that 'You are our peace'. It says
that 'You are not the author of confusion, but of peace'.
You say to us, 'Peace I leave with you, my peace I give
to you'. We covet all of the peace that You have for us.
We thank you that Your word is truth and we can stand
on that word. So in Jesus Name we rest in Your peace.
AMEN.*

It wasn't long after that when the two of them,
snuggled together in that small hospital bed, closed their
eyes and slept peacefully. Neither of them moved again
until a knock on the door woke them.

It took Genie a moment to realize where she
was and remember what was happening today. She
immediately looked at Gale who was still sleeping. As
carefully as possible, she slid out of the bed and went
to the door to greet the tall man who was being ever so
patient.

"Good morning. Mrs. Smith I presume?" He said
as he offered her his hand. "I'm Dr. Flynn. I will be the
attending doctor today on the ride with your husband."

Shaking his hand Genie replied, "Thank you
Doctor. Excuse us for not being more prepared this

morning. Neither of us slept very well last night."

"Certainly to be expected. I assure you everything within our control will be done to ensure a smooth trip. I'm here before the others to make sure Mr. Smith is ready and comfortable. If it's all right with you, I'd like to wake him up and get him situated in a chair for a while. It's going to be a long day on his back for him and I'd like him to have a rest from laying flat before we begin."

Genie already liked the man whose very size swallowed up space and seemed commanding. She appreciated his consideration for Gale's comfort today. "Let me call the attendants while you're waking Gale up. They can assist with that move." Genie went to the bed to press the button.

Gale was waking up as they approached and Genie took a moment to make the introduction. She explained how Dr. could translate Gale's blinks and then gave Gale a quick kiss as the attendants arrived.

"I'm going to freshen up while you are getting everything in place. My flight will be leaving an hour ahead of you. I'll be waiting when you arrive in Indianapolis."

"Absolutely. We'll have everything under control when you return." There was a reassuring nature about the doctor, which made it easier to walk away and leave him taking care of Gale.

She waved as she exited and Gale blinked twice back at her.

By the time she returned she had already washed up quickly and drank a cup of coffee one of nurses had given her. She was excited to see Gale was very comfortably sitting in his chair and the doctor was amusing him with years of crazy stories from his practice.

Everyone seemed very relaxed. Gale blinked a welcome at her just as the phone rang. Looking at her caller identification she saw it was Nissa.

"Good morning Honey." Genie answered.

"Hi Mom. How was your night?"

"It was restless. We're trying not to be anxious; it's difficult. We prayed and finally fell asleep. The doctor is here right now. How are things going at home?"

"We have already had a call from our Hospice here and they're going to make a delivery within the hour. A nurse will arrive closer to the time you guys will get here. She is planning on being here before you are. So...I think we're doing great."

"That's reassuring. I'm going to say good-bye to your dad soon and head to the airport. Pray for me. Leaving is going to be so hard."

"I know and I know you...Stop worrying. Everything is going to be wonderful. Dad is going to travel well. I feel like we're in good hands; God chosen hands."

"Well the doctor certainly has your dad relaxed right now. He has him up in a chair sitting in a different position. He'll be flat on his back until we get him home."

"Good. You're going to all be here before you know it. If you need us for anything, just call. Otherwise we'll be praying. Give Dad our love and we'll see you soon. Love you Mom."

"Love you girls too. Thanks for all you're doing. And thanks for the prayers." Genie said good-bye and went over to Gale. She kissed him gently and told him about the call.

"You seem to be cozy." She smiled lovingly at him as she smoothed her hand through his hair. "I'm going to have to leave for the airport soon. Are you okay with that?"

Gale blinked twice. Then looked at the doctor. Looking back at Genie he gave her their three blink code...I love you.

"I love you too." She kissed him one more time. "Okay...This is it. I'll see you at the house."

He blinked twice.

As she gathered her purse, phone and bag, the doctor was reassuring her they were going to be just fine. Turning she gave them one last smile, "Here we go!"

"We'll be fine. You relax and enjoy your flight." The doctor was looking confident. Waving Genie turned and walked out the door.

Her first stop was Pastor Dan's office. Knocking she heard his usual, "Come in."

Poking her head in she said, "It's me. I wanted to say good-bye before I head to the airport."

"I was just getting ready to head over to Gale's room. I'm glad you stopped. Are you doing okay?" He asked as he offered her a chair.

"I really don't have time to sit. I need to get to the airport and turn in our rental car before I check in. I couldn't leave without thanking you again for all you have done for Gale. The most important gift you have given him is your obedience to serve the Lord. Where would we be if he hadn't accepted the Lord's saving grace? As a family, we'll always be grateful."

"He is an easy God to offer. We have a great product to sell. I'm just thankful Gale was able to surrender his plan for God's plan. You'll stay in touch with me, won't you?"

"We will. And please know you are welcome anytime you can come and visit. I don't know how much time we have; but I'm planning on a gradual improvement once we get him comfortable in our home and he feels the love that will surround him."

"I have said it more than once, he's a lucky man to have a family like yours. It's been my gift seeing the love between the two of you. Together you've created a beautiful family. You're truly blessed. So many have never experienced the love you all have for each other."

"Thank you. I do feel truly blessed that God allowed us to reconnect. God is so good."

"Yes...Yes He is."

"Well then...With that I'm off. We could all use extra prayers today. I'll feel much better when this day is over and we're settled in."

"You have my prayers. I'll be praying with Gale before he leaves. Angels surrounding your airplanes, peace in your minds and joy in your Spirits." Hugging her, he prayed. *Father, thank you for your daughter. Be with her today and in the future. Give her strength to do the job You have put before her and help her to call on You daily. In Jesus Name. AMEN.*

✳✳✳✳✳✳✳✳✳✳✳✳✳✳✳✳

Eyan woke early. He lay in bed and was revisiting his talk time with Nissa last night.

He mused at the idea that conversation came so easily for her and yet he seemed to stumble over his words. It had begun to feel painful. He was thankful they were alone and he could work his way through this new territory without extra eyes and ears. Nissa was very patient with him. They had stopped to eat lunch.

"Eyan?"

"Yes."

174

"Are you okay?" Nissa asked after the waitress had taken their orders.

Taking a deep breath and looking into the face that seemed to exhibit confusion, he decided to be completely honest with her. "No...I don't think I'm okay." He answered.

"Are you sick?"

"Maybe."

The concern on her face almost made him feel sorry for the way he was handling this.

"What's wrong?" She asked.

He paused and decided to jump in. "I think I'm heart sick."

The confused look made him laugh.

"Heart sick? What do you mean 'heart sick'? Is something really seriously wrong?"

"I have to tell you this. I can't wait any longer."

"Go ahead." She nodded.

He reached over and took her hands in his. "I realized this while you were gone. I love you."

His words took her breath away. She slowly let it out. But she didn't say anything. She just kept looking at him.

"Did you hear me?" Eyan asked.

She laughed, "Yes...I heard you."

"Well?"

"Do you have any idea how long I've waited for you to say those words?"

"No. I don't think I do."

"Well I do. I knew I loved you at Noelle and Brad's wedding. I knew when I went back home to finish school. I knew when I came here to live. I knew every day I've worked with the you."

"You did?"

175

"Yes...I just didn't know when you were going to fall in love with me. I knew it was going to happen. I prayed for us every night and I reminded God if I fell madly in love with Him, He would give me the desires of my heart. So I did...And He did."

"Really? You were that confident?"

"Is God a faithful God who is true to His promises?"

"Yes. He is."

"Then what did I have to be concerned about. All I had to do was continue moving closer to him and wait for His timing."

"So his timing is now."

"Apparently it's now."

Eyan thought for a few minutes then said, "I'm thankful you were patient and you trusted Him."

"You were worth the wait."

"I'm sorry I took me so long to catch on."

"Not that long. We're young."

"We are young." The conversation had slowed and he continued rubbing circles on the inside of her tiny wrists as he stared into her eyes. He hadn't thought he would have this conversation tonight; but the timing just seemed right, "You know, it's always been my dream to go minister on a distant mission field. I've always wanted to go some place remote where no one has taken God's Word yet."

"I know."

"That's why I wasn't going to get involved seriously. I always figured a relationship would just get in the way of my dream."

She smiled and allowed him to continue. She knew where this conversation was going and she had already prayed fervently, asking God for direction. She

176

wanted to make sure the mission field was what God was calling her to and not just her following Eyan's dream.

He continued, "But now my heart is full of love for you and a desire to follow where God leads. I'm divided. I want to be considerate of your feelings. I need to know what your dreams are?"

"My dreams are simple. I've asked God to show me what He wants from me. I knew someday you would ask me this question and it was important I put God first. So if you're asking me, will I follow you where ever God leads, the answer is yes. Where you go, I'll go. We'll serve Him together. I'll try to be the best helper I can possibly be. I'll let God nurture my strong suits so I can contribute and I believe He'll place us where we'll make a difference. I'll stand by your side and serve Him with you."

"Really?" Eyan couldn't believe all of this had been going on and he'd been clueless.

"Really. I've even been setting my class schedule so my training will be beneficial to the calling." She shrugged her shoulders and giggled. "One of us had to be getting ready. During this time I was the only one who knew where we were headed."

Eyan was bursting with joy. He was beginning to realize He was going to have all he had longed for. He was going to have Nissa and his dream of living on a mission field was going to be shared by his mate. What could possibly be better?

"Well then...I think we need to discuss what that looks like?"

"What do you mean?" She asked.

"I can't very well go off to serve the Lord and take a single, young woman with me...Can I? After all, what kind of an example would that set?"

"Not a very good one." Nissa answered. Her stomach was starting to churn. Could this really be happening this quickly?

Right there in the restaurant, with the noise of the world silenced to their ears, Eyan stood from his chair, turned her to face him and knelt down on one knee. "Nissa Smith, I'm a little thick headed and it may take me a while to figure out what's best for me; but when I do, I don't waste anytime. If you'll be my wife, I promise I'll love you every day of our lives. I promise I'll protect you. I'll be your best friend, your lover and if the Lord is good, and we know He is, I'll be the best father to our children I can possibly be. I promise to serve the Lord with you and make Him the head of our house. We'll serve Him together. Will you marry me?"

Nissa was smiling even though the tears were sliding down her face. Eyan reached up and wiped the tears away.

"This a happy moment." He gently reminded her.

"I am happy." She answered.

"Do you have an answer for me?" He asked.

"Yes. Yes, Eyan Conroy, I will marry you."

"You will?" He asked again, wanting to make sure he had heard her correctly.

"Yes. I will." She laughed.

Time stood still for the two of them. He tenderly took her face into his hands and kissed her ever so gently.

She felt like she had just been captured. She thought of **Song of Songs** that Solomon had written. *"My lover is mine and I am his."* This was what she had prayed for and God was giving her the desires of her heart.

Eyan pulled his lips from hers, "No more of that

178

until I can kiss you thoroughly." Eyan said as he rose from his knee.

A patron from a nearby table yelled, "Well? What did she say?"

Eyan laughed and answered, "God is good. The lady said yes!"

The gentleman stood and said, "The man just found a bride", and he began to applaud. A round of cheers broke out around the room and their moment was shared by a restaurant full of strangers.

Nissa laughed as Eyan took a hold of his lady's hand, pulled her to her feet and spun her around. He raised his hand to everyone saying 'thank you'. Chuckling as he lowered her tenderly into her chair, he whispered into her ear, "the world loves a happy ending."

She smiled in agreement. "So do I."

The rest of the evening was spent discussing what their future looked like. As Nissa explained about the path they were taking with her dad, Eyan began to form a plan.

"Nissa, how much time do they say your dad has?"

"They haven't really said, at least not to us. We googled the disease and it's easy to see we aren't going to have him long enough."

"Well...If I'm understanding you correctly, even though his body is failing him, his mind is strong. That really is the saddest part of this disease. He must feel really bad he's already missed his first daughter's wedding. I assume his health couldn't handle a big wedding. However, I'm betting it would bring him great joy to be able to be at our wedding."

"What are you thinking Eyan?'

I'm thinking if you're happy with a small

179

wedding, maybe we should just have a family ceremony where he would be comfortable being a part of it. We could even have it in your living room."

"What?"

"If that isn't what you want, just say so. I don't care how we get married, just so we do."

"No...I love the idea. He would love it too. I'm sure of it. But Eyan, I don't know if we have enough time?"

"Then we had better get moving. We have a lot to do."

"What will the family say?" Nissa asked, suddenly embarrassed by the speed this was taking.

"Seriously...You have to ask? You know my mom. She'll have everything in place before we can go shopping for a ring. Speaking of which...Do you want me to surprise you or would like us to go together? Whatever you want is fine with me."

"I think I would like to go together. This may come as a surprise, but I don't really love diamonds. I would rather take that money and spend it on setting up our future. Matching bands are more my style."

"Are you telling me the truth? I can afford a diamond if that's what you want. The farm has made a good living for us over the years. I'm not much of a spender. Mom taught us how to manage our money well."

"Honestly Eyan, maybe someday I'll feel differently. For now, I would rather be frugal so we can get on the mission field quicker."

"You are amazing!" He answered.

"Don't you ever forget it." She laughed.

"Believe me...I know I've found a treasure. I promise to do everything in my power to make you

180

happy. I'll do everything in my power to have years and years of happiness."

"I am so happy. I've waited almost two years to hear you say these things to me."

Then he could see the shadow pass over her face. "Tell me what you are thinking." He asked her.

She hesitated only a moment and then shared her heart, "Here we are making plans to be married immediately and we just brought Dad here to live so we can take care of him. Mom and Anaya can't do this by themselves. How can I leave right away?"

He hesitated only a moment. "You can't. You have to be here to help. We'll figure it all out. Remember God already has a plan to prosper us. He won't harm us and He wants to give us hope and a future. So He'll make a way. We just have to be obedient."

"Look how you're already leading in wisdom." The pride was coming through in her voice. She loved this man.

Tucked comfortably in his bed, Eyan knew he had already spent enough time today reliving yesterday. It was time to get moving. He had told Nissa he would be at the house when her dad got there in case he could be of any help. They had decided they would wait to make their announcement until everyone was settled and he had some time to meet her dad and let him see he wasn't just a fly by the seat of his pants kind of guy when it came to Nissa. Although he was so excited he could hardly be contained, they would give her mom some room to catch her breath before dropping the bomb that they wanted to get married immediately.

****

Genie's plane had landed and she had already made connection with the ambulance through the airport's security office. All they knew at this time was the plane was on time and scheduled to land in 35 minutes. The continual watching of the clock wasn't helping her anxious spirit. She was sure the clock wasn't moving. Brad and Noelle had called her to say they were fifteen minutes out. She told them to park in the short term parking. Her plans were to meet the plane with the ambulance. Security had given her clearance so she could check on Gale and make sure he was doing okay. She just needed to see him. The kids said they would wait for her by the luggage claim.

Genie though of *II Peter* where it says, ***One day is with the Lord as a thousand years, and a thousand years as one day.*** Well right now it felt like she was in the thousand year mode. To God time may be flying past; but she was struggling with the speed she was living in.

A man in uniform came up to her and said, "Mrs. Smith, if you would follow me, the plane is about to land. I'll take you to meet the ambulance."

She jumped up and almost kissed him, "Thank you...Thank you."

He took her to a lower level of the airport on a back side away from the commercial flights. There, as they stood watching, the small airplane came in for the landing.

"Follow me please." The guard offered as he held the door. They walked through the tunnel that had been connected to the plane. She heard a noise behind her and saw the ambulance crew being escorted down the tunnel also.

"Mrs. Smith?" One of the ambulance attendants offered his hand.

"Yes." She responded back to his hand shake.

"I want to reassure you we've been in periodic contact with the staff attending to your husband. He has tolerated this move and is resting comfortably. I'm sure you're anxious; but please know he is traveling well."

Genie took a deep breath and expelled the air she was sure had been held in her lungs for some time. "Thank you. That does make me feel so much better. I've tried not to worry. It's been hard."

"Don't beat yourself up. We'd all be anxious."

The attendant's phone beeped and he looked at it. "Here we go." He motioned to her to precede him. "I'm sure you would like a few minutes to see for yourself all is well before we transport."

"Oh yes...Please? Thank you so much." She said as she hurried down the tunnel.

Entering the plane she saw a very relaxed bustle going on. The plane was small enough she could see in the cockpit where the pilots were sitting still filling out paperwork. They nodded to her as she said, "Thank you."

The doctor and nurse were doing a last check before handing him off to the ambulance crew. Stepping back they allowed her a quick moment with her husband. She walked up to Gale and kissed his forehead. "You doing okay? She asked as she lovingly smoothed his cheek.

He blinked twice.

She could see he looked tired.

He blinked their three blink code.

"I love you too. Brad and Noelle are here waiting for me. We'll be following you home. Everything is going well. I'm sure you'll be relieved when we get there. The girls have everything all set up; they are just waiting. You can rest soon. The hospice doctor and nurse are waiting for their patient."

Again, he blinked twice.

Genie felt Dr. Flynn touch her shoulder, she stepped back, "

"He has been a very accommodating patient. Everything has been very smooth. I'm sure he'll be ready to rest when you arrive at home. I'm ready to hand my patient over to this crew." Taking Gale's hand he said, "It's been my pleasure meeting you. I'm glad we had the opportunity to share this ride. I've already given my report to the ambulance crew and they're ready to transfer you. Live every day, Gale. That's what we should all do, cherish what we've been given."

She watched as Gale blinked twice.

"I'm sure my husband is very appreciative of all you've done. Thank you for taking such good care of him." Genie said to the doctor as she positioned herself out of the way. The ambulance attendants came forward and introduced themselves to Gale. They explained they were ready to shuttle him on home. Then they began the process of moving the stretcher and all of the medical devices very carefully.

"If you have any questions, Gale will answer you with eye blinks. Two blinks mean yes and one blink means no. Multiple blinks could mean he is excited about something. Good or bad."

"Don't you worry Mrs. Smith. We'll figure it out quickly enough. Everything is going to be fine." The head attendant answered with his little Indiana drawl.

"Right. Good." She answered as she watched them very professionally and carefully move him down the tunnel. She followed them through an open door that took them through a back way and when they exited there was the ambulance. Just waiting.

Before they took the stretcher to the back of the ambulance, Genie seized the moment to give him a quick kiss and say, "I'll see you at the house. I love you."

He blinked back three distinct blinks.

The attendant laughed saying, "You save that 'I love you' for us. We're your best friends on this ride."

Genie was thankful for everyone's sense of humor. Several times today it had eased the stress she was feeling. God really had sent all the right people.

Stepping back out of the way, the Security Guard suggested, "If you would follow me, I'll see you get back to the luggage claim. It can be confusing in these back halls to find your way around."

"Thank you. You've all been so kind."

"It's our pleasure to help."

There were several turns. Genie was grateful for the assistance. Without her guard she would have surely lost her way. When they opened a door and stepped out, there they were right beside the luggage claim and there stood Brad and Noelle. She saw them before they saw her.

Turning to the guard she said, "Thank you again. Especially for allowing me to see him. I'm sure none of this is normal protocol. I was so worried and seeing him relieved the stress I was feeling."

The guard nodded saying, "You're welcome. Good luck." He said as he turned to leave.

Noelle spotted her mother and headed her way with the luggage.

Brad gave Genie a big squeeze as he kissed the top of her head. "We're doing okay?"

"Yes. They let me see him on the plane and I was there when they loaded Gale into the ambulance. He seems to be doing quite well. He looks tired; but we'll take that. Thank God for his traveling mercies."

"Amen to that." Brad said. "Let's get you home before the ambulance."

"Great!"

Noelle put her arm through her mother's arm and they headed off for the final stretch. Neither of them knowing just how close they were to this journey coming to an end.

Chapter Eleven

I CORINTHIANS 13

11. When I was a child, I talked like a child, I thought like a child, I reasoned like a child. When I became a man, I put childish ways behind me.

THE AMBULANCE PULLED IN JUST A FEW MINUTES after Genie and the kids arrived. Noelle heard her mother say, "Thank you Father!"

"Amen to that." She offered in agreement. Genie put her arm around her oldest daughter and gave her a squeeze. She nodded her head, "Now we live."

Nissa, Eyan and Anaya had stayed back at the house with the hospice nurse. Theresa was going to be with them through the night to make sure Gale was comfortable and the family was all trained on the things they would need to know. The four of them joined Genie and the others.

"Mom," Nissa offered, "this is Theresa. She has been here setting every thing up for us. She's been wonderful. I think we're really in good shape to take care of Dad."

Genie turned and offered her hand to the nurse who looked so young yet her face showed a life that understood. "Thank you so much. They let me see him when they moved him from the airplane to the ambulance. I was told he traveled very well. He looked very tired to me. I think he will need to rest."

"It's nice to meet you Mrs. Smith. We'll get him settled as quickly as possible so he can do just that. How about you? How are you holding up?" Theresa sincerely asked.

"Oh...I'm fine. Or I will be when we get him settled in and comfortable."

"It won't be long now."

"I understood there would be a doctor here also?"

"Yes. The doctor has been in consultation with

the doctor on the plane and I believe with the ambulance crew. He called and said that everything had gone so well, he didn't believe he would be needed. If we need him we are to call and he'll come. I'm going to assess the situation once we have him settled in and then make that decision. I assure you that everyone has been working hard to make sure Mr. Smith is traveling comfortably. We're in good shape. I promise."

"All right. God has been doing great so far. He isn't going to leave us alone when we get this close."

"Here we go." Theresa made her way to the ambulance and Genie could see her having conversation with the crew. Minutes later Theresa was directing them to the bedroom at the back of the house on the ground level. Genie followed slowly behind giving them plenty of room to do what was necessary. The room was large. Plenty large enough for an extra twin bed against the opposite wall along with a couple of comfy upholstered chairs, still leaving room for all of the medical machines Gale needed daily. When she left home this room had been a computer room. With the attached bathroom and the slider door leading out to a small patio in the back of the house, it would be perfect for their patient. Lots of flowers and bird feeders were set up around the yard. This would be a wonderful place for someone to sit and relax as they were surrounded by God's creation. The room smelled lovely. Very earthy. There was a large bouquet of flowers sitting on a table with candles burning around the vase. The room was perfect. Genie was very proud of her girls, they'd done a great job getting everything ready.

Then she noticed on the other side of the bed was a new recliner very similar to the one that had been in Gale's room at the care facility.

190

"Where did you get that?" Genie asked Nissa who was now standing outside of the door by Genie.

"We told the nurse about him having one at the home and she suggested having one would be very nice for him so he had different options for positioning. Brad ran out this morning and picked it up for us."

Genie said to her family, that had all gathered outside of the room, "What a great idea. You've done such a great job. I couldn't have done better myself. Brad...Thank you.

No need to thank me. It was a team effort. I got the easy part. Eyan stayed here with the girls and together they moved all of the furniture in and out. That was the real work. They really deserve all of the credit."

"I couldn't be prouder of all of you. Thank you. So...so...much."

"I'm going to give your dad a quick kiss and let him know we're all here. Then I think he'll need to rest for a while. It's been a long day for him and he's been strong enough. A nap will do him a lot of good. I'll just check with the nurse and then I'll join you." She said as she entered the room.

Gale's eyes focused on her as soon as she approached the bed. Taking his hand she asked, "Are you comfortable Honey? It's been a long day."

He blinked twice.

"Tired?"

Two blinks.

"You rest for a while. We're all here and we aren't going anywhere. We can all visit when you wake up. Okay?"

Two blinks.

"I'm sure Theresa has a lot to teach us. She can do that while you're resting." Genie looked over at

Theresa and winked. The young nurse smiled back and again Genie could feel her kindred spirit. Yes...This girl understood loss. There was a compassion that emitted from her spirit that only comes from saying good-bye to someone you love. Genie knew she had a story.

"Theresa, is there anything you need?"

"No. We're in great shape Mrs. Smith. You and your family have done a fabulous job setting everything up. You have a beautiful home. Mr. Smith has a beautiful view to enjoy. I see days sitting on the patio watching the birds and hearing them sing."

Genie looked at Gale, "Please call us by our first names, Gale and Genie."

Gale blinked a yes.

"Very well. Thank you. You're both so kind."

"How are we doing?" Genie directed the question to Theresa as she attended to Gale's needs.

"We're doing great. You're right though, he has had a long day and I think as soon as I get everything set up and checked out, he'll rest for a while."

"Please join us. I'm sure we'll overwhelm you with questions. There is so much we need to learn."

"Not as much as you would think. The most important need, you all fill so easily."

"What is that?"

"Love." Theresa patted Gale's hand.

Genie responded with a smile at the man lying in the bed, "That's easy. He taught us that. And he is loved very much."

Genie kissed his cheek and said, "You rest. We'll be out here waiting for you. When you wake, we'll all have a good visit and then you can meet the boys."

Genie remembered to tell Theresa, "You will need to know he communicates well with his eyes. One blink is no. Two blinks is yes. Lots of blinks is excitement about something, good or bad."

"Got it." Looking at Gale she said, "I'm a quick learner."

He blinked twice and his eyes fell closed. He was already asleep before Genie turned and walked out of the room.

Theresa finished and followed her out with a maroon binder in her hand, closing the door softly as they left.

Genie escorted the newest member of their group into the kitchen where everyone was gathered around the table. The girls had put the extension in and the table was covered with food. There sat Angelina at the end of the room.

Angelina stood up, and coming to her friend, wrapped Genie in her arms. They held the embrace long enough for Angelina to send strength to Genie's travel weary body.

"I should have known you would come with food."

"Yes, you should have. It's the one thing I can do to help. You're all going to have to eat. I know how to feed."

"You certainly do my friend." Turning to Theresa she said, "Let me make introductions and then please have a seat and we'll eat.

"You don't have to feed me." Theresa instantly objected.

They all laughed before the rounds of, "Oh...Yes we do. You don't know my mom. We feed everyone. It's what Angelina does."

"Okay...Okay...I get it. I'll eat." She surrendered. She was outnumbered.

Genie made the introductions as they all sat down to eat and she asked Brad to pray.

Reaching to both of the people at his sides, he waited while they all followed his lead. When they were bonded by their circle, Brad began. *"Father, thank you for the safe travels today and for bringing Gale home to his loving family. We are grateful for Your faithfulness, grace and mercy. We ask You give Your strength to each of us as we journey on with him. May his days be rich and full, may his life be blessed and may we all see the beauty of life and not the darkness of death. Thank you for Theresa and be with us as we learn to attend to Gale's everyday needs. Help us to remember the greatest of these is love and that love covers a multitude of needs. Bless this food and the hands that prepared it. May it give us both spiritual and physical strength. In Jesus Name. AMEN."*

"Amen." They all echoed.

The table talk started out light as everyone filled their plates and then settled into the training they were desperate to have.

Theresa answered all of their questions calmly and assuredly. "It isn't going to be as difficult as you all think. Brad's prayer was spot on. Love does cover a multitude of mistakes. That's what your husband and dad needs more than anything else. I can tell you are going to excel in that area. Your gentle spirits will go a long way in making his time with you precious."

"Theresa, we have never asked this question; but, what kind of time do we have?" Genie's eyes shone with the desperation she was feeling.

"I wish I could give you the answer you're looking for. I've talked with the doctor who was treating Gale in Georgia and after reading his records, I see a very steady decline. ALS is not a pretty death. The best you can hope is for him to go to sleep and not wake up. His muscles have been on a steady decline for some time now. The disease frequently begins in the hands, feet or limbs and then spreads to other parts of your body. As the disease advances, your muscles become progressively weaker until they are paralyzed. It eventually affects chewing, swallowing, speaking and breathing."

She paused giving them time to process all she was saying, "Gale's progression has been swift. As you have seen, he has walked through all of those stages already. This is a disease of the nerve cells in the brain and spinal cord that control voluntary muscle movement. He received a feeding tube over a year ago because he was aspirating his food when he swallowed. My guess is you've watched him decline in weight. He was put on mechanical ventilation shortly after his feeding tube and has been in a state of decline ever since."

It was at this point that Genie felt it necessary to explain their situation to Theresa. "There is a story here you haven't heard. Almost 3 1/2 years ago, the girls and I came home to a letter from Gale saying he was leaving. He told us he had found someone else to love and though he loved us very much, had to leave to start a new life. We were devastated. The five of us had a wonderful life. Gale and I were very much in love and seemed very happy. We never could make any sense of it. He saw to it that we were taken care of. The house was paid for and given to us and a check came every month. It was all handled through an attorney and we never saw Gale again. That is until we received a call from a mutual friend who happened to be in the care facility where Gale was living and saw him. Michael called us and we flew down the next day."

195

"I see. He was going to protect you from the ugliness of ALS. He loves you all very much."

"We're just thankful God's timing is perfect. He could have died by himself and we would have never known just how much he did love us. We understand why he thought this was the best way. We simply didn't agree. So we told him we were bringing him home. And here we are."

"It certainly makes sense with the time line in his records. He must have known about his disease for a year before he left. He was diagnosed about 4 1/2 years ago."

"Is that significant?" Nissa asked.

"It is in the sense that death often occurs within three to five years of diagnosis. Only one in four patients survive for more than five years after finding out they have this debilitating disease."

"Are you saying we could have less than six months?" Genie asked.

Theresa thought for a moment before answering, "I'm saying I think you should live every day with as much love as you can. At this point, every day is an extra gift of love. None of us are guaranteed tomorrow. Especially someone who is in the kind of condition Gale is in."

"What you're saying is we could lose him at any point. Right? Isn't that what you are trying to tell us?" Nissa pressed on.

Theresa nodded, "Yes." Theresa allowed a pause before continuing. "It's more important to look at the quality of time spent together, than it is to count the minutes. Say every thing you need to say. Don't leave anything unspoken. Love like I've already seen. You are excellent at that. Make the most of the time you have instead of worrying about what is around the corner."

The room was quiet. Genie was looking into the faces of the people she loved. She was looking for assurance they were not going to lose the man they had just found. No one said a word. There were no words of comfort and the silence became uncomfortable.

Until Eyan broke the somber moment. "Then I suggest Theresa is right and we should live each moment as if we may not have another. That being said, Nissa and I have an announcement to make."

Nissa looked at him as if she were clueless. Eyan waited for her to show him she was on board. It took her a few moments before the reality of what he was about to say set in. When it did she broke out in a big smile and nodded her approval.

"What is it?" Genie couldn't imagine what they were thinking.

Taking Nissa's hand in his and bringing it to his lips to gently kiss it, Eyan said, "We want to be married; we want to be married immediately so Nissa's dad can be a part of our celebration. Due to the circumstances, he missed Brad and Noelle's. Imagine what it would mean for him to be able to share in this family moment. Besides now that I woke up to my feelings, I don't want to waste a minute of our life together."

"What?!" Was heard around the table.

The two young people were smiling ear to ear, obviously enjoying the moment.

Brad broke out in a huge laugh as he pointed at his brother.

Genie saw the look of love on their faces and joined in the laughter, "Will I never have a daughter who takes her time and plans a wedding? Will we always have weddings on the run?"

Angelina jumped in with, "Maybe you will now that my sons are all spoken for."

A round of hugs and kisses broke out. Congratulations were shared by all

Genie pulled her daughter into her motherly arms and kissed her forehead. "I don't have to ask, I can see the love in your eyes. I'm so happy for you."

"I knew God was going to give Eyan to me. I just had to wait for God's timing. When we left, suddenly he began to realize what a piece of his world I was. He loves me Mom and I have loved him from the very moment we met."

"He is a special young man. I know you'll be very happy. I've watched how Brad loves Noelle and our family. The boys have been taught the importance of family. You'll be in good hands. I'm excited for you. See there...When you wait for God's best, dreams really do come true."

Theresa observed as an outsider. She was watching love in motion. It was a beautiful dance full of rhythm and grace. She was right about this family... They knew how to love. Yes...Gale was in good hands.

As the gang quieted, they began to ask questions.

Nissa answered with, "I don't know why you're all surprised. Did I not tell you almost two years ago I was going to marry Eyan. We just had to wait for him to figure it out."

Eyan laughed, "She's right. Nissa's been a part of my life almost every day since you guys moved here and I didn't know what an important part until you left a few days ago. When she was gone, a part of me left with her. It may have taken me some time to figure it out; but when I did, it made complete sense. I was in love. I think I have been the whole time. It was just that our

198

lives were so easy and I was comfortable. Then one day, it wasn't. I was miserable."

"I can vouch for that. He came and talked to me about it. It really was quite painful to watch him come to the reality of what he was experiencing." Brad threw in.

They all had a good laugh on Eyan.

Nissa said, "We had decided to wait until Mom had a chance to catch her breath and rest a little. Given what Theresa has shared with us tonight, maybe we had better move ahead as soon as possible."

Genie, with the fatigue of the trip closing in on her, began to feel overwhelmed. They could all see the change on her face. The joy of the moment was slipping away.

"Mom...Don't panic. We're thinking we would just have a small ceremony right here in the living room. That way it would be comfortable for Dad. It doesn't have to be anything extreme."

Eyan reached over and took Nissa's hand in his, "Neither one of us care about a big wedding. Having you all here is all that matters to us."

Angelina asked, "Can I jump in?"

They all laughed knowing by asking she was only being polite, "You all have so much on your plate, why don't you let me take care of arranging the wedding. I love to do stuff like that anyway."

"Awesome." Nissa thought it was a great idea.

"Genie, is that okay with you? I know you didn't get to do much planning for Noelle's wedding. This really does seem to be a pattern with my boys. When they make up their minds they just bulldoze ahead." Angelina really wanted Genie to understand she was just offering and if Genie had other plans that was okay too. "I'll do whatever you want me to do."

"Thank you Angelina. This has taken me by surprise. Don't get me wrong, I'm completely thrilled for the both of you. I just need some time to see what this looks like here and how we can fit your dad into the plan."

Noelle offered a solution, "Here is just a thought. Dad didn't get to see my wedding and I understand Nissa wanting to do this quickly so he can be here. We have dresses. We could all wear what we wore at my wedding. I would like Dad to see how beautiful we looked on that day. The difference would just be I would wear Nissa's dress and she could wear my wedding dress." Looking at Nissa she said, "It's just an offer. I certainly understand if you want to get your own dress and do things your way."

"No...It's a perfect idea. I love it. Let's do it. It's like Dad could be a part of both days then." Nissa was really excited about it. "Plus, we don't have to worry about days to go shopping and get alterations done. Noelle and I are the same size. We can easily swap dresses."

Genie looked at Angelina and said, "I guess you have a wedding to plan. I think we can make this work."

"Nissa and I will go tomorrow and apply for our marriage license. We can stop by and order a cake and flowers. We'll use the same shops we used for Brad and Noelle's. Then we'll pop over and order tuxes for Brad and I. It will be simple and beautiful."

"Aren't you forgetting something?" Nissa asked.

Eyan thought for a minute and said, "Oh right. Pastor Travis. We'll stop and talk to him too."

"And..." Nissa continued.

Thinking harder Eyan came up blank, "Help me here...That's your job now Helpmate."

She held up her left hand and said, "With this ring..."

"Oh that...Yup...We'll take care of that tomorrow too." Again, he kissed her hand. "We have a busy day ahead of us tomorrow. After we talk with Travis, we'll call you with a locked in date and time. In fact, he had better be our first stop. I'll call him tonight and find out what time he can see us. Hopefully in the morning."

Genie asked, "What about after the wedding? Where will you live?"

"We haven't really had time to work through all of that. This decision to get married happened yesterday. I do know Nissa wants to be here near her dad so she can spend as much time with him as possible. I also know she wants to be able to help you with his care."

"Well then, why don't you set up house in the basement for now. It's comfortable and there is a bedroom and bathroom for your privacy. You don't have to, it is just a thought." Genie offered hoping the kids weren't going to think she was being pushy.

"Oh Eyan...I'd love that for now."

"Okay then. See how it all comes together. Everything will be perfect." Eyan really did understand Nissa's need to be close by.

Genie remembering Theresa, looked over at her and laughed, "What must you think of all of us? You must think we're all nuts."

"Oh my goodness no. I think I have just been privileged to watch a well oiled machine in motion. I've never seen anyone plan a wedding in ten minutes. You guys are amazing."

They all laughed.

Theresa continued, "I also think this is one of the best ideas I've ever seen come out of a Hospice situation.

Gale is so fortunate to have you all in his life. It can be a great idea to give a loved one something to live for. This is perfect. It may be just what he needs. He'll love this.

Genie smiled at the young couple so excited sitting across the table from her and said, "Yes he will. We will too."

Chapter Twelve

I CORINTHIANS 13

12. Now I see a poor reflection as in a mirror; then we shall see face to face. Now I know in part; then I shall know fully, even as I am fully known.

THAT NIGHT AFTER THE EXCITEMENT AROUND THE dinner table, the whole family filed into Gale's room when he woke up. They helped Theresa move him from the bed to the chair so he could be more a part of all that was happening. Introductions were made and everyone joined in the camaraderie. Including Gale. Genie loved watching her family together. She also loved that Gale was getting the chance to see how their family and Angelina's had blended together into one. God had brought them together through Brad and Noelle and he was keeping them together with the union of Eyan and Nissa.

After lots of conversation and having the opportunity to laugh together, Eyan stepped forward and kneeled down beside Gale's chair.

"Mr. Smith, I know this is going to seem like a strange time for what I'm about to ask you. It certainly isn't the conventional way of moving forward. Under the circumstances, we feel it's important. Nissa and I love each other and with your permission, we would like to be married here at the house in the next few days. We want you to be a part of our union. We want you to share in our day. This means a lot to your daughter and she means a lot to me. I'm asking would you bless our marriage?"

Gale looked to Genie for her affirmation. He was touched; yet, he didn't know this man who was asking to take his daughter. Who was he? Was he worthy of Nissa's love? Looking at Nissa, he could see she loved this man. The look on her face told that story. Is this something he should approve of? Then he thought...

They are including me in something I don't deserve, the privilege of watching Nissa get married. I missed Noelle's wedding because of choices I made. Here they are giving me a second chance.

Genie's eyes told him everything he needed to know. She had already read his mind and her look of love told him there was no need for him to go in that direction. She nodded her approval to him and smiled. He understood how lucky he was and what a gift he was being given.

Looking Eyan in the eyes, he blinked twice very deliberately.

"Thank you Mr. Smith. I promise to love your daughter with the love of Christ. I understand the gift I've been given and will treasure her forever. I'll make you proud of me. I will honor you and your family as you all become my family."

There wasn't a dry eye in the room. Everyone understood the true commitment Eyan was making not just to Nissa; but to Gale, Genie and the girls. He was letting Gale know he, and Brad, would be there to take care of his girls forever. They would never be alone.

These were important words to a man who was dying; to a man who knew he wouldn't be the one to take care of those whom he loved. There was a peace in seeing the men who God had brought into their lives. Gale could see these were men who knew God, who understood the importance of family and covenant and who would be there for the duration. Gale could do nothing more than thank God for his enduring grace and mercy. He was reminded that God's faithfulness reaches to the mountains. *Thank you God. Thank You God. Thank you God.*

Angelina's heart swelled with love for her sons.

They were good men. Their dad would have been very proud. She certainly was.

Though she hadn't wanted to leave Gale, Theresa insisted Genie go to her own bed and get a good night of sleep. It had been a long day for both of them. With Gale's already weakened body, she wasn't comfortable leaving him just yet. But, she also knew the days ahead of them were going to be full and she would need all of her strength. After all, she was going to become the main caregiver of her husband. The girls would be there to help. But Genie wanted to make sure that Gale hung onto his dignity and the girls hung onto the best memories of their dad that this situation was going to allow. Tonight she would rest and prepare for the task she had chosen.

Their first full day at home was a blur of activity. Genie was feeling more in control of herself. She had slept surprisingly well in her own bed, even with Gale just down the stairs.

Theresa was doing her best to show Genie everything she was going to need to know. Genie was trying to make sure she absorbed all of this new knowledge. She was learning about the breathing machine that pushed the air into Gale's lungs; the importance of turning him and watching for bed sores and she was becoming proficient with the feeding tube. Then there was the care of his catheter and the correct way to use the Hoyer that helped lift and transport him into the chair and then back into the bed. Genie felt like she had been taking notes all morning. Theresa patiently explained what would be crucial to get right and what would be laughing moments if done wrong. She had been a great teacher, reassuring Genie regularly that she could do this. By the end of the day, Genie almost believed that to be true. She was feeling confident and the bedroom had been transformed into a medical facility. Theresa made sure to stress that Hospice manned the office 24/7. No matter what time, if there was a problem or just a question needing clarification, someone would get a message to a nurse to call back.

"You're not in this alone. We'll be with you as much or as little as you would like." Talking directly to Gale she said, "Remember, this is your journey and you can walk it any way you want. We are only here to assist you where and when you want assistance."

Gale blinked twice. He knew what she was saying. He was doing the dying. It was his choice how he did it. Well...That wasn't really true at all. It wasn't his choice to die. He wanted to live. With every thought he wanted to live. It was his body that was calling the shots. His body was dying. As sharp as his mind was, it couldn't stop it. So there were lots of things he wasn't going to get to do his way.

He was grateful for the love of his family. He wasn't sure now why it had seemed so important to leave them. If he could go back, he wouldn't have missed one second of their lives together. That was then and this was now. He knew there was no going back. The only way he had to go was forward. Forward didn't look so good.

Theresa was going over last minute questions. The time had come for her to leave. Gale was comfortable. Genie seemed very competent with her new role. All of the emergency numbers were handy in the maroon binder. Theresa continued, "There will be someone stopping by tomorrow to help with any personal care you may want assistance with. Also, someone will be in contact with you about sitting services. If you want to run to the store or just get away for a few hours, we have people on staff who volunteer to just come and stay for a few hours."

Genie, looking at Gale answered, "I'm not going anywhere. We're here now. We're going to spend our days relaxing and being together." She patted Gale's hand.

"Genie," Theresa became very serious, "Gale would not want you to neglect yourself. You won't be any help to him if you don't rest also."

"I understand. I do. I have the girls and there are always Brad and Eyan if I need muscle. You've set us up for success. We're going to be very comfortable. We'll be fine, both of us...I promise.

Theresa knew when she had said enough. The truth was, she didn't believe they were going to have a lot of time together. They should enjoy every minute they could. This was their time for healing...And their time to say good-bye.

Taking his hand Theresa said, "Gale, I'll see you in a couple of days. You're in great hands. They all love you very much. You're a very fortunate man. God has given you an amazing family, enjoy every minute." She smiled and walked to the door.

Genie followed her out and led her outside. "Thank you again for everything. You've been very kind."

"It really has been my pleasure."

"Can I ask you a question before you go?"

"Certainly."

"Why do you do this. I sense there is a story."

209

Taking a deep breath she replied, "You're very intuitive. There is a story. Six years ago, I was a woman in love with a wonderful man. My husband and I had been married for three months when he was hit by a drunk driver. He laid in a coma for another three months before complications of an unstoppable infection raged through his body. My life crumbled. A year went by and I couldn't pull myself out of the deep, dark depression that had become my life. My sisters insisted I go to counseling. I went just to get them to leave me alone. Out of that I realized my life had not ended that day in the hospital. The group of people who were in my grief group convinced me that if I wanted to find a way to go on, I needed to find a way to make a difference in other people's lives. I went back to private nursing care and realized I was good with people who were facing end of life. So here I am. Everyday I still see Tony in his hospital bed and it still feels like yesterday. I go on because I feel like someone needs me."

"You had no children?"

"I was three months pregnant when the accident happened. I miscarried when I was told. Just another of the guilts I had to learn to live through."

"You are so young. Have you not thought about marrying again?"

Theresa laughed and shook her head no. "He was the love of my life. When you have experienced the best it is hard to settle for seconds. I measure all of the men I meet against Tony. That's a hard act to follow."

Genie understood exactly what Theresa was saying. It was the very reason she had never dated since Gale had left. She measured men against the standard Gale had set for her. They never could compare. "I get that. I'm going to pray for healing for you and an opportunity to find happiness again."

"Well, if that's God's will, then it will be so. Thank you Genie. Call us if you need anything." With that she hugged Genie quickly and walked to her car.

Genie closed the door and leaned against it. She listened for just a moment. Faintly she could hear Gale's machine rhythmically pushing the air in his lungs. She was alone. Just her and Gale. The girls were all out. Anaya was at school making arrangements to be absent when necessary. Nissa was taking care of wedding plans and filing papers to be on medical leave from work. Noelle was home with Emma. She knew soon the house would be full and the quiet would be gone. But for now... Just this moment...She was alone. *Father, can I do this? Can I be strong enough for Gale and the girls? Who will be strong enough for me?*

> *Remember my words to you, my daughter.*
> *The Lord is my shepherd, I shall not want.*
> *He makes me lie down in green pastures.*
> *He leads me beside quiet waters, he restores my soul.*
> *He guides me in paths of righteousness for His name's sake.*
> *Even though I walk through the valley of the shadow of death, I will fear no evil, for You are with me; Your rod and Your staff they comfort me.*
> *You prepare a table before me in the presence of my enemies, You anoint my head with oil; my cup overflows.*
> *Surely goodness and love will follow me all the days of my life, and I will dwell in the house of the Lord for ever.*

His words from Psalm 23 had immediately come to her remembrance. The words were water to her soul. He would be her strength. He would fill her with everything she would need. He would lead her down paths of peace and quiet where he would see she was renewed. All she had to do was keep her eyes focused on Him. What did the words say? He would guide her and she would not be in want. She thought of green pastures and the feelings of life. Each sentence was full of rest and relaxation. In the calm of the days, He would fill her up with the energy she would need to face each challenge. Even when they were taking that last walk into the valley, they could go there with confidence. He would be there with them guiding them through uncharted territory. His love and His mercy would be with them as long as they remained under the protection of His wings. That was exactly where Genie was going to stay, safe and sheltered by the Father's loving arms.

She went back into Gale's room and found him to be sleeping. She watched him breathe, she soothed the hair from his head, "Sleep my love. The Father is watching over us." Grabbing the Bible on the table by the lamp, she pulled the chair closer to the bed and opened to the Psalms and began to softly read. As she read, the room filled with a peace and she could feel the Father's presence flooding over them. *Thank you Father. Thank you.*

✲✲✲✲✲✲✲✲✲✲✲✲✲✲✲✲

The chaos of the afternoon and evening was coming to a halt. Everyone had been in and out of Gale's room. They all had stories to tell of the adventures of the day. Especially Nissa and Eyan. Their day had been full of wedding plans and preparations. They had to share every moment with Nissa's dad. It was fun just to watch his excitement about every plan they had made.

The first stop of their morning had been with Travis and Rebecca, who weren't surprised at all by their announcement. They admitted they had wondered what had taken Eyan so long to figure it out. The two of them had seen the love growing out of the friendship that was developing from the very beginning.

After hearing Nissa's story about her dad and what had happened, they understood the importance of moving quickly. Their immediate concern was for Gale and his relationship with Christ. Nissa was relieved to be able to tell them he was a believer. She shared all about the wonderful Pastor at the facility and how he had nurtured that relationship. She told of his caring nature and how her dad had responded to him. They had become friends and he had led her dad to the Lord.

"We'll come and visit with him and your mother as soon as possible. We certainly want to help in any way we can. Your mother is such a sweet person. It'll be important to come along beside her and lift her in prayer. We want to be there for all of you." Rebecca said.

"Thank you so much. It seems so strange. We grieved the loss of dad and we moved on. At first we were so angry and then, after finding our own relationship with God, we began to pray for dad. We did it so we could find peace in our own lives. The unforgiveness we were harboring was only causing us bitterness. We always prayed God would put someone in Dad's life so he could find the love of the Savior. Now here we are, reunited; yet, preparing to say good-bye all over again. Sometimes life just doesn't make any sense. However, if it hadn't been for the way all of this played out, Noelle wouldn't have run away, we wouldn't have ended up here and Brad and Eyan would not have become part of

213

our family. God always makes something good out of the craziness this world has to offer. So regardless of the pain we lived through, I guess I'm thankful." Nissa laughed.

"That's a very mature way of looking at the challenges you all are facing. I have to say I'm very proud of you and your family. You have certainly been an example for all of us on forgiveness." Travis complimented her.

"Now let's see what we can figure out about this wedding. These Conroy boys don't mess around. Once their mind is made up they kick into high gear." He jokingly added.

They spent a couple of hours working through the arrangements and decided they would get married on Sunday after the church service. They were in agreement the ceremony should be traditional and sweet. More of a dedication of their lives to Christ and His service. Travis was totally on board with traditional, but 'sweet'? "What does that mean?" He asked.

"You'll figure it out and it'll be an awesome day." Nissa said.

Travis wasn't sure about that request. He was going to have to spend some time thinking about 'sweet'.

Travis and Rebecca were pleased to learn the young couple still intended to pursue a ministry on the mission field after...well after they were no longer needed at home.

While Eyan and Nissa shared the excitement of their day, Emma lay cuddled up in her Grandpa's arms. Genie seized the moment to capture the love in pictures. Grabbing her camera she took several pictures of the two of them. She chose her angles carefully to be sensitive to Gale's feelings. Showing him the pictures of sweetness that followed his granddaughter everywhere she went, he relaxed a little. He seemed to grow comfortable with the pictures Genie was always snapping of him and the girls, or he and Genie together.

The moments she loved charted their coarse. This was an important part of their lives. She had always taken lots of pictures. If this was how their life together was to end, then it was going to be a captured journey of love. After all, the life of their Savior was a picture of love even though his last days were pain and suffering. The beauty of that picture has carried on for over 2000 years. Genie wanted Gale to understand he was still a vital part of this family and long after he was gone, he would be remembered for the love he had given to each of them. The three years he was separated from them, wasn't going to change the role he played in their lives.

Father, I am so thankful the girls and I found You and discovered how to forgive Gale during that time of separation.

She thought about forgiveness. In the Bible, in the Old Testament, forgiveness was connected to sacrifice and was delivered by the priests who offered the sacrifice of blood. The sacrifice was appropriately connected to atonement, or covering over, of the sin. In the New Testament, when Jesus Christ came and died on that cross, He became the atonement, or covering, for all sinners who would call him Lord. He delivered sinners from a penalty divinely and righteously imposed. His blood covered it all. We were forgiven.

Genie thought about **Matthew 6:14-15 For if you forgive men when they sin against you, your heavenly Father will also forgive you. But if you do not forgive men their sins, your Father will not forgive your sins.**

When the girls and she were first learning about
215

God and His love, forgiveness was a huge stumbling block for them. They were all filled with bitterness and anger because of the turn their lives had taken. They had a choice to make. Did they remain broken and bitter, or forgive and be healed? Jesus' words were a constant reminder of what God was calling them to do. They wanted God's forgiveness and as great step followers, it was clear to them. Step one. If they would forgive. Step two. God would forgive them. So they did.

This was a go to for them *I John 1:5-9 This is the message we have heard from Him and declare to you: God is light; in Him there is no darkness at all. If we claim to have fellowship with Him yet walk in the darkness, we lie and do not live by the truth. But if we walk in the light, as he is in the light, we fellowship with one another, and the blood of Jesus, His Son, purifies us from all sin.*

If we claim to be without sin, we deceive ourselves and the truth is not in us. If we confess our sins, He is faithful and just and will forgive us our sins and purify us from all unrighteousness.

Forgiving for them required an ongoing decision to let go of the offense against them and give up the inclination for vengeance, retribution or the entertainment of negative thoughts toward their offender. In this case it was the man they loved, her husband and the girls' father. They had also come to realize that forgiveness was not forgetting or condoning. They had accepted that forgiveness for them would not necessarily bring reconciliation. They believed that due to Gale's choice they were in an inactive relationship and may never have the opportunity to interact with or confront their offender. They had to learn to forgive through the love of Christ. It was a process that had taken time to complete. It had been work. They had to work on their hearts, regardless of what was going on in their dad's heart.

Because of their decision to forgive, now they were living the outcome of grace. Their family had been restored. It wasn't in a way they would have chosen. However, they knew God's plan was perfect. So here they were, walking a hard, sad path and trusting God to make it perfect.

As the evening was drawing to an end, everyone began to say good-night. Brad and Noelle picked up the sleeping Emma and headed to the car while Nissa walked with them to the door to say good-night to Eyan.

Genie found herself alone in Gale's room with her youngest daughter.

"Mom," Anaya said, "If you would like to get some sleep, I'll stay here with Dad."

"I'm..." Genie stopped in mid stream of telling Anaya no, when she realized maybe Anaya was offering because she needed some time alone with her dad. So she changed her answer. "I'll spend the night here in the room; however, if you would like to sit with him, I could use some time to tidy things up and take a shower. If you're okay for a while, maybe I'll even take a little nap."

"Sure!" Anaya's enthusiasm told Genie she had been correct.

"Okay. Thank you Honey." She kissed Gale and then her daughter on the head and left the room.

Anaya pulled a chair up to the bed and rubbed her dad's hand. Stroking it with love she said, "Hi Dad."

He blinked twice.

"I've been wanting some time for just the two of us."

Two blinks again.

217

"You aren't too tired are you for us to talk a bit?"

"One blink.

"I just wanted you to know how much I love you. I know we got off track for a while; but I don't want you to think about that time. I understand why you did what you did. You loved us enough to sacrifice the time you would have with us to protect us from what you were afraid was coming. I get that. I just wanted you to know I admire you for your strength. Not everyone would have been brave enough to face a scary future by themselves. I remember as a little girl, you always put our needs first. You were there when we wanted to play, you were there when we needed to cuddle up on your lap and you were there when something in the night scared us and we needed to know we were safe."

As tears rolled down both of their eyes, Anaya reached for a tissue and wiped the tears from her dad's eyes. "Now stop or Mom won't let me sit with you again by myself." She laughed and he blinked twice.

"I don't know...I just wanted you to understand I forgave you a long time ago for leaving. Even before I knew about all of this. We all did. God helped us do that. I don't want you thinking about anything except how much we love you. I wanted you to know you were a good daddy and I am who I am today because of you and mom."

He blinked twice.

"Daddy...I will always be your little girl. Even when the years have separated us and we are waiting to be together again, my memories of having a great dad will carry me through. And when God sends me the perfect man to spend the rest of my life with, I know he will look just like you. He will be the best husband and the best dad. Just like you." She laid her head down on his arm and let him feel the love she had for him. They laid there for the longest time just enjoying their moment alone. No need for words, just an understanding of two hearts.

Anaya raised her head and looking into the eyes of the man who she loved said, "I feel your love Dad."

He blinked three times.

"I love you too." Anaya answered back.

When Genie returned that is where she found them wrapped in the love of each other.

Gale looked at Genie and blinked twice.

"You're welcome." She said.

****

The next couple of days passed in a flurry. The daily activity was becoming routine and there was a flow to their schedule. Feeding, positioning changes, daily time spent on the patio. Gale loved that time. Just to sit and watch the wind blow was a blessing for him. The singing of the birds and the chatter as they communicated from tree to tree brought him such pleasure. Genie wanted those times to go on forever. She knew all too soon they would be gone. She wasn't a nurse; but she could see the effort it took for every move that was made for him. She also noticed there was a difference in his breathing. It seemed more labored. She was glad it was a nurse day.

In the midst of their everyday tasks, add the preparations for the wedding day; it was a busy life they were living.

Genie had taken out her dress from Noelle's wedding and tried it on making sure it was going to be perfect for Nissa's day.

219

Her panic happened when she realized they hadn't gotten anything for Gale to wear. She quickly called Nissa.

"It's okay Mom. Eyan took care of that. He ordered Dad a tux also. We called home while we were at the rental store and Anaya looked at some of his shirts and pants to get a size. So we're good. He will be as handsome as ever on Sunday."

"Oh, Nissa! Thank Eyan for being so considerate. You know your dad was always so meticulous about his appearance. That will mean so much to him."

"Hey we couldn't have him bringing me into the room in sweats or pajama pants could we?"

"You're such a thoughtful person. I'm so proud of you. All of you girls. You've grown into wonderful, loving, caring women. Eyan is getting a real prize."

"Mom...I feel like I'm the luckiest girl in the whole world."

"That's how I felt the day I married your dad. It was the most special day for me. I want Sunday to be that day for you also. I just wish..."

"Stop right there. Sunday will be everything we have ever wanted. The people who mean the most to us will surround Eyan and me with their love. We'll profess to God our love to him. But most important, Dad will be there. I couldn't ask for more."

Genie took a moment to shed a few tears. Nissa knew what was happening in the quiet coming from the other end of the phone.

Genie finally said, "It'll be beautiful."

"Yes it will."

$$* * * * * * * * * * * * * * * *$$

Later that afternoon Genie opened the door to the Hospice nurse. "Come in."

Giving Genie a hug, Theresa asked, "We haven't received any calls, I'm assuming things have been going well for our patient?"

"It has. This has been a wonderful time for all of us. We're thankful."

"Good."

"I'm a little concerned though."

"Why so?" Theresa asked.

"I'm not a nurse; but I don't like the way his breathing sounds. It seems more labored. And when we move him, I think he seems weaker. I know that sounds strange since we do all of the movement anyway. I don't know...It's the only way I know how to describe it. He just seems weaker to me."

"Well then let's take a look. Then we can talk about it."

Theresa was half way through her exam when Gale woke from his nap. "Hello sleepy head. It's Theresa, your Hospice nurse. Remember me?"

Gale blinked twice trying to clear the fog from his mind that seemed to be a constant friend as of late.

"It looks to me like these girls have been doing a wonderful job assisting you. I hear they haven't dropped you once."

Gale blinked multiple times acknowledging her humor.

Completing his check up she said to him, "I'm hearing a rattle in your lungs that I didn't hear on the day you arrived. Are you feeling a little struggle as you take breaths?"

Gale blinked twice.

"Do you understand what that is?" She asked.

221

Genie was at the foot of the bed watching his every blink.

Gale blinked twice.

Genie knew what was coming. She didn't want to hear Theresa say it. Taking a deep breath she steadied herself.

"Those muscles are getting weaker. Even with the assistance of the ventilator, you're having trouble sustaining and moving the air around."

Again, he blinked twice.

He knew what his nurse was going to say. It was just Genie who had been in the dark.

"I think our time is getting close Gale. Your body is betraying you. I'll turn up the oxygen today and see if we can't slow it down some. We'll try to make you more comfortable. My suggestion to you would be to enjoy every minute you can with your family. I wish I could give you more. They're a wonderful, loving family and you can be very proud of how you raised them. I can tell there is a lot of love between you all."

He blinked twice.

"That makes this even more difficult, knowing you have to say good-bye doesn't it?"

Again...Two blinks.

Genie realized the tears were falling down her face. She wanted to scream NOOO! We just found each other. We need more time. The words would not come. She had to be strong for Gale. She had to make this passing as easy on him as it could be. She thought about Sunday. *Please God...Give us Sunday. Let Nissa have her dad there. Give them that moment.*

Gale looked at Genie and blinked three long blinks.

She couldn't trust her voice. She mouthed the

words back as she choked down the tears that were falling despite her attempts to stop them.

Theresa moved about the room attending to the needs of her patient, giving Genie the time she needed to accept where they were headed.

Genie, sitting beside Gale, took his hand and laying her head down on his bed, cried as silently as she could. She needed just a moment to release the pain that was welling up inside of her.

God how can I do this?

I am with you always. Even until the end of time.

But...I don't want time to end for us.

There is a time for everything, and a season for every activity under heaven: a time to be born and a time to die.

We need more time.

Man does not control events. The race is not to the swift or the battle to the strong, nor does food come to the wise or wealth to the brilliant or favor to the learned; but time and change happen to them all. Remember your creator in the days of your youth, before the days of trouble come and the years approach when you will say, "I find no pleasure in them" before the sun and the light and the moon and the stars grow dark, and the clouds return after the rain; when the keepers of the house tremble, and the strong men stoop, when the grinders cease because they are few, and those looking through the windows grow dim; when the doors to the street are closed and the sound of grinding fades; when men rise up at the sound of birds, but all their songs grow faint; when men are afraid of heights and of dangers in the streets; when the almond tree blossoms and the grasshopper drags himself along and desire no

223

longer is stirred. The man goes to his eternal home and mourners go about the streets. Remember him-- before the silver cord is severed, or the golden bowl is broken; before the pitcher is shattered at the spring, or the wheel broken at the well, and the dust returns to the ground it came from and the spirit returns to God who gave it.

Genie understood what God was telling her. The time was coming when Gale's spirit would return to God and she couldn't stop that from happening. He knows our days. She understood that. However, the human part of her was never going to be ready to say good-bye to the man she loved. Especially after losing the time together that they had to a disease they hadn't asked for. She also knew because of Gale's relationship with His Creator, and his judgment affirmed, meaningless would not be the last word. He would live again and someday she would be with him worshipping God together in spirit. The knowledge that this was not final, gave her the strength she needed to continue on.

Raising her head and looking deeply into the eyes of the man in front of her, whose body was deserting him, she said, "I love you...Forever."

Three long blinks.

Chapter Thirteen

I CORINTHIANS 13

13. And now these three remain: faith, hope and love.

THE DAY DAWNED WITH THE HOPE OF SUMMER right around the corner. Though morning was still cool the sun was shining and the beauty of God's creation was everywhere to be seen. The birds were doing their mating dances and games of chase swooped up and down before your eyes. The spring flowers had burst forth into the new colors of summer as flowering bushes waved in the breeze. The scent of Honeysuckle was blowing through the air and the house windows were opened to let the smell of new life waft it's way from room to room.

The house was a bustle of busyness. Angelina was there bright and early with mouth watering smells emitting from earthenware that was now laid out on the kitchen counter. Plates sat in ready position for hungry people waking up from a night of slumber. As each one came seeking the prize at the end of the aroma, Angelina went on about her way carrying bins of secrets that would transform the living room into a sanctuary of peace and reverence. Their offers of help refused, this was a service she could fulfill as the morning of ritual was playing out.

Genie, already in Gale's room preparing him for the exciting day ahead of him, worried about the weariness she could see in his face. They both knew. Yet, neither communicated the truth in hopes of refusing acceptance.

Soft knocking on the door drew their attention. "Come in." She called.

"I have Gale's tux for the wedding." Eyan held the bag up for Gale to see.

Genie could see the pleasure in Gale's eyes as

Eyan entered carrying the tux they would lovingly dress the father-of-the-bride in. As he looked at her, she could see the relief flood through his eyes.

Immediately sensitive to his feelings she said, "Oh Honey...You didn't think we would have forgotten you. Did you? Eyan made sure you were included when he picked his out."

Gale blinked twice from teary eyes.

"You are more than welcome. In a house with this many women...We men have to stick together." Eyan laughed.

Genie's heart was breaking for the man who wanted so badly to be a part of every minute of this day; who wanted to smile and laugh; who wanted to be able to voice 'I love you' and walk his daughter to her groom. Yet this terrible disease had robbed him of the ability to do any of those things.

Eyan hung the tux on the closet door. "I'll let you guys get ready; do you need any help?" He asked.

"Thank you Eyan." She said as she lovingly kissed his cheek. "You go and get yourself ready. We have everything covered here." Genie answered the young man who was noticeably anxious to get on with the day.

"Yup...I have this girl getting ready to marry me and she's going to be gorgeous. I'm going to have to step up my game to look good enough to stand beside her in pictures."

Gale blinked multiple times letting Eyan know he understood exactly what he was talking about."

Eyan nodded back at him, "Sure you get it. Look at this beautiful woman who has been by your side. It isn't hard to see where Nissa gets her beauty from. When a woman sets the standard that high, a man really has to

228

work at not messing up the pictures. Right?"

Gale blinked over and over his agreement.

"All kidding aside, the two of you sure made a beautiful family. Beauty on the inside and out. I hope Nissa and I are...someday...that lucky."

"Eyan...Thank you. That was sweet. When the time is right, the two of you will raise a wonderful family. They'll be a beautiful blend of the two of you. Gorgeous, determined and a little sassy."

"You're right. I'm going to have to work on her little sassy spirit. I'll tame that right away."

Genie gave him her look of pretend concern.

He laughed, "Just kidding. I love that girl's sassy spirit."

Relaxing Genie smiled, "I hope so!"

"Well...You guys get ready and I'll see you in a few hours."

"Love you Honey." Genie welcomed the warm squeeze from her soon to be son-in-law.

Eyan took Gale's hand and gave him a firm shake.

Gale blinked back.

As the door closed behind him, Genie felt a peace cover her. All was going to be well. Looking at Gale, she could see him studying her. "Are you wondering what I'm thinking?"

He blinked twice.

She came over and carefully crawled into the bed beside of him. Leaning on her side, she stroked his cheek. "I'm thinking we did create a beautiful family. The girls are loving, compassionate and fun. Add to the mix Brad and Eyan. We couldn't have asked God for two more perfect young men. They'll take care of our girls and love them completely. The best part is that the homes our grandchildren grow up in will teach them to love and serve God. What more could we ask for?"

Gale's eyes became teary.

Looking deep into his soul she said, "Yes we could ask that you would be here to see it. We could ask for more time."

As they lay in the solitude of the moment, they shared their sorrow. As the tears flowed freely, they both released the sadness that lay so close to the surface. Both of them wanting so much more; yet knowing all too soon, their time together would come to an end. Time slipped by until the tears were spent. Accepting they couldn't change the inevitable, grasping onto truth and trusting in a loving Father, they knew it was time to press on.

She kissed him tenderly as she snuggled close to his face. "We had better get you ready. Yes?"

He blinked back.

So she started the process of transforming him into the handsome man she had married almost twenty-four years ago. As she cleaned and dressed him, she talked about their wedding day, she told of her feelings and the excitement she felt and she shared feelings that she was the luckiest woman in the whole world because Gale Smith had chosen her. They shared this intimate moment as she tenderly prepared him for their daughter's wedding.

When all was done, he was exhausted. "Now I have to get ready. Why don't you rest while that happens and when it's time, I'll get you in your chair so you're ready for your daughter."

He blinked his agreement and was almost asleep by the time she closed the door.

Please, Father, give us time? She pleaded as she leaned against the door realizing time was slipping away all too quickly.

Going into the living room to see if Angelina needed any help, she was amazed at the transformation. The room was a beautiful array of flowers and white twinkling lights. She had created an alter around the fireplace and rearranged the furniture so that all eyes would be on the bride and groom. There were pillars holding bouquets of flowers. They gave the room a wispy look and the overhead ceiling fan created just enough movement that the flowers looked as if they were waving in the wind. The sweet aroma made you feel as if you were in the middle of a beautiful garden.

"Angelina...You are amazing! Everything looks so beautiful. I'm not going to want it to change. Can't it stay this way forever?"

"I don't know about that Honey. In a few days those flowers won't look or smell so good."

"Well...For today they're perfect. Thank you."

"You're welcome. How's Gale today?"

"Getting ready was very wearying for him. He's resting for now. Can I help you with anything?" Genie asked, giving her friend a loving hug.

"No. I was just finishing up here and the food is just waiting in the kitchen. Michelle and Shawn are taking charge of everything in there. They have all of the dishes set out on the dining room table. It'll be set up at the appropriate time in a self-serve format. I think we just need to get ourselves ready."

"I can't thank you enough. You have really made this day a beautiful memory for the kids. I couldn't have done any of this under the circumstances."

Putting her arm around her friend Angelina said, "This was nothing. What is making the day is the fact that Gale will be here and is able to share it with them. That is the memory they'll cherish forever. None of this

231

will really matter in the end."

"So true. Not just for Nissa, but for her dad also. For him to be able to share this day with them, means more than words could have even expressed."

She started to cry.

Angelina took her into her arms and asked, "You okay Honey?"

"I'm losing him so quickly. I see him weaker and weaker. We don't have long and I'm not ready. We lost so much time. I want it back."

"Shhhh. That's the funny thing about time...We never feel like we have had enough. You can't focus on what you aren't going to have, you have to grab every minute of what you do have. Treasure each moment and love like there isn't a tomorrow. None of us know if tomorrow will come. But when it does, we have to know we made the most of the days before. Love by the minute and don't worry about the future."

Genie dried her eyes, "Thank you my friend. You are so right. I'm going to love every minute of today. Each moment will be a picture moment to tuck away in the recesses of my mind."

Angelina, turning her friend, said, "Now let's go get ready. We're not presentable for a day this special."

They both laughed as they walked arm and arm out of the room and headed up the stairs. As they reached the landing the doorbell rang.

Genie wondered as she hurried to the door, *Who would that be ringing the doorbell?*

Opening the door, she was shocked to see her sister. "Debbie," she yelled.

The two women stood embracing each other as if time had stood still. Both giving and receiving strength. Taking a moment to understand the heartache in the way that only sisters can connect.

"You didn't think I would miss this did you?"

"Oh Debbie, my life has been so full of Gale's needs I didn't even think about calling you. I'm so sorry. I feel like I live in the center of a tornado and the world spins me round and round."

"Hush. I understand. The girls called me. I told them I would be on the first flight in today. Brad came to the airport and picked me up. I told them not to tell you. I just wanted to sneak in and help where I could."

"I'm so glad you're here. I need you so much." Genie said as she again fell into the embrace of her sister. "How long can you stay?"

"Actually...I'm here for as long as you need me. I explained the situation to my boss and he said, 'go!'. It will give me some time with Gale also."

"I'm afraid not much. It's going so quickly. Every day he is weaker."

"The important part is he's here. You're all together."

"That's right. We're going to love each other as much as we can."

"Right now though, we have a wedding to get ready for. Is there anything I can do?"

"Oh my goodness no. Angelina has all of that covered. I'm so glad you're going to be able to get to know her better. She's amazing. She's decorated the living room and has the food all set. We were just on our way upstairs to get ready. Come on, the girls are going to be so happy to see you."

The next two hours were spent pampering and fussing as all six women did hair and makeup, painted their nails and dressed in beautiful gowns. They were just finishing when there was a knock on Nissa's bedroom

233

door. "Come in if you aren't Eyan." Nissa called.

In through the door came Brad. "Is everyone decent?" Called his male voice.

"We sure are." She answered back.

In he came with the photographer who had taken the pictures at their wedding.

Nissa squealed, "Pictures?"

"Absolutely...We couldn't let the day slip by without recording it for history." Angelina answered.

"Thank you so much."

The delight on Nissa's face was all of the thanks Angelina needed.

The photographer was already snapping pictures and capturing the surprised expressions on everyone's faces. That is, everyone except Angelina.

Looking at the time, Genie went over to Nissa and hugged her daughter tightly. "I can't believe the time has come for me to send you off to create a family of your own. Where did it all go? How did you become a beautiful woman ready to embrace a new life? I wish we could have celebrated this day more. I want you to know I'm so proud of you. You're an amazing woman. You are loving and kind. I'm so happy for you. Eyan is going to love you everyday and the two of you will build a wonderful home full of love for each other. That home will be full of peace and the joy of the Lord as you go with excitement wherever He sends you. But know this, no matter where you go, you'll always be our daughter. We will always be so proud of you. Today your father and I send you off into the arms of the man you love." Genie held her as if never wanting to let her go; but realizing it was time to release her into her own future.

"Mom, I love you and Dad's the best gift today."

Noelle jumped in, "Speaking of gifts. We have something for the new bride."

Anaya pulled the box from under the bed. "Here you go. This is from all of us. A send off into womanhood."

Noelle added, "I just wish we could have spent the day embarrassing you in the store like you got to do for me." The girls shared a laugh as Nissa opened the package.

Inside was an array of beautiful lingerie, some new cologne and a box of expensive chocolates.

"Nissa held up one of the exquisite pieces. "Oh my goodness. It feels like silk. It's beautiful. Thank you all so very much."

Anaya coaxed, "Dig a little further and check them all out."

Nissa did as requested and looked at each piece with excitement. Then she found it. On the very bottom was a two piece something, tastefully skimpy.

"What is this?" Nissa laughed.

Noelle jumped in, "In the marriage bed everything goes. Sometimes it's fun to feel just a little naughty. You know...We like to please our man. Believe me, Eyan will like it."

Nissa blushed as they all laughed, enjoying the moment. Then she started to cry. "I'm so happy. I can't believe my dreams are about to come true. I'm going to be Mrs. Eyan Conroy." The girls grabbed each other and began to giggle and dance in a circle. Genie cherished the moment remembering years past and the bond that her girls shared. She was so thankful. Her heart was bursting. Even though she had missed the moment of shopping with them, she was so pleased they had made the effort to make sure Nissa didn't miss the joy of the gift. She caught the eyes of her two daughters and sent them a 'thank you' smile.

"You guys are wonderful. You know this all happened so fast, we haven't even had time to think past the moment of the wedding."

"I think you have all done extremely well just getting this far. You all amaze me. But maybe this is the time for me to give you my gift?" Debbie suggested.

"Oh...Aunt Debbie, you are my gift. I'm feeling so blessed to have all of the important people in my life here with me today."

"It was quick notice, though I am starting to expect that from you girls. Because of that I didn't have a lot of time to think about it. I checked with Noelle and she helped me a little. Brad and Eyan are already in on it. I didn't want to do something that had already been taken care of."

"What is it?"

Debbie handed her niece an envelope and Nissa asked, "Should I wait for Eyan?"

"No...He already knows." Noelle offered.

"Okay" she said as she opened the envelope. Inside was a printed certificate for two nights in a hotel in Indianapolis."

"Aunt Debbie. It's perfect. We seriously hadn't even talked about what we were going to do tonight. I love it." She hugged her aunt saying, "I love that you're here more than any gift."

"I'll tell you the same thing I told Noelle, there isn't anywhere else I'd rather be. I was there when you were born and I will celebrate with you as long as God allows. You're my family. I love you more than life. I would move mountains to be at these moments."

Nissa hugged her aunt.

Turning to the others in the room she said, "I'm so happy. It almost seems wrong being this happy knowing that Daddy is...

She didn't finish the sentence.

Genie took hold of her daughter and gently spoke, "This is one of the most important days in your life. Your dad feels so blessed that you were willing to rush through this moment so he could share it with you. He is happy and he wants you to be happy. We're all going to embrace each minute and recognize the gift we have in each other. So be happy. We're all going to be happy. This is the day that the Lord has made and he has, in our world, made it just for us."

"Thanks Mom...For everything."

Genie kissed her daughter and said, "I'm going to go and get your dad settled in his chair. Then he'll be ready whenever you are."

Nissa kissed her mom one more time saying, "I've been ready since I met Eyan."

All the girls were grabbing tissues and wiping their eyes carefully. No one wanted smeared mascara as they shared the easy spirit of Nissa's love.

****

When Genie entered the room, she was delighted by the sight. There was Brad, Eyan, Pastor Travis and Rebecca all entertaining Gale. Everyone was laughing.

"I must have interrupted a humorous moment," she said.

"Good thing you did. I may need to be rescued. Brad's decided it an appropriate time to share with Gale any crazy thing I may have done, all the way back to kindergarten. If this keeps up, Nissa's dad isn't going to want us to get married." Eyan stepped over and gave her a quick kiss on her cheek. "I think you came at a perfect time."

"I can't imagine anything he could say that would cause us to change our minds. Besides, I just left a room full of beautiful women and I promise you there is one of them that would not let anyone stop this wedding."

Brad jumped in, "Well then, there was the time..."

"Enough all ready." Eyan stopped him.

Genie could see from the look on Gale's face he was thoroughly enjoying himself. She walked to the side of his bed and smoothed his hair.

He blinked three times.

"I love you!"

"Boys, if you are ready to get this ceremony on the road, I had better get her dad in his chair so he can escort his daughter."

"Can we help?" Eyan offered.

"Nope...We have this." She said looking at her husband.

"Okay, then if there is a girl ready to get married, I guess I should go get in my place."

"Yes you should." She answered.

The men headed for the door when Eyan turned back. Going to the bed and hugging Genie one more time then taking Gale's hand in his, Eyan said, "Thank you for making Nissa the woman she is. I love her very much."

Genie's eyes filled with tears yet another time. "You are very welcome. Thank you for loving our daughter."

Eyan squeezed Gale's hand.

Gale blinked twice through eyes also wet.

Smiling from ear to ear, Eyan said, "Let's do it."

238

And out the door they all went.

Genie looked at Gale saying, "He's going to make Nissa a fine husband. They should be very happy wherever God takes them."

Gale blinked twice.

"Are you ready?"

Again, two blinks.

Genie brought over the Hoyer and began to get everything in place. They were just finishing when Nissa knocked on the door. "Can I come in?" She called.

"Yes Honey...Absolutely. Come in."

Nissa opened the door and stood in the entryway. Genie watched for Gale's reaction.

Because his eyes were filled with tears, Genie's did too. "We are such cry babies any more." She said.

Gale watched his daughter enter the room. He thought, *She is stunning. Noelle must have looked the same way. I wish I could tell her she's so beautiful.*

"Daddy, do you like the dress? This is the one that Noelle wore also."

Gale blinked multiple times.

"Am I beautiful?"

He blinked over and over again.

She came to his chair and kneeling, laid her head in his lap. "I'm so glad you're here and you're going to give me away. Nothing could be more special to me today."

Genie reaching over and picking up Gale's hand laid it lovingly on Nissa's hair. The photographer came in just in time to capture the moment. She knew the picture she saw through the lens of the camera would be special to the three of them. A moment of private love. Gale's hand looked so natural stroking his daughter's hair. Only they would know.

Nissa could hear the music playing. "I think that's our cue. She kissed them both one more time."

As they exited the bedroom, the girls began a slow stroll in front of Nissa to Mendelssohn's Wedding March. As it reached the spot where the bride enters, Nissa walked beside her dad holding onto his hand while Genie pushed the wheel chair slowly down the aisle that Angelina had created with flowers. This was the first time Nissa had seen the transformed living room. Later she would be thankful for the pictures; because at this moment she only had eyes for the man who was waiting. She would always remember that Eyan was grinning from ear to ear. She smiled back and then they were both giggling. Their happiness was so contagious the rest of the room shared in their joy.

"Eyan and Nissa came to my home and told me they wanted to be married this week, they said they wanted something traditional and sweet. I think we have just shared the sweet moment." Pastor Travis announced.

"Now for the traditional." He continued with the ceremony until the part where he asked, "Who gives this bride away?"

Genie said, "Her father and I."

Gale looked into his daughter's eyes and back at Pastor Travis then at Eyan. He then blinked twice, very distinctively.

Nissa knelt down to his level and taking his face in her hands, she kissed him. "I love you." She then turned to her mother and smiling, kissed her also. "Thank you."

Genie nodded and then backed the chair into the circle of family that was surrounding the couple in front of them who were so in love.

Eyan stepped forward and reached out his hand

to Nissa. Taking his hand and stepping forward as if saying, I'm leaving my old life behind and stepping into the future with you. Eyan kissed her hand and they turned to face Pastor Travis.

Travis looked at the two young adults standing in front of him and said, "Love seeks the highest good for others. It's not based on emotions or feelings. It's a decision to be committed to the well-being of others without any conditions or circumstances."

For God so loved the world that He gave His one and only Son, that whoever believes in Him shall not perish but have eternal life.

Jesus said, *"My command is this: Love each other as I have loved you. Greater love has no one than this, that he lay down his life for his friends. You are my friends if you do what I command."*

Dear friends, let us love one another, for love comes from God. Everyone who loves has been born of God and knows God. Whoever does not love does not know God because God is love. This is how God showed his love among us: He sent His one and only Son into the world that we might live through Him. This is love: not that we loved God, but that he loved us and sent His Son as an atoning sacrifice for our sins. Dear friends, since God so loved us, we also ought to love one another. No one has ever seen God; but if we love one another, God lives in us and His love is made complete in us.

Pastor Travis continued, "Love had its perfect expression among men in the Lord Jesus Christ. Now, today we are looking for that perfect love to be expressed through the love that you will share with each other."

"Will you turn and face each other for your vows?"

There they stood, holding hands, looking deeply into each others eyes. The love they shared so new and fresh. The expectations of the future unmarred by human hands or pain and suffering.

"The vows that you are about to express are a commitment to each other. Those vows should be seen as an unconditional oath where you are binding yourselves to each other without expecting anything from the other. A pledge that neither man nor either of you can annul. These vows will be made in the presence of God with your loved ones as witnesses. Is your love strong enough to vow that love and commitment to each other?"

Looking at each other they answered, "It is."

Travis held the paper so that Eyan could read the vows and said, "Eyan Connor, will you make your vows to Nissa?"

Eyan looked at the vows and then at Nissa saying, "I, Eyan Michael Conroy, take you Nissa, to be my wedded wife, to have and to hold from this day forward, for better for worse, for richer for poorer, in sickness and in health, to love and to cherish, to honor and obey, 'til death do us part; according to God's holy ordinance and thereto I pledge you my love and faithfulness."

Pastor then held the paper so Nissa could see it and said, "Nissa Smith, will you make your vows to Eyan?"

Nissa's voice never wavered as she lovingly said, "I, Nissa Smith, take you Eyan, to be my wedded husband, to have and to hold from this day forward, for better for worse, for richer for poorer, in sickness and health, to love and to cherish, to honor and obey, until death do us part; according to God's holy ordinance and thereto I pledge you my love and my faithfulness."

Travis asked, "May I have the rings please?"

Brad and Noelle laid the beautiful rings on the Bible Pastor was holding.

He continued, "These wedding ring are an outward symbol of an inward expression of your commitment to one another. They signify a never-ending and immortal love. The circle is the symbol of eternity, with no beginning or end. Will you exchange your rings?"

They had chosen two matching bands simple yet elegant.

Eyan took Nissa's ring first and placed it on her finger. Nissa did the same for Eyan.

"By the power that is vested in me by the State of Indiana, I now pronounce you husband and wife. Eyan, it's time, you may kiss your bride."

Eyan looked deep into Nissa's eyes and said, "I will love you forever." He slowly leaned in and embraced her leaving no doubt that he was sealing their union.

Applause broke out around the room.

They laughed and kissed again.

Pastor Travis said, "I would like to be the first to introduce you to Mr. and Mrs. Eyan and Nissa Conroy."

Applause again. Then Rebecca turned the music on and the excitement in the room over flowed.

Chapter Fourteen

I CORINTHIANS 13

13. But the greatest of these is love.

Genie was in Gale's room by his bed watching him sleep. His breathing labored and sporadic, even as the respirator breathed rhythmically in and out, in and out. Theresa had already stopped by. She was so excited to hear about yesterday's wedding day. The aroma of the flowers alerting her senses as she stepped into the house. The living room, so beautifully adorned, a tell tale sign of Angelina's decorating talents. However, her enthusiasm waned when she saw Gale.

How was his day yesterday?" She asked full of hopeful anticipation.

"He did really well. It was a long day, full of lots of emotion. We all enjoyed every minute. There was so much joy and he was at the center of it. Nothing was left unsaid."

"And today?"

"What you see right now is what I've seen all night and day. He hasn't woke up at all. I don't like the way his breathing sounds. He doesn't seem to be resting well. Yet he hasn't opened his eyes one time."

She patted Genie shoulder, "Maybe he has peeked them open when you weren't in the room."

"I've been by his side all night. The only time I left was early this morning when I went into the bathroom for just a moment."

"Genie, you have to take care of yourself too. You need a break. I'll sit with him and you go and rest for a while. Take a walk. Get something to eat. Soak in the tub."

"I can't leave. Something isn't right. I can feel it in my spirit. Tell me what to do. How do I make him fight? I need him to fight." The fatigue of the desperate vigilance was catching up with her.

Theresa put her arms around Genie's shoulders and gave a reassuring squeeze. "He did fight. He has been fighting. His body has put up an amazing fight. Now he's tired. We've talked about this before. His body is betraying him and those muscles are not going to be able to do their job. We can manually help with some of the voluntary muscles; but not all of them. We reach a point where the voluntary muscles just won't respond anymore."

"What happens then?"

Theresa wanted so badly to be able to tell her all would be better; she knew that wasn't true. "Why don't I do my medical evaluation and then we'll talk. While I'm busy in here, I think it would be a good idea for you to take a break. You're going to need to be strong for your family."

"I can take a break later. I'll have plenty of time to take a break. Oh Theresa...I'm not ready."

"We're never ready. Sometimes it helps to just go off by yourself and have a good cry. It settles the nerves and releases the pent up stress."

Genie understood what she was being told. Yet every nerve in her body screamed 'don't leave'.

"I can't...I can't leave him. We just found each other again. He's spent too much time alone already."

Theresa walked up close to Genie and wrapped her arms around her. "I understand your feelings. I would have hung on forever and Tony would have hated it. I needed him to be by my side even if it meant he would never really live again. I just needed him. The truth was, he would have hated life that wasn't lived. It was my needs and my fears that yearned for him to stay.

246

He was really already gone from me. I just couldn't let go."

Genie softly cried, "It's so hard."

"It is hard. It will be one of the hardest life moments that will ever be forced into your journey. The good news for you is that you have the hope of eternity. Someday, because of the choices you've all made, you'll be together again. This life is just fleeting. Though it seems so long as we walk through the darkness, the light at the end of the tunnel shines brighter than we can imagine."

Genie knew Theresa was right. She also knew that Gale was going to be moving towards that light. His struggles were coming to an end and she didn't need a medical exam to tell her.

"I'm sorry. Today just seemed to come too quickly. I knew yesterday was a gift. He was already struggling. I think he used any reserved energy he had to be a part of the wedding."

"He wouldn't have had it any other way. If yesterday was all he would have had...It would have been enough. He would see it as a gift."

"I know. It's just so hard. This is going to be harder than losing him the first time."

"This time you know the answers. You know he loves you all very much...He will always love you. God's timing is never wrong."

"I'm trying to be strong, I really am."

"You're doing a wonderful job. Gale knows how much you and the girls love him. The opportunity to be together during this time has been a blessing for him that he hadn't planned on."

Genie understood and agreed with all Theresa was saying. She knew they had all been blessed in

247

having this opportunity. It made her think of something she had heard a pastor say once, *When we wait for God, we get God's best.*

She and the girls had waited on God for their healing. They had trusted him to take away the pain and brokenness. He had been faithful. Then when they were in a good place, He gave them back Gale so they could be a family again. It had been a gift. It had been time they would always treasure; a time for complete and total healing. They had been given time to love.

Genie knew their time together was coming to an end. Gale had fought the good fight. He was now looking towards the prize of Christ Jesus. He had earned the right to rest in the Father's arms. There would be no more struggle to breathe; his body would be at rest. In fact he was promised a new name, a name given to the victors. Gale was victorious. The body that had held him captive would be no more and his spirit would soar with the angels.

Father, help me not to be selfish. Give me the strength to release his weary soul to you. Help me to be strong for the girls and find peace in his passing. You have been there for us through the storm now carry us through the valley. Help us to find the mountain top again. We need you. In Jesus Name. AMEN.

Do you not know?

Have you not heard?

The LORD is the everlasting God, the Creator of the ends of the earth.

He will not grow tired or weary and His understanding no one can fathom.

He gives strength to the weary and increases the power of the weak.

Even youths grow tired and weary, and young

248

men stumble and fall; but those who hope in the LORD will renew their strength.

They will soar on wings like eagles; they will run and not grow weary, they will walk and not be faint.

Trust my daughter. Trust Me.

Theresa was walking through her medical check list, speaking to Gale with loving, compassionate words. Genie decided to call the girls. She knew in her spirit it was time. They would want to be here to say their final good-byes.

As she softly closed the bedroom door, she saw Anaya coming down the stairs. Opening her arms to her youngest daughter, Anaya wrapped her arms around her mother and softly cried.

"Is he going to leave us?" She asked tearfully.

"I'm afraid so."

"We need to call the other girls."

"I was just on my way to do that."

As they were speaking, the entry door opened allowing in Brad and Noelle.

Seeing Genie and Anaya standing there crying Noelle stopped in mid walk, "Is he..."

"No Honey. But I was just going to call you. I don't believe it will be long. Theresa is with him now. We need to call Nissa and Eyan."

"I just talked with them. Nissa couldn't sleep so they got up and started back. They're about 10 minutes out." Noelle offered.

"Good."

Silence.

Brad, his heart breaking for the women he loved, stepped forward, opened his arms and said, "Come here."

The three girls came into his embrace feeling the comfort of his love. They stood for a time letting the tears fall and just being held.

Then he began to pray, *Father, we ask for your peace. We ask for strength. We thank you for a gentle passing from this world into the next for Gale. We know You have already sent his angels to escort him so he won't be alone. Let these final moments glorify you on a life well lived. In Jesus Name. AMEN.*

As they finished praying, Theresa opened the door. Turning in expectation, they eagerly hoped for good news; yet knowing their wants weren't to be.

She began, "He is resting comfortably. His body is slowing down. Blood pressure is lowering. There is a discoloring of his lower extremities. Dying is a process and his body is just walking through that process. I wouldn't anticipate it to be a long time; maybe a couple of hours. That's just a guess. You know we live not on our own timing, but on God's. That would just be my best guess from my medical training. Your important focus is on the fact that the hearing is the last body function to leave. Gale can hear what you're saying. He will know you're with him. This is your time to love and encourage him on his final journey as he leaves this world behind."

"We have been doing that." Anaya said.

Theresa smiled at the sad girl, "Yes you have been. And you've done a great job. He knows he was loved. You have been an amazing example of love and caring. He's a very lucky man. He knows that."

"Is there anything else we need to know?" Noelle asked.

"No. It appears to be an easy passing. He's relaxed and comfortable."

"Are you leaving?" Genie asked.

"I will do whatever you want." She answered.

"I think I would like to know you're here."

"Then I'll stay. I'll just be out here. If you need me call. I can check on him periodically if you would like. Or we can just let nature take it's course. Whatever you want." Theresa finished.

"As long as he's comfortable, let's just let him rest. If we need you we'll call." Genie made the decision.

Noelle offered, "Angelina will be here shortly with Emma so you won't be alone."

"Oh good. She's such a sweet baby."

"One more thing, I just want to remind you that on the ventilator, his body will continue to breathe, even after he is gone."

"How will we know?" Nissa asked.

Theresa answered, "You'll just know. Then call me and I'll listen for a heart beat. We'll check the signs. The body will tell us."

Genie was turning to go back to Gale when the door opened one more time and Eyan and Nissa were there. Genie went to her daughter and wrapped her in arms of love. She whispered, "He's still with us; but his time is near."

"Oh Mom...I'm not ready."

"We'll never be ready. This isn't our choice. God is calling him home. He's going to follow the call. All we can do now is love him into the arms of Jesus."

"I'll try to be strong. It's just so hard."

"We'll all be fine together. I'm going to go and sit with him and let the others fill you in. We'll just spend our time in and out sending him our words of love and letting him feel our hugs."

"Okay."

Genie smiled at her family as she turned towards the door and left them.

The room was dimly lit by the light coming

from the closet and bathroom. She decided to light the candles that were placed around his room. They were sage scented and gave the room a manly, earthy smell. The girls had picked them out. She noticed they were soybean candles so they would burn clean and the room would be toxic free. Her senses seemed to be memorizing everything. There was a stereo system so she chose a CD of old hymns and turned the music on softly in the background.

Sitting down in a chair close to his bed, Genie took the hand of the man she loved. Leaning close to his ear she said, "We're all here. You aren't going to be alone. Thank you for the gift you've given us. Having this time together was better than anything you could have ever done. Our family was put back together and we've cherished every minute. Nissa will always remember her daddy bringing her down the aisle to the man she loved. It's every little girls dream and you made that come true. You were a great daddy and husband. As your wife I felt loved and cared for. When you were with us, I felt like the luckiest woman on earth. You always made me feel like I was a queen and we created three beautiful daughters who have become amazing women who will honor us. You were the head of our family. You led us well. You made sure we were taken care of. No one could've loved us more."

She continued whispering into his ear.

"The regrets are few. But in the end the most important step we made was to love Jesus. Someday we'll all be together again because we made that decision. I don't want you to think about regrets. We know the choice you made to leave us was because you thought you were protecting us. We will always know you did it out of love. We understand. We don't blame you for anything. We love you. God was good. He always is. He brought us all back together."

She stroked his hand as she continued, "Our season is coming to an end. I'll try to be strong for you and the girls. You taught us how to do that. You resembled strength. It took a strong man to walk away knowing he would struggle by himself. I'm just so thankful we've been reunited and you don't have to be alone."

Genie sat looking at the man in the bed and realized the tremors had stopped. His body was no longer fighting itself. He was laying still. There were no muscle jerks, no flailing arms or kicking legs. In front of her was a man resting in peace. It was comforting to know there was no fight going on inside of him that he couldn't control.

A new strength was growing inside of her. God was answering their prayers in the form of the picture in front of her. There was peace in the storm. Gale's body was relaxed and she was comforted by his calm. Though she didn't want to do this, she now knew she could.

"Sweetheart, I love you. I will be here right to the end. We're in this together. But I want you to know you have my permission to leave with your angels. I want you to be at peace. I know you'll be waiting for us on the other side and we'll all be together again. Our separation will be just a fleeting moment before we're reunited. I'll be strong for the girls. You taught me how. Just rest and walk in the light. Leave this broken body that I love so much. I will be encouraged to know that you are soaring to the heights and nothing can hold you back." Kissing his hand, Genie stood to sooth his hair and nuzzle his cheek and forehead.

She cherished the feel of him; the smell of him.

She could still smell his cologne from the day before. She breathed in that smell trying to permanently embed it into her memory. Yes...She would miss so much about who he was. But she was ready to let him leave this body that was holding him captive. She could say good-bye to give him that freedom. God would help her do that.

As she stood giving him all of her love, the girls and their husbands came into the room. The girls all spoke words of love and encouragement to their daddy who gave them life. Even the young men who had only known him briefly were able to encourage with their words of commitment and promises to take care of his girls.

The time seemed to tick slowly at the same time that it seemed to fly. Hours felt like minutes and minutes felt like hours. They could all see the sweet passing of his life into the heavens. They laughed, they cried, they loved. It was a time of sweet memories revisited and promises of a beautiful future ahead. Gale had to be proud of his girls and blessed to call them his. They honored the man who had loved them beyond life, his life. He was going to leave this earth knowing he had made a difference and the world would be a better place because he had existed. He was leaving a legacy behind.

As the music played 'Amazing Grace', with those he loved standing around his bed, the body of Gale Benjamin Smith gave up its spirit. They knew. Genie looked at the clock. It was 1:16 p.m. She didn't have to be told. You could feel the spirit of the room change. Leaning forward she laid her lips on his forehead to feel his warmth one last time. The tears fell. Not for what they would not have; but for the love they had. The love of God, the love of family and the love of a man who was

254

willing to sacrifice all for his girls.

Brad's voice broke the silence with "*Into your hands we commit his spirit. Go in peace and love and may the grace and mercy of the Father remain with us. AMEN.*"

Epilogue

Jeremiah 29:11

For I know the plans I have for you,
declares the Lord,

plans to prosper you
and not to harm you, plans to give
you hope and a future.

Then you will call upon me and come
and pray to me, and I will listen to you.

You will seek me and find me when
you seek me with all your heart.

I will be found by you,
declares the Lord,

and will bring you back from captivity.

I̲T WAS A BEAUTIFUL DAY. THE SUN WAS SHINING and a refreshing breeze was blowing through the slider's screen door opened to allow the smell of the honeysuckle to sweep through the room. The melodious sound of a hummingbird as it hovered, suspended in time, just outside of the room caught Genie's attention. She thought of the day Gale and she had sat in the peace of God's creation just two weeks earlier. Closing her eyes she was able to capture the memory for a fleeting moment.

Her mind traveled what seemed such a long ways to capture the smell of him and the feel of his hand in hers. She treasured those memories and a tear slid down her cheek. She longed for more...More time... More memories. Yet, they were not to be. Their season had come to an end. Still the desperate cravings of her humanness went unquenched.

Most days she was able to focus on the life they had lived together. Today as she sat working at her desk attempting to close the pages of their life journey, doing the paperwork that inevitably came with death, she struggled to stay in the moment of peace. The world required a different journey than the heart wanted to take. There was such a business to dying.

Fortunately for her and the girls, a call to the attorney who had helped Gale to mastermind his plan of protection, proved to be very helpful. Gale had everything in place. His plan had been for burial after his death. Then they were to receive another letter. This letter would have given them the whole story. The truth of his final days. That way he would have protected all of them from the ugliness of what his passing would have been. Thank goodness for God's grace. His ways are always better than our ways.

However, the attorney had been able to fill in blanks that had been left unanswered. Gale had the financial part of leaving this earth in order. He had made sure they were taken care of even in his absence.

He took over much of the paperwork that Genie had thought she would have to try to figure out on her own. Because they were never divorced, some of what Gale had in place changed. However, the attorney knew she had never signed the papers. It actually made so much of it easier. Genie was grateful she could give him the end of a happier story than the one he expected. His closing words to her were, "He loved you all very much."

That was something the girls and her already knew. Gale's love for them had transcended even death. Even his own. He had made sure they knew how much he had loved them. He had made it clear in his letter he wrote to them.

God's grace was that they had been reunited and his words of love came as no surprise. For that she would be forever grateful. The time they shared would be cherished. But more importantly, Gale died knowing his family had forgiven him and loved him even before they knew the whole truth.

Genie and the girls had learned the lesson of the freedom of forgiving. They had walked through the bitterness and hurt, the pain and anguish and the brokenness and despair. They were the fortunate ones. Coming out on the right side had allowed them to be ready for the best God had to give them. It had prepared them for a reunion they couldn't even have imagined.

258

Their family had been restored. That was the God they served. He was a God of restoration and His ways would always be higher than their ways.

With a thankful spirit she would be able to face the future. She knew God was in control and she could walk with confidence into the unknown.

A knock on her door brought her back from her wanderings.

"Mom?"

"Come in Anaya." She answered.

"Just checking in to see what you're doing. Noelle just called and they're on their way over. Angelina wants us all to come over to the restaurant to have dinner. She's just tried making a new recipe of strawberry rhubarb pie and she thinks we should come be her guinea pigs."

Genie laughed at the thoughtfulness of their new family. This journey had brought them to a comfortable place in life. Though her heart was sad, God had made sure there was a way to carry on. Genie would always be thankful for a God who had a plan for her life and that His plan would never cause her harm.

Genie smiled at her daughter and said, "Well then we should go. I don't know about you, but I want ice cream on mine. If I'm going to eat the calories, I want to load them up."

Anaya laughed, "Sounds good to me."

By the time they were ready, Brad and Noelle were pulling into the driveway. Climbing into the seat with Emma positioned between them, Genie was already counting her blessings. Did her life look different than she had envisioned? It sure did. A few years ago her plan was to grow old with the man she had always loved. The man who had helped to plan her future. It wasn't meant to be and in that there was sadness. However, joy comes in the morning. God promised it. His promises are true. She believed them. Praise God for His mercy. It endures forever. Amen and Amen.

Thoughts

From

The

Author

I HOPE THAT ALL OF YOU HAVE ENJOYED THE TIME you've spent journeying with Noelle, Brad and their families. You've been a part of their history as they began a walk that continued through four books.

In the first book, **SAVING NOELLE**, we learned of God's love for us. We discovered His willingness to chase us no matter how far we run. God never wants His children living in their darkest hour. His Word, The Bible, tells us He is the lamp that lights our way. He doesn't want us to stumble and fall. However, if we do, He is there to pick us up and carry us if He must. Noelle ran, not knowing who He was. In her running, God made a way for her to find Him. You see He will never leave us out there by ourselves. Separation from God only happens by our choices not by His. Noelle's choice was to accept Him as her Lord and Savior. Through God, Noelle found salvation and eternal life.

God gave others the opportunity to receive their blessings when He opened the doors for them to help Noelle and they walked through. Angelina was willing to share the saddest time of her life. Through that willingness to be obedient, even when it hurt, Noelle was able to find her way to a loving Savior. By finding Him, she was able to make the decision of life for her baby. God opened his arms wide and Noelle came broken and spilled out eagerly captured by His love.

Through that process, God rewarded Angelina for her faithfulness to serve Him. The life she saved became her own grandchild and Noelle became her new daughter. God's plans are always more than we can imagine. His abundance is above and beyond. There was no way for Angelina to know the direction God was going to take her family. She walked in blind faith. She chose to serve a living God. She had prepared herself for an opportunity like the one that presented by serving on a daily basis. It was such a deep part of who she was, that when God directed Noelle to her home, she was obedient without question.

Do you hold onto God daily? Are you practicing His ways so that when you're called you can answer? His ways are not always our ways. Only by obediently following Him daily can we be sure that we don't miss the opportunities He sends our way. Those opportunities may not look like anything we can imagine. Just as the blessings we will receive, will be more than we can comprehend.

As we moved into **PERFECT LOVE** the second novel in the CARRIED BY ANGELS SERIES, we saw how God was masterminding Noelle's healing and giving her a future. The Lord gave us His promise in

Jeremiah 29:11

"For I know the plans I have for you," declares the LORD, "Plans to prosper you and not to harm you, plans to give you hope and a future. Then you will call upon me and come and pray to me, and I will listen to you. You will seek Me and find Me when you seek Me with all your heart. I will be found by you," declares the LORD, "and will bring you back from captivity.

It was Brad's plan to make sure he was waiting on the Lord and because of his obedience, we watched as God gave him a future. God used Noelle, broken and desperate, to fulfill the desires of Brad's heart. God used Brad to open the door to an amazing new life in the Lord for Noelle and himself. After all, it would

264

have been easy to ignore the call of God in the situation where Brad found himself. Yet, he chose to love in the perfect and flawless love of the Lord. There was no fear for Brad as he embraced the feelings he had for Noelle. Why, because of God's promise, His love is perfect and His word tells us in *1 John 4:18 There is no fear in love. But perfect love drives out all fear, because fear has to do with punishment. The one who fears is not made perfect in love.* He chose to have God as His shield and take refuge in Him. Brad was willing to surrender his control. He let God arm him with strength and he stood on his ROCK...JESUS CHRIST.

I marvel at how God works. Let's look at the Prophet Elijah. He showed unconditional loyalty to the Lord and God took care of him. Elijah called forth a drought in the land to punish the nation for its idolatry. Yet God had him go to a place of peace where he could drink and God sent ravens to feed him. Then when the brook dried up because of the drought, God sent him to a widow who was going to eat her last meal with her son and then die for lack of food. Elijah told her, under the direction of the Lord, to feed him first. She obeyed and made that last meal for Elijah and the Lord made her meals plenty. See how God used someone who was desperate to minister to Elijah. God gave the widow a chance to be obedient which then allowed God to bless the widow and her son. You can find this story in *I Kings 17:1-16.*

Brad and Angelina saw blessings because they were willing to be obedient and walk in the perfect love of the Lord. Noelle was blessed because she too surrendered all to the Lord.

In the third book, **FORGIVING FREEDOM**, we watched as the opportunity for forgiveness tears open healed wounds. Just like faith is a verb, so is forgiving. It requires an action that is not always comfortable. Brad and Noelle, with a bright new future looming ahead of them, walked into the darkness to see true freedom abound. We saw the story line broach yet another principle near to God's heart... Forgiveness.

In **SAVING NOELLE**, the choices Noelle made came out of her bitterness towards her father's leaving. Those choices became self-destructive. Her harboring the offense caused an unforgiving spirit and took her down a road of depression, fear, and family separation, almost to the point of death. By not forgiving her father, she may have felt she was getting even or causing him some of her same pain. Actually, the person hurt the most from unforgiveness was always her. What Noelle and her family did as they refused to forgive was invite satan into their lives where he would create an atmosphere of destruction.

It was through finding a personal relationship with Jesus and beginning to pray for their father, that they were able to stop the enemy's attacks and find the joy he had stolen from them. Through God's grace and mercy they were able to forgive their father and watch as God restored the peace in their lives. Once they closed the door on the sin of unforgiveness, God was able to move forward and open the door on their life of abundance.

Book four, **REDEEMING GRACE**, shows God's protective plan for this family unfold. As Noelle and her family's lives became full of His love, He gave them the opportunity to heal by reuniting their family. The twists and turns surprised even me and is an example of how much he loves us and wants only the best for us.

It was my pleasure to open up pages in the lives of these characters you have come to love. I hope as

God wrote their story, you saw them rise to the occasions created for them. My prayer will always be God's principles will live out on the pages of these books and you will be able to find him in the midst of the words.

Closing the final page on their lives is bittersweet. I've come to love the characters and who they were created to be. They became very real to me. Especially Noelle as she represented a combination of the four broken women who shared their stories of abortion with me that started us on this journey. God's plan in these stories has always been healing for those whose decisions about life have left them carrying burdens of guilt and regret. He wants you to forgive yourself. There has a life of abundance just waiting for you. God loved you so much that He sent his Son to die on the cross. There is no place in your relationship with him for the burdens of guilt. He wants you to walk in freedom. Let His mercy and grace cover you and rest in the protective healing of His arms.

If these stories have left you desperate to know the love of our God and you want to surrender your life to Him, I would love to pray with you right now. It doesn't matter where you are in your life, God will find you when you cry out to Him. Now is the time. It's never too early or too late. He's just waiting for you to come. He won't push His way in. He wants it to be your choice to love Him. He gave you free will. He didn't create you to be a robot. It has to be a choice that you make. He wants it to be your choice to love Him. I'll say it again, He is a God of relationship and His relationship with you was important enough that He gave the life of His Son for you. If you're ready to receive His love that knows no boundaries, just repeat this prayer with me: He is listening.

Lord Jesus, I come to You completely surrendered. I realize that I need a Savior. I confess that I am a sinner and I need You. I want to be Your child and heir to Your eternal kingdom. I believe You died on the cross for my sins. I believe You were dead and buried and on the third day You rose from the grave. Thank you for cleansing me from my sins, for removing them as far as the east is from the west. I am grateful that You see me white as snow. Thank you for making me new. My old ways are gone and now I am a new creation bought and paid for by the precious blood of Jesus. I am now Your child and I will never be separated from You again. By praying this prayer I have sealed my place in Heaven forever to live with You. I acknowledge I could never be worthy without You and that only by Your blood, and Your grace, and Your mercy can I be free. Thank you for forgiving me and for loving me as Your own. In Jesus Name. AMEN.

If you just prayed that prayer for the first time, congratulations. On the other hand, maybe this was a recommitment because you had slipped away from your first love and wanted to rededicate your life back to the God who loves you. Do not feel guilt. He loves you wherever you find yourself in life. He is standing with arms opened wide to welcome you. Find a Bible. Begin to read His word. Fill up the hole that only God can fill. He wants nothing but the best for you.

Do not let satan come in and steal from you anymore. He'll try. He doesn't want you living in freedom. Satan's words are pain, suffering, destruction, anger, bitterness, resentment, jealousy, all words that destroy your life. Close the door on your old life and open the door on your new life.

2 CORINTHIANS 5:17
Therefore, if anyone is in Christ,
He is a new creation; the old has gone,
the new has come.

2 CORINTHIANS 5:20
We are therefore Christ's ambassadors,
as though God were making His appeal through us.
We implore you on Christ's behalf:
Be reconciled to God
God made Him who had no sin to be sin for us,
So that in Him we might become the righteous of God.

For now…God bless you and yours and may all of your dreams come true as you encounter the Living Lord.

God loves you…

Be CAPTURED!

Brenda Conley
Angel Wing Ministries

Jeremiah 29:11
For I know the plans I have for you

These books continue to be my obedience to serve God. It has always been my desire that whoever reads these words will find a burning passion to know my Savior more

I would love to hear from you.

Communicate with us on

Facebook

at

Angel Wing Ministries.

or

bconley9446@yahoo.com

PROVERBS 16:3
Commit to the Lord
whatever you do;
And your plans will succeed.

God Bless

Notes

Notes

Carried By Angels
Series

BOOK ONE
SAVING NOELLE

BOOK TWO
PERFECT LOVE

BOOK THREE
FORGIVING FREEDOM

BOOK FOUR
REDEEMING GRACE